It was a scene right out of a horror movie, and Harry couldn't believe it had really happened...

The scene inside the unit was surreal. There was splattered blood everywhere. Both cage doors stood open and the Yeti were gone. The body of a man was askew on the floor, his limbs mangled, his face a mass of gore, and he lay in a large pool of dried, dark blood. Two men in khaki sheriff's uniforms were in the unit, one bent over the body, the other took photographs. Papers and equipment were scattered in disarray throughout the unit. Harry's stomach revolted and he pushed down the urge to vomit.

"Oh my god," exclaimed Dixie in a low groan. "What in god's name happened here?"

The man bent over the dead body looked up then stood. Dr. Radner stepped around an overturned stool.

"Sheriff Calder, this is our departmental chairman, Dr. Harry Olson and his wife, also Dr. Olson."

Harry shook hands with Calder and Dixie smiled faintly at the man. Harry pointed to the body. "Who?"

"Jimmy Winkleman," Radner said, shaking his head. "So sad. I'm going to have to call his folks."

"Yes," Dixie said. "I remember him from our previous trip."

"What happened in here?" Harry asked. "The place looks like a bomb went off."

His stomach reeled. The strong smell of iron permeated the unit, making his nausea even worse. His body felt light, as if floating, his head spinning. It was like the time he was coming out from under anesthesia after his appendectomy when he was in high school. He floated on a cloud, half-conscious of this world, half not.

Dr. Harry Olson, an American paleoanthropologist, and his wife, Dixie, have returned from the mountains of Mongolia with two live Yeti, a male and a female. A team of scientists in Harry's anthropology department at California Pacific University are now trying to uncover a link between human and Yeti genetics. But when the Yeti escape, Harry's in a race against time to recapture the animals, knowing only too well how terrible the consequences will be if the creatures make it off the desolate high-desert facility and reach a human city…

KUDOS for *Yeti Unleashed*

In *Yeti Unleashed* by Richard Edde, Harry Olson and his wife Dixie have come back to the US from Mongolia with two live Yeti, a male and a female, which are being held at a secure facility in the high desert in Nevada. Scientists are studying their DNA, trying to find out how closely related the Yeti are to humans. But the Yeti escape, and Harry has to recapture them before they get closer to humans than they are supposed to be, and he ends up with a massacre. The story is well written with a lot of additional subplots and plenty of fast-paced action. It will keep you on your toes all the way through. ~ *Taylor Jones, The Review Team of Taylor Jones & Regan Murphy*

Yeti Unleashed by Richard Edde is the second book in his *Yeti* series. This time, Harry Olson and his assistant Dixie, who is now his wife, have brought two live Yeti back from Mongolia to be studied at a research compound in Nevada. While the facility is run "by the book," accidents can always happen, and people make mistakes. Now the Yeti have escaped, and Harry is determined to recapture them before law enforcement can slaughter them—and before the Yeti can slaughter any humans they might encounter. Filled with fascinating science and mind-boggling possibilities, *Yeti Unleashed* tells a chilling tale of human misjudgment and the sometimes fatal consequences a mistake can have. ~ *Regan Murphy, The Review Team of Taylor Jones & Regan Murphy*

Yeti Unleashed

Richard Edde

A Black Opal Books Publication

GENRE: PARANORMAL THRILLER/ROMANTIC ELEMENTS

YETI UNLEASHED
Copyright © 2017 by Richard Edde
Cover Design by Jackson Cover Designs
All cover art copyright © 2017
All Rights Reserved
Print ISBN: 978-1-626946-15-6

First Publication: FEBRUARY 2017

Published by Black Opal Books **http://www.blackopalbooks.com**

DEDICATION

*To My Parents
Robert and Jeanne*

"Man's mind, once stretched by a new idea, never regains its original dimensions." ~ *Oliver Wendell Holmes Sr.*

"It is absolutely necessary, for the peace and safety of mankind, that some of earth's dark, dead corners and un-plumbed depths be let alone; lest sleeping abnormalities wake to resurgent life, and blasphemously surviving nightmares squirm and splash out of their black lairs to newer and wider conquests." ~ *H. P. Lovecraft*

"Things exist either because they have recently come into existence or because they have qualities that made them unlikely to be destroyed in the past." ~ *Richard Dawkins*

Prologue

Deep in a recess on a remote salient of the Altai Mountains, a large, hairy creature sauntered to the opening of the cave in which it lived. Large snowflakes swirled as an angry blizzard howled and covered the ground in deep drifts. A blue-gray sky filtered through dense clouds, caused the landscape to appear as if viewed through a blue filter. Except for the wind screeching outside the cave, no other sound echoed in the mountains. The towering hulk stood in the opening and stared into the muted world beyond. A thick vapor belched from its maw while its eyes glowed deep red, flickering as it looked around.

After a long moment, it stretched out its huge, muscular arms and shrieked a shattering growl. Then it stepped from the cave, ambled through the deep snow, and disappeared into the mist.

❧❧❧

In the small village of Tenduk, located atop a high plateau in the mountainous Altai region of Mongolia, the Buddhist monastery was the center of daily activities. Most of the village merchants earned their meager living by selling their wares to the monks who worked and prayed in the ancient cloister. Roofed with terra cotta tiles, the monastery was a large multi-storied affair with many smaller living quarters terraced around the main temple building. The buildings—interconnected through a series of steps and stairways made of rocks and a few rickety wooden bridges—enabled the monks to pass easily between the various levels. The main stone-and-mortar structure was in the form of a stepped pyramid of three rectangular stories, three circular terraces, and a central pagoda forming the summit.

The plateau was part of a valley in the Altai Mountain range, its rugged, snow-capped peaks providing shelter from bitter winter storms. The steppe, as the plateau was called, formed part of the Mongolian-Manchurian grassland, covered over a quarter million square miles, and forged a crescent around the Gobi Desert. Its dominant flora consisted of medium to tall grasses, monopolized by feather grass. The steppe was where Mongolian nomads grazed their herds of camels, goats, and yaks, where they had done so for generations.

The formation of Altai mountainous region began almost two hundred millions years ago. During this period, the earth's crust was extremely unstable and fluid so the area formed the bottom of a deep sea where numerous layers of sediment accumulated. From about 150 million years ago the region experienced a process of denudation. As a result of the active tectonic processes which took place during the Paleozoic period and which were accompanied by violent volcanic activity, the sea disappeared from the area and the land rose in height. Mainly, the tectonic process, with its vault lifting, formed the modern structure of the Altai region. The most up-thrust occurred in central Altai with a maximum rise of three to four thousand meters.

Traditional Mongols worshipped heaven or *the clear blue sky* and their ancestors. They followed ancient northern Asian practices of shamanism, where human intermediaries placed themselves in a trance then spoke to some of the numerous infinities of spirits responsible for human luck or misfortune. In 1578, Altan Khan, a Mongol military leader with ambitions to unite the Mongols and to emulate the career of Chinggis, invited the head of the rising Yellow Sect of Tibetan Buddhism to a summit. They formed an alliance that gave Altan legitimacy and religious sanction for his imperial pretensions and that provided the Buddhist sect with protection and patronage. Altan gave the Tibetan leader the title of Dalai Lama, which his successors still hold. Altan died soon after, but in the next century the Yellow Sect spread throughout Mongolia, aided in part by the efforts of contending Mongol aristocrats to win religious sanction and mass support for their ultimately unsuccessful efforts to unite all Mongols in a single state. Monasteries were built across Mongolia, often sited at the juncture of trade and migration routes or at summer pastures, where large numbers of herders would congregate for shamanistic rituals and sacrifices. Buddhist monks carried out a protracted struggle with the indigenous shamans and succeeded, to some extent, in taking over their functions and fees as healers and diviners and in pushing the shamans to the religious and cultural fringes of Mongolian culture.

಼಼಼

Abbot Bo Zhing greeted the new day as he had for years—sitting in his favorite chair on a ledge, his face pointed toward the rising sun. A deep rugged valley dropped away from his perch, its vegetation dappled in hues of gold and yellow. It was a brisk morning, in spite of the sun's warming rays on his kashaya, his brown robe of Tibetan origin. He sat under a small pagoda, arms folded, chanting his morning prayer.

"I am a link in Lord Buddha's golden chain of love
that stretches around the world.
I must keep my link bright and strong.
I will try to be kind and gentle to every living thing,
and protect all who are weaker than myself.
I will try to think pure and beautiful thoughts,
to say pure and beautiful words, and to do pure and
beautiful deeds, knowing that on what
I do now depends my happiness and misery.
May every link in Lord Buddha's golden chain
of love become bright and strong
and may we all attain perfect peace."

His prayers completed, Abbot Zhing rose and walked with measured steps to the small dining hall where he would greet his fellow monks. There was much excitement among the men the past few days for there had been a sighting of a strange beast higher in the mountains. Ever since the American scientific expedition earlier in the year, speculation mounted that a family of large creatures lived in the remote mountains near the monastery.

Zhing remembered well the overcast day when a small group of scientists from the expedition arrived, their leader inquiring about an ancient skull they heard was kept there. The skull was an artifact that the monks had kept in a deep secure vault for generations. What it was, exactly, no one seemed to know. There were rumors, of course. Zhing had heard them during his many years as a monk in Tenduk. This part of Mongolia was rife with stories of strange creatures that roamed the mountains. Proof of their existence was always vague, inconsistent.

Hesitant at first, Zhing finally acquiesced and showed the skull to the leader of the expedition, Dr. Harry Olson. The man and his small party said they were a team of scientists, digging for early human fossils in the Altai Mountains and had unearthed a group of bones that were neither human nor animal. He hoped the skull might shed light on the mystery. The doctor and his colleagues were very polite, took measurements of the skull, and left.

Then tragedy struck.

Four evil men, one with a long scar on his face, pursued the expedition team to the Tenduk monastery, demanding the whereabouts of the scientists. They murdered the senior abbot, Lama Yang. Why, Zhing did not know, but it was a brutal and senseless killing. Much later, he learned that one of the female scientists was taken captive by a large animal and dragged deep into its mountain lair. With the help of the Mongolian Police, it took the all the expedition could muster to effect her eventual rescue.

Zhing knew it was the Yeti of his youth.

Before the scientists left Mongolia, Zhing talked by phone with the expedition leader, Dr. Olson. He promised the scientist to notify him if and when he or his fellow monks came by any information of creatures lurking in the mountains. The scientist needed the information for his research, and Zhing liked the man's easy manner, his seemingly genuine pursuit of knowledge.

For decades there had been rumors and supposed sightings of the famous Yeti, a large, hairy, shy beast that roamed the remote regions of the Altai. According to legend, the animals lived in caves in the high altitudes and ventured to the lower altitudes in search of food, mostly vegetation growing in the valleys. Through the years, sightings were common but the physical evidence of such a creature was never found.

The Yeti were reputed to be six-foot-tall, bipedal creatures, covered in reddish brown fur, with anthropomorphic facial features, including pronounced brow ridges, flat noses, and no chin. And, unlike the Himalayan Abominable Snowman, their behavior was considered far more human than ape-like. They were said to inhabit the mountains of central Asia and the Altai Mountains of southern Mongolia. Modern accounts documenting footprints, as well as native traditions dating back hundreds of years, attested to the existence of the Yeti, including the exchange of trade goods between remote Mongolian villages and the creatures. Drawings of Yeti also appeared in an ancient Tibetan apothecary handbook, with the following comment:

> *The book contains thousands of illustrations of various classes of animals including reptiles, mammals and amphibia, but not one single mythological animal, like its medieval European counterparts, which often listed many fantastic animals in its medical books. Being that every creature in the Tibetan medicinal book are well-documented actual species, with the exception of the Yeti, gives some validity to the creature's existence.*

Speculation that Yeti may be something other than legendary creatures was based on purported eyewitness accounts, alleged footprint finds, and interpretations of long-standing native traditions, which had been anthropologically collected.

Now, there was talk. Excited talk. Even whispers among the monks. Zhing needed to know if this talk could be substantiated with sightings and facts or was all just idle chatter. Today in the dining hall he would find out.

Hopefully.

He strolled into a large, brightly lit room filled with wooden tables and straight back chairs. The buzz from the monks gradually diminished at their seeing him standing at the head of the tables.

"Namasta, my brothers," Zhing said.

"Namasta," was the uniform reply from the men seated at their tables.

"Brothers," Zhing began, "I have heard talk recently of the Yeti. I am here to learn if the talk is founded in fact. Have any of you actually seen such a creature?"

No one ventured a raised hand.

"Have any of you talked with someone who claims having seen such an animal?"

The dining hall erupted in one continuous buzz, everyone speaking at once and raising hands.

Zhing spent the better part of an hour listening to his brother monks describe their experiences and, in the end, decided that there was enough credible evidence to call Dr. Olson. Later, he walked down to the village butcher shop to use the region's only phone.

Chapter 1

Dixie was near panic. Sobbing, her tears mixing with the dust caked on her face, turned the mess into a dried-mud facial. It was difficult to open her mouth with the dried mud, and the dust choked her—breathing was difficult. It was surreal being in this place. Like a dream. No, a nightmare.

She knew she was going to die.

At first, when the large creature grabbed her and carried her off, she put up a fight, but its strength easily overpowered her. Its hot, fetid breath, smelling of rotten garbage, quickly overwhelmed her senses, while its eyes, piercing, red, glowing, were like embers in a dying campfire. Most of all, she remembered its fangs, long, pointed, and stained yellow and brown.

At first, she waited in fear for the beast to sink those long canines into her neck and was surprised when the monster only dragged her to a cave and deposited her in a small room. Later, it tied her to the wall, using crude straps made of dried vines, and there she hung, like a piece of crude art. The monster knew what it was doing, acting almost human.

Imprisoned and in a state of exhaustion, she watched the creature and its comrades...was that the right word?…come and go in silence. Was it a hallucination that they seemed to be an extended family? One male creature appeared dominant over the others, acting as their leader, while a smaller female was never far from his side. In her tortured mind, she thought they completed a family unit, although the exact nature she could not say. But they did appear to be some sort of primate unit, for they knew each other and worked together. They grunted some sort of language that only they understood and, to her surprise, seemed to show affection for each other. At one time, she thought she saw the male caress his mate.

The creatures came and went without paying her much attention. They seemed content to have her confined and helpless, hanging there. They gave her no food or water. As the hours dragged on, she weakened to the point of losing consciousness, and it was as if she were in a dream, looking down upon her body. But then, one of the hairy beasts would amble into the little room, shove its ugly face into hers, and snarl, its hot breath smelling of rancid meat. But not one of them harmed her. It was as if they were studying her, like in the movie, *Planet Of The Apes*. Or, maybe, she was just a piece of art, stuck on the wall for them to enjoy.

Nearing total collapse, she lost her fear of being devoured and accepted her predicament. She remembered the moment she realized she would not survive, because no one in the expedition had the faintest idea where she was. When the end came, she hoped it would be quick. She thought of her parents, her dead brother, and Harry. She would miss Harry and realized she was in love with him. Not overtly religious, but spiritual in her own way, she felt that there was some sort of soul's existence after death, although exactly what it was she couldn't say. But she knew it would be a good existence—of that she had no doubt.

That and Harry were the only thoughts that gave her any comfort.

By the second day of her imprisonment, the creatures hardly noticed her as they came and went. The excruciating pain in her arms was replaced by a numbness, a fact for which she was grateful. Sometimes the large male sauntered up to her, stared for a moment or two, then turned and left. He didn't snarl anymore. None of them touched her, except one of the young females did feel her breasts, as if they were something she had not seen.

By the third day, she developed frank hallucinations. Dehydrated and weak, she was near collapse with only short lucid periods interspersed with those of unconsciousness. At one point, there were bug-eyed snakes spewing from the cracks between the rocks and their tongues flicked at her, mouths hissing. When a tongue touched her, it burned and left a mark. She tried reciting the twenty-third Psalm but couldn't remember the words…

ᗧᗤᗧᗤ

Dixie woke with a start, gasping for breath, pulse pounding.

It was the nightmare again. The nightmare that would not go away. That time as prisoner of a group of Yeti deep in a Mongolian mountain cave now served as the womb of her sordid dreams, birthing nightmares that visited on a regular basis.

She reached out and noticed Harry was not beside her. The clock read two a.m. She sat on the edge of the bed, filled a glass of water from the carafe, took a deep breath, and tried to quell her racing heart. Since returning from the ill-fated Mongolian expedition, she had finished her doctorate in anthropology, after which she and Harry were married. Harry had been her professor and mentor at California Pacific University. Now, she was an assistant professor in her own right, a position her new husband secured for her.

Sitting in the dark bedroom, she noticed a small shaft of light emanating from their study on the far side of the house. She donned her robe and sauntered down the hall ,where she found Harry bent over his desk, a cluster of papers spread out before him. At the sound of her approach, he turned and smiled.

"Couldn't sleep?" he said. He sat in his pajamas, held out a tanned hand, took hers, and pulled her to him. "Did I wake you? I tried to not make any noise."

"No, you didn't. It was the nightmare again," she said, running a hand through her tussled hair. "I must look a sight."

Harry pulled her onto his lap and laughed. "You look marvelous, honey." He kissed her on the cheek and smiled. "I love the way you look. Now, it was the nightmare again?"

"Of course. It's always the same. I'm back in that damned mountain cave and those creatures have strung me up and are pawing over me. I can see their eyes—like glowing coals—and smell their breath. The smell of rotting flesh and death."

"Baby," Harry said, brushing a strand of blonde hair from Dixie's cheek, "you had a horrific experience and were close to death. It's no wonder you're having nightmares. It's called post-traumatic stress. But I think it will get better with time. I really do."

"You don't think I'm losing my mind?" Dixie climbed off Harry's lap and sat in a chair near the desk. It was quiet in the house, except for the ticking of the old grandfather clock in the hallway.

"Absolutely not," Harry said. "If I thought that, I'd

have had you examined by a psychiatrist. No, Dixie, no. What you're going through is a perfectly normal reaction, given all that happened."

"But it's been almost a year," she said, tears welling up in her eyes. She didn't want to break down and cry or become hysterical.

"But the nightmares aren't nearly as frequent. You've said so yourself. That speaks volumes."

"I hope so. I sure wish Professor was here."

"Me too," Harry said, leaning back in his chair, the concern on his face relaxing. "His sudden death was quite a shock to everyone. I couldn't believe it when it happened. The man was like a father to me."

"And me," Dixie said. "I didn't realize I could miss him as much as I have."

"His heart attack was completely unexpected. But I guess, when you're older, anything can happen. I was glad that he was able to see us married. I know that made him happy."

Doctor Julius Kesler had been chairman of the Anthropology Department at California Pacific University and Harry's boss. He was the lead scientist of the expedition, led by Harry, into the Altai Mountains of Mongolia in search of hominid fossils. Dixie had been Harry's chief assistant. Dr. Kesler, or Professor, as his associates affectionately called him, took Harry under his wing, and Harry responded to the man's tutoring by becoming a rising paleoanthropologist and heir-apparent to Professor's position whenever the man decided to retire.

But the expedition was interrupted and prematurely ended when a ruthless relic hunter and his band of armed security forces arrived on scene, intent on stealing what the team uncovered. However, everyone's plans did an about face with the appearance of large creatures known previously only through legends. In the end, they turned out to be Yeti, akin to the Abominable Snowman, Almas, or Bigfoot, and terrorized anyone who came close to their habitat.

The fate of their expedition made international news and catapulted Harry's reputation into the stratosphere. Early one morning, one of the Yeti seized Dixie and carried her to their lair deep within a system of mountain caves, where they kept her bound and imprisoned. In a desperate bid to find and rescue Dixie, Harry, along with aid from the Mongolian Police forces, tracked the Yeti to the cave system. After fending off several attacks by the large creatures, Harry and the police found and rescued Dixie and began their exit from the large underground cave.

But the Yeti followed.

In a daring escape that involved blowing up part of the cave system, Harry and Dixie made their way to the surface. The final, violent confrontation with their pursuers ended with one man dead and their leader arrested.

Back in the States, Harry's fame spread through academic circles. He appeared on talk shows, lectured at various universities, wrote a paper with Dr. Kesler. Amidst all the hoopla, he and Dixie were married and she finished her doctorate. After a honeymoon and some much-needed rest, Dr. Kesler argued that they should return to the Altai and bring back tangible evidence of the Yeti's existence. After receiving a call from the monastery abbot, informing them of the Yeti's whereabouts, they once again mounted an expedition to locate them.

They were successful beyond their wildest dreams. Not only were they able to find a group of the creatures, with the help of local labor, they managed to capture a pair of Yeti. They returned to the States with a male and a female, which they kept at a special facility in the Nevada mountains. It had been dangerous work but sedating the two animals, using tranquilizer darts, made the work easier and somewhat safer. They secured cages and placed the Yeti on a freighter going to San Francisco. Sadly, a few months later, Professor Kesler succumbed to a fatal heart attack while working in his university office. Harry and Dixie were stunned.

"He was a great man," Dixie said, her voice near a whisper. "And a good man."

"One thing is for sure," Harry said, "it won't be easy to replace a man like him. He was a giant in our field. And so well liked. With all the competition, that's unusual in academia."

"I remember him as a kind person, always patient with students and faculty alike. I miss him, honey."

"Me too."

The couple sat in silence for a few moments, then Dixie sighed. "I tell you this, sweetie, two trips to the Altai are about all my nerves can stand. I'm not sure I'm up for another. I couldn't believe Professor left you his house here in San Mateo. It was unbelievable."

"Yes, it was. I was overcome. I never suspected anything like this and Professor never spoke about it."

"He had no other family?"

"Not that I am aware of," Harry said. "He spoke once of a lost love but he never married. Never had any children."

"No brothers or sisters?"

"I guess not. If he did, they have died, quite possibly. What little money he had accumulated he left to the university."

"It's such a lovely house," Dixie said. "I love the view of the bay."

"More than I ever could afford."

"Well, now that you are chairman of the department, you deserve a house like this. I'm glad the president followed Professor's wishes and made you chairman. You've worked hard for a lot of years."

"I never expected to get the job under these conditions—with him dying, I mean. It's an honor, to be sure, but I'm finding out that there's a lot of work involved. And internal politics."

"Yeah, that new archeologist wants his own lab. What's his name?"

"Bernard Wickingham. That's Dr. Wickingham, excuse me."

"He does seem to be eaten up with self-importance," Dixie said, now offering a smile. "Pretty stuck on himself, I've noticed."

"I've told him time and again that there's no available space for a lab. And being the newest faculty member, there's no money either. I've told him, 'get a grant and we'll see.' But he doesn't seem to understand."

"Well, honey, he's new. Time may mellow him. It did you."

Dixie laughed and winked at her husband. She loved poking the bear now and then.

"Very funny, my dear. Very funny."

But she could see the corners of his mouth turn up in a faint smile. She stood. "Coming to bed soon?"

"Yeah, in a little bit. I'm about finished here."

Dixie bent over his chair and peered over his shoulder. She put a hand on the back of his neck and massaged his tense muscles. "What's all this?"

"Something I found in Kesler's files," Harry said. "Something profoundly unusual."

"Yeah?"

"It has to do with the Primate Research Facility. You know how Professor and the woman who is the head of the DNA lab, what's her name?"

"Dr. Rawlings," Dixie said. "Chloe Rawlings."

"Yes. Professor and Dr. Rawlings took on a long-term project to decipher the Yeti's complete genome. It was one of a number of things we were studying with the animals."

"So?" Dixie said, leaning farther over his shoulder to study the papers on the desk.

"If I'm reading these notes correctly, they may have discovered a segment of mitochondrial DNA identical to that found in humans."

"Harry, are you serious?" Dixie's tone was now clipped with an anxious edge.

"I can't be for sure, but I need to speak with Dr. Rawlings then make a trip to the facility and check it out. It's been over a month since we've been up there."

"You're saying that there is a segment of Yeti DNA in our own genome?"

Harry nodded. "I don't know. These notes aren't that obvious. It seems that there are two identical segments of DNA, one in the Yeti and the other in the human genome."

Her eyes narrowed. "What would that mean?"

"I'm no genetics expert, honey, but it might mean we are related to the Yeti in some way. Similar to the way humans and Neanderthals interbred thousands of years ago."

"Wow," was all Dixie could say.

"That's why I need to get up to the research facility soon."

"Well, when you do, I want to go along. I want to look at our Yeti again."

"I would have thought—"

"I need to, honey," Dixie interrupted. "Each time it gets easier. It's just in my dreams that they come for me, that they take me away."

Harry turned in his chair, pulled her onto his lap, and

caressed her cheek with his hand. Her blonde hair fell in tussled curls above her shoulders and her dark eyes were moist.

"I understand, sweetie. Let's go to bed."

He turned off the desk lamp, and Dixie followed him into to their bedroom where she fell into his arms and a contented sleep.

Chapter 2

The Primate Research Facility was an extensive compound, located in the East Humbolt Mountain Range in Elko County, Nevada. It was an isolated part of the state, far from any major roads or highways, towns, or other conveniences. The nearest town was Grant, thirty miles to the south. The facility itself, perched atop Cinder Mountain, was reached by a one-lane dirt road and consisted of several buildings containing research laboratories and living quarters. The Primate Research Facility was Professor Kesler's crowning achievement, his last erection, Harry loved to joke. From the outset, the facility, built as a place where scientists could process their archeological and paleontological specimens, grew and became a state-of-the-art hominid research laboratory, doing genome and DNA sequencing projects on all sorts of primates and hominid fossils.

The huge teaching and research laboratory had ten research laboratories, including one that also functioned as a darkroom. The laboratories were outfitted with four-foot hoods, chemical resistant counter tops, and seamless flooring, and had its own hot and cold water, gas, compressed air, vacuum, and both 110v and 220v electrical outlets. Laboratory facilities included multiple two and three-room suites, each with a dedicated procedure room and animal holding room and a dissecting suite with its own procedure and animal holding rooms. The building also contained two biosafety level three laboratories for in-vitro work. BSL-3 labs were suitable for work with infectious agents that might cause serious or potentially lethal diseases as a result of exposure by the inhalation route. The BSL-3 laboratories were located away from high-traffic areas. In those labs, air moved from areas of lesser contamination to areas of higher contamination, such as from the corridor into the laboratory. Air movement was single pass—the exhaust air not recirculated to other rooms—and was HEPA filtered. In addition, there was a freezer room, autoclave processing area, decontamination air lock, storage space, and shower-out facilities.

All electrical outlets in the building were centrally protected from voltage surges and spikes, and some outlets in each room were on the building's emergency generator. The building also contained a room designed for the processing of field samples that was outfitted with silt traps and special sinks for washing and sorting samples. A lecture room and general laboratory and a class analytical chemistry laboratory supported teaching operations. The building contained a small library, a computer laboratory, a conference room, and administrative offices.

The main building was a self-contained, stand-alone facility—all materials, including waste products, were managed on site for increased safety. The specially designed structure had its own steam plant, two sources of water and power, a backup generator, autoclaves, and an effluent decontamination system. There were also redundant systems for both supply and exhaust air with inward directional airflow.

Primate Research Facility scientists possessed unique expertise in gamete biology, reproductive toxicology, lifespan health, regenerative medicine and gene therapy, the application of in-vivo imaging tools and technologies for translational research. Investigation of the genetic basis of human diseases had been a major focus of effort at the Primate Research Facility since its inception. Nonhuman primates made outstanding models for the study of the genetics of disease because they were so similar to humans in their biochemistry, physiology, anatomy and behavior. As researchers in many areas of biomedical research focused greater attention on the genetic basis of disease susceptibility and rates of progression, the use of nonhuman primates as animal models for these genetic processes became standard procedure. The value of nonhuman primates as models for human genetics and genomics, and as tools for comparative genetic analysis, was now recognized throughout academia. This was one reason why the National Human Genome Research Institute had already approved the complete whole genome DNA sequencing of nine species of nonhuman primates—chimpanzee, rhesus macaque, marmoset, baboon, squirrel monkey, tarsier, mouse lemur and galago—and was considering others.

The facility dormitory and conference center provided a large space for year-round housing and conferences. This building had two floors, on which all rooms were fully furnished. The first floor contained an apartment for the facility director, along with a kitchen and dining area. It also contained a large TV/conference room with a capacity for twenty-four, a pool room, laundry facilities, and storage space. The second floor contained numerous bedrooms and bathrooms.

The Animal Care Unit held caging, bedding change stations, and sinks and was organized as individual rooms accessed from a corridor system. The Procedure Rooms were located next to the housing rooms and were a primary setting for research activity within the unit. The animal care area contained barrier elements—airlocks, lockers, pass-through autoclaves—that provided the primary barrier and access control that separated the controlled animal care environment from external influences. The cage washing area was the hub for all cleaning, sanitizing, and husbandry activities, duties that were performed by the animal care technicians. These areas were dominated by equipment-generated heat and moisture. The major equipment items included pass-through rack washers, pass-through autoclaves, bedding dispensers and dump stations, and bottle washing and filling stations. A quarantine room for suspect and incoming animals that could be a source of infection was located in this area as well.

Down the hall and isolated from all clean areas was the necropsy/perfusion room - a critical support function used for post mortem procedures on sacrificed animals. There were containment facilities—facilities for working with potentially infectious biological agents—that operated under negative pressure to prevent the escape of air to the general environment. Wastes and effluents were separately contained and decontaminated. Sophisticated control and monitoring systems and equipment were employed to achieve closely controlled and regulated air pressurizations and flows.

Air flow and air exchanges along with temperatures were alarmed and monitored. Finally, there was a veterinary care clinic that provided lab and care functions such as surgery, clinical chemistry, and histology.

Animal Care Unit technicians provided routine daily care for all laboratory animals housed in the facility, along with daily observation and provision of food and water. Environmental conditions for each species were maintained, and temperature, humidity, and light cycles modified, as required by experimental design.

The director of the Primate Research Facility was Dr. Miles Radner, a man in his forties with a Harvard PhD. Kesler hired him after the man made a startling discovery in Indonesia, linking the ancient Denisovans to the extinct Neanderthals. Harry didn't much care for the man. His pompous and condescending attitude toward his colleagues seemed uncalled for, given the fact the man had not done anything noteworthy since his earth-shattering revelation ten years earlier.

However, Harry had to admit that Radner had used his notoriety and influence to equip the research facility with the latest in genetic, forensic, and archeological testing equipment. It was a state-of-the-art facility—nothing like it on the West Coast. Besides the usual DNA sequencers, he had managed to equip the many labs with a Solexa Genome Analyzer, a quantitative PCR analyzer, a Galaxy Luminometer, numerous incubators, a mass spectrometer, and a cell sorting system. One recent advance was an enrichment method called whole-genome capture. It involved the use of RNA probes that were based on current human DNA. To eliminate the capture of contaminating DNA, mostly from microorganisms that were invariably present in ancient tissue samples, the RNA probes only bound to small fragments of ancient human DNA. Next, magnetic tags attached to proteins that bound the RNA probes, allowed for the isolation of as much ancient DNA as possible from the limited samples.

The researchers who developed this particular method reported that they could previously only isolate and sequence about two percent of the ancient DNA available in any given sample. However, using the RNA probe method allowed them to increase their reads to up to sixty percent.

All in all, the Cal Pacific Primate Research Facility had become a place where brilliant young scientists wanted to work or spend a year doing post-doctoral research.

And now, with Harry's discovery that someone at the research facility may have linked the Yeti to modern humans, he needed to unravel the current state of research and find out why he had been kept in the dark by Professor and Dr. Radner. The Yeti were his and Dixie's discovery after all, and they were responsible for bringing the pair to the primate facility in Nevada. And they had risked their lives, not only with the original Yeti discovery, but also in the expedition to bring them back.

So his blood simmered as he struggled to analyze the reasons for keeping him in the dark. Kesler's papers shed no light on why he had not confided in either him or Dixie. There was no indication as to the timeline as to when Professor learned of the possible DNA similarity. It could be recent, just prior to his untimely death. Harry hoped that was the reason for his apparent secrecy. But he needed to uncover the truth for, after all, he was the chairman of the Anthropology Department and the Primate Research Facility was his responsibility.

Dr. Olson reclined at his desk in his office at California Pacific University that was located on the outskirts of San Francisco. It was a fine office, belonging to his former boss, Julius Kesler, and it offered a magnificent view of San Francisco Bay. Below, a large boat made its way up the channel toward the Palo Alto docks. The sun was bright and Harry felt good.

He spent the morning with administrative duties, first going over the progress of the department's graduate students then lecturing to his class in Basic Field Methods. Afterward, he ate lunch with Dixie in the faculty dining room and listened to her explain why one of her students was not doing well in her anthropology class. He feigned interest over their meal together then returned to his office, eager to study Dr. Kesler's papers once again.

Harry gazed out at San Francisco Bay. The boat was gone, its long pearlescent wake dissolved in the blue ocean water. He missed the old man as if he were family. His own father was a rude, abusive, drunk who never worked and ranted that Harry would never amount to anything. So, from his first contact with Dr. Kesler, Harry had become enthralled with anthropology and became, after years of dedicated work, a paleoanthropologist. Professor became his surrogate father, in addition to his mentor. It was a complex relationship—teacher, mentor, father figure, friend, and confidant. And Professor treated Harry different from his other students. He was kind but demanding, like a loving father, and Harry responded to the man's tutelage with a drive and passion for research and fieldwork.

When the Mongolian expedition became a reality, Professor chose Harry to be the team's leader. Too old to be scurrying over rough terrain, he allowed Harry to be his eyes and ears on the ground.

Within a month, they unearthed an ancient Russian airplane containing a box full of bones. As the team worked at uncovering the meaning of their discovery things began to unravel after their encounter with the Yeti. One of the creatures abducted Dixie forcing a change in the team's priorities—finding Dixie and bringing her back safely. And with the help of the Mongolian authorities, they had been able to do just that. In the process, they discovered a branch of human evolution never thought possible.

That first expedition had been complicated by his mother's illness and hospitalization. Her heart required an emergency pacemaker, making her critically ill for a number of weeks. To add to the stress of dealing with her long distance, he was informed of her progress through his estranged brother, Max. Two years older than himself, his brother was the son whom their father loved best, whom their father thought was the greatest, and with whom Harry never spoke. Max worked on Wall Street and boasted an entitled attitude, one condescending to those he met. But through it all, Harry and Max eventually renewed their relationship and his mother's health gradually improved.

Once Harry and Dixie returned to the States, Professor, excited by the incredible scientific ramifications, urged Harry and Dixie to return to the Altai Mountains and bring back evidence of the Yeti's existence.

At first, Dixie wanted no part of returning to the place where she nearly lost her life but Professor's gentle pressure and logical arguments, in the end, convinced her to accompany her new husband. It became a harrowing ordeal.

Mongolia was a large landlocked country between two larger countries—Russia and China. Located on mountains and plateaus, it was one of the world's highest countries, with an average elevation of five thousand feet. Mongolia suffered temperature extremes, and the huge Gobi desert dominated southern Mongolia. Genghis Khan's Mongol horsemen conquered much of Asia and Europe during the thirteenth century. Mongolia became a communist country in 1924, but in 1990 multiparty elections were held. Poverty still was a major concern, but copper, cashmere, and gold exports helped the economy.

The Altai Mountains were a mountain range in East-Central Asia, where Russia, China, Mongolia, and Kazakhstan came together, and were where the rivers Irtysh and Ob had their headwaters. In the Mongolic language, the name, Altai, meant the Golden Mountain. Bordering a broad grassland plain, the mountains ranged from two thousand meters to the 4500-meter summit of Belukha, the double-headed peaks that towered over the region. On the east and southeast the great plateau of Mongolia, the transition being effected gradually by means of several minor plateaus, flanked this range. This region was studded with a number of large lakes.

The people of the Altai steppe were herders, dependent on sheep and goats, cattle and yak, horses and camels. In the present as in the past, families moved in groups about four times a year, in order to seek fresh grasslands and pastures for their animals. In general, the trajectories followed in these moves according with traditions established over many decades. With the aid of his old friend, Semyon Stepan of the Mongolian State Police, who was promoted to the rank of Major and was now Chief Stepan, Harry put together an expedition back to the Altai. Using his former foreman, Cheng, and Abbot Zhing's information, he and Dixie returned to the original mountain where the Yeti were first encountered. Cheng had been his guide and site foreman, and Dixie hoped that one day the young man and his wife would find their way to San Francisco to live. Back in the mountains after a long, difficult trek that brought painful memories flooding back to Harry, they located a different entrance to the cave system. Using fresh cut hay as bait, they succeeded in luring the creatures out into the open where Harry used a dart gun to subdue and tranquilize two animals. But it was not without a struggle. Sadly, one of the workers had been badly injured when a rope used to bind a Yeti broke, and he sustained a skull fracture.

The sedated animals, a male and female, were bound then loaded into cages for the transport home. Keeping the creatures alive on the helicopter trip back to Ulaanbaatar was a difficult task and several times the female almost died. Dr. Gerald Siscom, the veterinarian at Cal Pacific's Primate Research Facility in Nevada, met the team in Beijing where he inspected the animals, then, along with Cheng, transported them to the port city of Tianjin, where they were loaded onto a freighter bound for San Francisco. Harry and Dixie flew home. The creatures were immediately shipped to the Primate Research Facility and placed in quarantine cages until Dr. Siscom deemed them disease-free. Federal inspectors arrived to certify Siscom's evaluation.

Except for occasional outbursts from the Yeti, who screamed and rattled their cages with their oversized hands, a pair of graduate assistants assigned to the Yeti and responsible for obtaining blood specimens eventually established a routine. Those times were the most dangerous, for the creature had to be sedated and the assistant required entering its cage and coming into close contact with it. To prevent inadvertent escape, they closed and locked the cage while the assistant drew the blood sample and while Siscom stood by outside the cage with the tranquilizing gun.

Two graduate assistants were selected to spend a year at the Primate Research Facility doing genetic research. Millie Harbaum and Jimmy Winkleman, both in their last years of graduate studies and needing a research project to finish their doctorate, were living and working at the facility. They were selected after a lengthy process of applications and interviews.

Harry received monthly reports from the facility director, Dr. Miles Radner, who detailed the progress of the various research projects and the work of the graduate assistants who were under his tutelage. According to the latest report, interestingly, the female Yeti seemed to develop an attachment to Millie, the graduate assistant assigned to her. Millie often came to the unit after work hours to check on her Yeti. Jimmy, the other graduate assistant, didn't have the same relationship with his Yeti, as the creature growled and snarled each time Jimmy approached its cage. It watched everyone in the cage area with wide, red glowing eyes.

As Harry sped along the coast on Highway 101, a setting sun provided for a soft golden glow over the bay and its waters turned languid. Dixie was home and it would be good to relax and chat about their day's activities. He had things to discuss.

Chapter 3

Dixie busied herself preparing dinner, one of Harry's favorites—lasagna. She had made a large pan the previous weekend and put it in the freezer so now she was heating it in the oven. Her teaching and research duties at California Pacific University didn't leave much time for household chores. Those she relegated to the weekend. Her Anthropology 101 class required a lot of preparation, and she still didn't have a lot of confidence in her lecturing abilities. Her afternoons were spent in the lab, helping graduate students prepare and restore specimens from the field.

She grew up on Long Island, in a big house with two servants. Her father was a well-to-do Wall Street banker so she attended Smith College on her father's money. She took up smoking pot during her freshman year while pledging a sorority and the marijuana led to stronger drugs. Each afternoon, a small group used to snort cocaine in each other's rooms. She lost interest in college, dropped a lot of weight, and argued with her parents all the time. When she flunked her courses that spring, her father had her tested for drugs and that ended her semester-long party. Reluctantly, she agreed to go into rehab, however, she didn't excel in the program until tragedy

struck. Her younger brother, Bill, was killed in an auto-
mobile accident, and the shock devastated her. Bill had
been on a pedestal, a special brother. He knew of her
struggles with drugs but was never judgmental, although
he begged her over and over to stop. He was handsome,
funny, and she loved him more than she loved herself.
After his funeral, she never ventured out of the house for
many weeks. One day, feeling lower than she ever had,
she realized no one could help but herself. Bill was right,
her downward spiral would only result in her death. Finally, she vowed to begin again in earnest. Returning to
Smith on probation, she attacked her studies with renewed zeal.

The first semester back was the hardest. She struggled
with her studies, having to relearn how to learn. But then
she made the Dean's Honor Roll the remainder of her
time at Smith and, upon graduation, moved to San Francisco to get away from her parents. She enrolled in the
graduate school at California Pacific University. Interested in biology, she elected to study human evolution and
anthropology. When she took a course taught by Dr. Olson, she flourished under his patient tutelage. Although
she first thought him rude and callous, she later found
him to be highly intelligent but shy. For four years, she
worked hard writing a doctoral thesis he would be proud
of. During those years, and while on the Mongolian expedition, she realized she was in love with Harry. And
much to her surprise, he fell in love with her, something
she never thought would happen in a million years.

Since their wedding, she had never been happier. She
led an idyllic life—an academic with a great job, married
to a wonderful man who cared for her.

She heard the door open and close and hurried into the
living room to greet Harry. He dropped his briefcase on
the sofa and plopped into an overstuffed chair.

"Hi, sweet," he said. "Something smells good."

"Lasagna from last weekend. It's in the oven. How did your day go?"

"Got time to talk?" Harry said.

"Come to the kitchen, honey, while I finish with dinner. We can talk there. And you can grab us a couple of beers on your way."

Harry followed his wife into the kitchen, found the beer in the refrigerator, opened them, and sat at the dinette table. The small table was situated in a nook off the kitchen and had a commanding view of the bay. Shadows fell over San Mateo and its docks. He took a long gulp of his beer and watched as Dixie served up the lasagna.

"So what's up?" she said, sitting across from him and picking up a fork.

Harry talked as he ate, speaking between mouthfuls. "Remember I said Professor had papers suggesting that Yeti DNA was linked to modern humans?"

"Sure," Dixie said, taking a swallow of her beer. She watched as Harry's steel-eyes seemed to light up as he talked. "But you never mentioned how."

"Comparable to the way Neanderthal DNA is similar to humans. The Neanderthal mitochondrial DNA sequences are substantially different from modern human mitochondrial DNA. Researchers compared the Neanderthal to modern human and chimpanzee sequences. Most human sequences differ from each other by on average eight substitutions, while the human and chimpanzee sequences differ by about fifty-five substitutions. The Neanderthal and modern human sequences differed by approximately twenty-seven substitutions, a much closer relationship."

"I suppose so. Harry, you know genetics isn't my strong suit." Dixie continued to eat lasagna.

"But you can understand what I'm saying, right? The

Neanderthals are related to us but not exactly like us. And they are closer to us genetically than chimps."

She nodded.

"Well, according to Kesler's papers, the scientists at the Primate Research Facility sequenced the genome from the female Yeti. It differs from the human genome by only thirty-five substitutions."

Harry waited for Dixie to say something and when she didn't he continued.

"So the Yeti are farther from human than Neanderthals but closer than chimps. Most likely they are an early form of hominid, not animal primate."

"You mean the *Homo* genus?" Dixie said, now alert and leaning forward.

"Most assuredly *Homo* and closely related to the common human ancestor in some fashion. But could be an *Australopithecus* or *Ardipithecus* variant, not a *Homo*. No one knows at this point. One thing is for certain—the Yeti is definitely a hominid."

"And Professor had this information?"

"It appears so, yes."

"And he didn't confide in you? His chief assistant? The man he hoped to take over the department helm when he retired? What do you make of that?" Dixie's voice turned hard and irritated, her brown eyes flashed sparks.

"Now, honey," Harry said, "don't go getting riled. Professor may have had a good reason, or he didn't receive the information until just prior to his death. I just don't know at this point."

"Still, it makes me angry. After all that we did for him. Risked our lives and all." Dixie's voice was now bellowing. She scrapped her leftover food into the trash and dumped her plate into the sink with a flourish. She returned to the table and downed the rest of her beer. "I'm still having nightmares for Christ's sake," she continued. "You would think the least he could do would have been to share the information with you. This is potentially earth-shattering, right?"

"A new species of humans? I should say so."

"Wow, honey. Think of it. We might have discovered a new species of humans, not dead, but living today, tucked away in a far corner of the world. It's fantastic!"

"Not so fast, there's still a lot of scientific work to be done, checking and rechecking, corroboration, all of that tedious, boring stuff."

"Still, a heady possibility. And to think Professor kept this to himself."

"That's why I need to go to the facility and check it out. Once I know what's going on, I'll be better able to decide what to do."

"I'm going, too. I have a vested interest in these Yeti, you know."

"Of course, honey."

ღ�യღჟ

Dr. Miles Radner put down the scientific journal he was reading and called his veterinarian, Dr. Gerald Siscom, and his Chief of Security, Bruce Drayton. He lit his pipe and puffed until both men were ensconced in the leather chairs opposite his mahogany desk.

"What's up, boss?" said Drayton, slouching in his chair.

"Bruce," Radner said, irritation showing in his voice, "I've asked you not to call me that but to address me as *Dr. Radner*. Please don't force me to remind you again."

"Sorry—er, Dr. Radner."

Siscom, the facility veterinarian, smiled and massaged an ear in silence.

"I've asked you both here to inform you that Dr. Olson, our departmental chairman, plans to visit next week so I want the place immaculate and running like a top. Gerald, all the animal facilities need to be shining and spotless. The containment policies need to be current and in compliance with AAALAC regulations."

Siscom nodded. He was a short man with muscular, tanned arms. His hawk nose was set between two wide eyes. "We are ready for an inspection at any time, Doctor, so nothing needs to be added before Dr. Olson gets here."

"Fine, fine," Radner said, puffing on the pipe. "Bruce, same goes for you and your team. IDs for every staff member need to be in order, and I don't want Dr. Olson getting on the compound without being stopped. Understand?"

"Yes, sir. Understood."

"I'll see to it that the scientific areas are running smoothly so his visit will, hopefully, be short and sweet. That will be all, gentlemen."

After the men had left, Radner relaxed in his chair and looked out his office window toward the desert plains below Cinder Mountain. Waves of heat filtered up from the desert floor, causing the ground to shimmer.

He was a thin, hyperactive man who wanted desperately to climb the academic ranks and into national prominence. The news of Olson's visit caused his stomach to churn and pump bile into his throat. Radner would just as soon be left alone to run the Primate Facility as he saw fit.

Born and raised in New England, he went to college at Yale on an academic scholarship then received his doctorate from Harvard University in genetics, with special emphasis on DNA sequencing. His parents ran a laundry in Queens, and he was always considered the school nerd, a fact that pushed him into a fair number of scrapes while in high school. His mother worried about his health constantly, a fact that caused him to become somewhat of a hypochondriac. His father, a heavy-set chain smoker who never shaved, did his best to keep food on the table. At suppertime, he wanted to know what Miles learned that day in school and chided him if he had nothing to report. Mother worked most of the day in the laundry but came home early to get supper on the table. They were poor but getting by.

Still, he excelled in his studies and soon obtained a degree in zoology, then at Harvard, his doctorate. He spent most days in class and most evenings washing dishes in a sorority house then to his small room for study. Awkward with the opposite sex, Radner had a few women friends but none that he ever loved or bedded. He was forever worried about his health, took a large number of vitamins, and used the Internet to research his symptoms.

Radner opened a cabinet, removed a bottle of twenty-one year-old Canadian whiskey, and poured a healthy measure into a snifter. Savoring the liquor's aroma as he swirled it in the glass, he reflected on an awkward moment while in graduate school with a girl he had invited to his apartment. He was eager to show her the latest draft of his dissertation while she was eager to show him her breasts. Which she did. He stood there, papers in hand, while she toyed with herself. As he was unable to say or do anything, she finally laughed and left, leaving him feeling stupid and childish. After that, he limited his discussions with women to public places, restaurants or the university.

It pained him, however, to know that he was not well-liked by the facility staff. At times in his past, he had attempted to change his personality, to become more outgoing, engaging, and smiling but after a few miserable weeks of putting on a false front, he lapsed back into his dour character. Radner didn't much like the man he was, but he was powerless to change his basic nature, so he opted, instead, to remain his usual timorous, devious self.

He didn't much like Harry Olson either, whom he believed was not an academic in the classic fashion, and had assumed leadership of their department solely on the strength of his friendship with Julius Kesler. Olson was younger than Radner and he thought Olson a johnny-come-lately whose reputation was based on his encounter with the Yeti, hardly a scientific endeavor. And Olson's tall, rugged, handsome looks put him off as well. The women at Cal Pacific all seemed to dote on him, a fact that irritated Radner further.

No, he wasn't looking forward to Dr. Olson's visit. He hoped it would go without a glitch and the man would leave as soon as he completed his inspection, for Radner wasn't in a mood to entertain his boss. He needed to review procedures and current experiments with Millie and Jimmy, his research assistants, and wrote himself a note to do it in the morning. Now he wanted to relax until dinner in the dining hall.

Chapter 4

D r. Bernard Wickingham sat alone in the paleontology lab, bent over a bone specimen of *Mammuthus primigenius*, the wooly mammoth. The appearance and behavior of this species were among the best studied of any prehistoric animal because of the discovery of frozen carcasses in Siberia and Alaska, as well as skeletons, teeth, stomach contents, dung, and depiction from life in prehistoric cave paintings. Mammoth remains had long been known in Asia before Europeans knew them in the seventeenth century. The origin of these remains was long a matter of debate and often explained as being remains of legendary creatures. Georges Cuvier identified the mammoth as an extinct species of elephant in 1796.

The woolly mammoth was roughly the same size as modern African elephants. Males weighed up to six tons while females averaged up to four tons. A newborn calf weighed about two hundred pounds. The woolly mammoth was well adapted to the cold environment during the last ice age. It was covered in fur, with an outer covering of long guard hairs and a shorter undercoat. The color of the coat varied from dark to light. The ears and tail were short to minimize frostbite and heat loss. It had long, curved tusks and four molars, which were replaced six times during the lifetime of an individual. Its behavior was similar to that of modern elephants, and it used its tusks and trunk for manipulating objects, fighting, and foraging. The diet of the woolly mammoth was grass and sedges. Individuals could reach the age of sixty. Its habitat was the mammoth steppe, which stretched across northern Eurasia and North America.

The woolly mammoth coexisted with early humans who used its bones and tusks for making art, tools, and dwellings, and the species was also hunted for food. It disappeared from its mainland range at the end of the Pleistocene Age, ten thousand years ago, most likely through climate change and consequent shrinkage of its habitat, hunting by humans, or a combination of the two. Isolated populations survived on St. Paul Island until around seven thousand years ago and Wrangel Island until four thousand years ago. After its extinction, humans continued using its ivory as a raw material, a tradition that continued today. It had been proposed that the species could be recreated through cloning, but this method was, as yet, infeasible because of the degraded state of the remaining genetic material.

Wickingham labored to extract enough material for DNA replication and analysis, an intricate and delicate process, subject to degradation even before putting it in the thermal cycler for the polymerase chain reaction. He hoped to map the mammoth's entire genome. His research led him to suspect that the full woolly mammoth genome was over four billion DNA bases, which was about the size of the modern-day African elephant's genome. Although the current dataset consisted of more than four-billion DNA bases, only 3.3 billion of them, slightly larger than the size of the human genome, currently could be assigned to the mammoth genome. Some of the remaining DNA bases might belong to the mammoth, but others could belong to other organisms, like bacteria and fungi from the surrounding environment that had contaminated the sample. His colleagues at the Broad Institute of MIT and Harvard used a draft version of the African elephant's genome to distinguish those sequences, that truly belong to the mammoth, from possible contaminants.

The lab door opened. Dixie entered and ambled over next to Wickingham and the counter on which the thermal cycler sat.

He looked up at her, a weak smile on his face. "Hello, Dr. Olson. Spying on me?"

He laughed and Dixie laughed along with him. "Why Bernard, how did you guess? Faculty always spy on each other, it's written into our job description."

Bernard loaded the thermal cycler and didn't respond.

"So, what's happening here?" she continued, observing him work.

"Well, Dr. Olson, you know I've been working on my wooly mammoth genome project all year. I getting ready to make the specimens so I can put them in the DNA analyzer."

"Bernard, we are fellow faculty here. You don't have to be so formal. Please call me Dixie." Wickingham nodded. "How is the project going?" she asked.

As if prompted into a lecture, Wickingham spelled out his project.

"Contaminants have been the main problem, most likely from bacteria growing in the bone itself. Trying to get a clean enough sample has been the hardest part of the project followed by sorting out any possible contaminants. But we are slowly making headway, Dixie. My colleagues at MIT and Harvard help out a lot with ideas. They previously sequenced the woolly mammoth's entire mitochondrial genome, which codes for only thirteen of the mammoth's roughly twenty thousand genes but is relatively easy to sequence because each of the mammoth's cells has many copies. In their most recent project, the MIT team sequenced the mammoth's nuclear genome, which codes for all the genetic factors that are responsible for the appearance of an organism.

"The two methods combined have yielded information about the evolution of the three known elephant species—the modern-day African and Indian elephants and the woolly mammoth. They found that woolly mammoths separated into two groups around two million years ago, and that these groups eventually became genetically distinct sub-populations. They also found that one of these sub-populations went extinct approximately forty-five thousand years ago, while another lived until after the last ice age, about ten thousand years ago. In addition, the team showed that woolly mammoths are more closely related to modern-day elephants than previously was believed."

"That's extremely fascinating, Bernard." Dixie sat in a chair near the cycler as it started. "Who is working on this with you?"

"Dr. Rawlings."

"Chloe Rawlings?"

"That's her."

Wickingham took a notebook and wrote. As he did he caught a glimpse of Dixie out of the corner of his eye. She possessed an alluring demeanor and smelled great. *Shouldn't come around young male faculty wearing that perfume*, he thought. Her blouse under her lab coat was cut low over the tops of her breasts and he caught himself gawking so he went back to his writing.

Dixie rose and headed for the door. She stopped, turned, smiled.

"If there is anything I can do to help, Bernard, let me know. We newbies have to stick together."

He glanced up from his work, nodded, then watched Dixie leave the lab. He did a slow burn. *Newbies? You're not a newbie. You're married to the chairman, so you've got it made. I'm stuck in this graduate lab for my research. A faculty member having to work in a student lab. How humiliating.*

Wickingham sat back, his eyes riveted in the door where Dixie earlier stood. The image of the tops of her breasts was fixed in his brain. A faint trace of her perfume still hung in the air.

Yes, that Harry sure is a lucky man.

ᏇᏬᏇᏬ

The office of the President of California Pacific University overlooked the small campus doted with cherry and dogwood trees. A large parking lot reserved for faculty and staff surrounded the Administration Building on three sides. Beyond the lot a large group of organized protesters paraded, many carrying large signs.

STOP THE CRUELTY!
DOWN WITH ANIMAL RESEARCH!
RELEASE THE ANIMALS!
END GHOULISH TINKERING!

Dr. Reginald Pauling, Cal Pacific's president, stepped away from the large window, a frown on his tanned face, and shook his head.

"I tell you, Harry," he said, taking a seat at his desk, "these protests grow louder, more frequent each month. I had the police run them off campus property but they have set up shop next to us. Not good publicity, I'm afraid."

"Well," Harry said, taking a sip of coffee from a Styrofoam cup, and smiled. "Science has weathered these storms before, Dr. Pauling. I'm sure we can again."

"They didn't start until you brought the Yeti back, and we housed them at the research facility. When word got out, these folks showed up."

"Who are they, do you know?"

"Some animal rights group called the Federation Against Animal Research."

"Not very original," Harry said, setting his coffee down and going to the window. Below, a group of around two dozen men and women marched with their placards. "They seem peaceful enough. What do you plan to do about them?"

"Nothing much I can do. At least not now. But when you visit the facility I want you to be able to report back that everything up there is being done by the book. I don't want to give these people any ammunition they can use against us. Understand, Harry?"

"Absolutely, Dr. Pauling. No one wants that more than I. And Dr. Radner is a top man. I'm confident he feels the same way."

"Good intentions notwithstanding, Harry, it is imperative that the animals be cared for properly and the experiments done in a humane fashion—like I said, by the book. If there is a problem up there and it should make the news, not only would it spell the end of the Primate Research Facility but it would seriously impair the university's endowments. And that we cannot afford."

Harry moved away from the window and returned to his chair. "I understand, fully, sir. All of our interests are at stake here."

"I'm glad you understand, Harry. You taking your wife?"

"Couldn't keep her away, Dr. Pauling. These are her

Yeti, you know. She worries and frets over them something fierce."

"She's a brave young woman." President Pauling stood, took Harry's arm, and escorted him to the office door. "Please give her my best. I look forward to your return."

❧❦❧

Bruce Drayton limped over to a golf cart, hopped in, and began a tour of the Primate Research Facility's outbuildings. A narrow gravel roadway connected the buildings and the cart's tires made a crunching sound as it rolled over the small rocks. Heading west, he passed by the main storage building where the facility's material was stored, from food for the primates, dry goods for the kitchen, unused lab equipment, batteries, tires, tools of various kinds, pallets of bottled water, lumber, and all types of electrical fixtures and wire. He opened the overhead door, switched on the large fluorescent lights, and looked around. All was quiet and in its place.

Closing the door, he resumed his tour and moved on to the fuel garage where drums of diesel and regular gasoline were stored. Next came the repair shop that housed a complete electronic repair laboratory and behind it a mechanics workspace. The metal building that housed the sixty-kilowatt diesel liquid-cooled generator stood across the roadway from the fuel garage. Drayton tested the generator every Friday at noon.

After assessing the buildings at the West end of the compound, Drayton reversed his course and headed to the dormitory behind the main building. A short breezeway connected the two buildings with an overhead wooden latticework that provided shade from the brutal summer sun. The dormitory had two floors, with the first containing Dr. Radner's apartment along with a kitchen and dining area. Also the first floor also housed a large TV/conference room, pool room, laundry facilities, and storage space. The second floor contained fifteen bedrooms and six bathrooms.

Drayton jumped from the cart and hurried into the dormitory for a quick inspection. Satisfied the staff were all working at their daily jobs and wearing their ID badges, he returned to the golf cart and drove the short distance to his office building at the front of the compound. A high chain-link fence surrounded the Primate Research Facility with video surveillance cameras mounted at certain strategic points along the perimeter. His office and apartment was situated in a small building behind a metal gate that served as the compound's entrance.

Inside, Drayton sat at his desk and glanced over the bank of video monitors connected to the security cameras that provided a view of the facility's perimeter at the top of Cinder Mountain. A bright sun beat down like a hot fire turning the mountain's surface into an oven. The air conditioning system seemed to work overtime, keeping the compound cool, especially the animal care units. The security chief took a notebook and checked off items as he had found them during his rounds, a daily log of conditions on the mountain facility. Everyone wore their ID badges and all seemed normal. The Primate Research Facility was secure.

Drayton was tall and lean with long arms and oversized hands. He possessed a penetrating gaze that caught most people off guard. He massaged his aching right leg, which pained him more than usual. The thigh still contained the bullet from a gun battle with a gang drug dealer while he was on the Houston police force. Because of the wound, he limped and was forced to take a disability retirement. After a disagreeable divorce, it was easy to obtain his private security license when he moved to California. He wished he could see his two adult children more often but with them living on the East Coast, the visits were few and far between.

He decided to locate the veterinarian, Dr. Gerald Siscom, and make some inspection rounds in the animal units and labs. He found the man, sitting with his feet on his desk at one end of the Animal Care Unit, chatting with one of the animal care technicians. He smiled as Drayton entered.

"Hello, Bruce," the veterinarian said and waved off the technician, who disappeared through a side door.

"Hello, Jerry. Got time to make a quick walk-through of your units and labs? I need to assure myself all is ready for this visit."

"No problem. We can do it now."

Dr. Siscom rose and retrieved a sterile white paper coverall, hair covering, and mask from a cabinet. He handed them to Drayton. "Put these on and we'll be off." The veterinarian also donned a coverall along with a hat and mask.

Once they were appropriately attired, Siscom led the way through the side door and down a short hallway lit by strong fluorescent lights. He opened a door into a room with several scrub sinks and a magnetic floor pad that would remove any loose particles from their shoes.

"We need to wash up before entering," Siscom said, and he began washing his hands with the antibacterial soap.

Finished washing, the veterinarian pushed a button on the wall next to a door. With a loud *whoosh* the door slid open and the pair entered an air lock, waited for the door to close behind them, then opened the front door, which opened with another *whoosh*.

Drayton limped into a brightly lit room filled with four

cages on each side of a short aisle. Inside each cage was a chimpanzee, each of whom promptly came alive with squawks at the arrival of the visitors. One of the chimps jumped onto the front of its cage and hung there, its large brown eyes peering down at Drayton as he walked by. A nauseating aroma, a mixture of animal chow, animal odor, and urine greeted the security chief, pushing his rolling stomach into his throat. At the end of the aisle, they entered another air lock then passed into another animal care unit.

Immediately, Drayton sensed it was a different place.

The two cages were much larger than those belonging to the chimps, the bars different—larger, stronger—and the room was not as brightly lit. The temperature of the unit was much lower, in fact, downright cold. Drayton wished he had brought a sweater.

It was the unit that housed the Yeti.

In each cage paced a large, hairy creature, their large red eyes fixed on the pair. A bolt of anxiety shot through Drayton as he gazed up at the gigantic beasts. They snarled when the men entered the unit.

At one end of the unit a young woman in a white lab coat sat at a small desk, writing. Dr. Siscom approached her as Drayton followed.

"Millie," he said. "How are you"

Millie Harbaum was one of two graduate research assistants spending a year at the facility. She was plump with dark Italian features, long slender fingers, and green eyes that sparkled at Siscom's approach.

"Fine, Dr. Siscom, fine. I see you brought the Gestapo with you."

Drayton placed a hand over his heart and frowned. "Stop it, Miss Harbaum. You're killing me," he said.

Millie laughed, her head tossed back. Her eyes sparkled. "Just kidding, *mein furher*."

"Millie, please," Drayton pleaded.

"All right, Mr. Drayton. I'll ease up for now. What do I owe the honor of this visit from our security chief?"

"Dr. Olson is paying us a visit sometime in the next few days so I'm making some last minute rounds. Everything shipshape here, Millie?"

"Of course it is. Like always."

"Can you take us through the labs, please," Siscom asked. "Just a quick walk-through will do. And prepare yourself—Radner will come through later."

"That little weasel?" Millie said. "Jesus, the man gives me the creeps."

"Millie!" Siscom said. "He is our director. A little respect is due."

"I dunno," Millie said. "I think we need to do a genetic analysis on the man. Not sure he's human. Gosh, what if we found otherwise?"

Millie laughed and led the men through an air lock and to the other labs in the facility.

Chapter 5

Harry sat in Dr. Chloe Rawling's office that was just off her DNA laboratory and was separated from it by a bank of floor-to-ceiling windows. From her desk, the head of Cal Pacific's DNA lab could look out over the myriad of machines and computers, humming away, doing genetic analysis of all kinds for many different faculty. She was tall, had blonde hair that fell in loose curls on her shoulders, and wore wire-rimmed glasses. Harry always thought she was an attractive woman and remembered Professor telling him, much to his dismay, that she was married to her lab. Today, she wore khaki slacks and a pale blue silk blouse. No perfume that he could tell.

"Care for a cup of coffee, Dr. Olson?" she said, as she poured a cup from a carafe on her desk.

"So now I'm Dr. Olson, Chloe? It was Harry, remember, when I worked for Professor. And, thanks, I'd love some coffee."

Dr. Rawlings handed Harry the Styrofoam cup, poured another one, then sat at her desk, smiled, and nodded. "Fine, Harry. That seems quite a while ago, doesn't it? Professor Kesler's death happened what, six months ago? Ages."

Harry nodded. "Yes, about that. I miss him, Chloe. I do miss him."

"Yes, he was a great friend. We used to eat our lunch together when he first came to Cal Pacific. Did you know that? You did? Then he began eating in his office and rarely ventured into the faculty cafeteria so I saw less of him the last few years."

"I know he held you in high esteem," Harry said.

"It's nice to hear. The last lunch we had together was when he was doing the DNA analysis in some of the bones you uncovered during your first Mongolia expedition. A long time ago."

Harry set his coffee on the desk and shifted his weight in his chair. "I came to ask if you knew anything about the Yeti genome, Chloe. Professor had some papers suggesting that its genome had been sequenced. Know anything about that?"

Dr. Rawlings shook her head. "Nothing much. I know they're working on it up at the Primate Facility. But they have their own sequencers and analyzers there, so I wouldn't necessarily know anything. They wouldn't keep me informed as to their progress. What were in his papers?"

"Just that the Yeti genome had been sequenced and that it, possibly, was closely related to modern humans. Or some distant hominid. The papers were vague on most points."

Dr. Rawlings took a sip of her coffee and thought for a moment. "If the complete Yeti genome has been sequenced—which would be a major achievement in its own right, as in lining up all the individual sequences in their proper order—but if it has, I seriously doubt anyone could have done the comparative analysis with the human genome in the short length of time the Yeti have been at the facility. It takes a lot of hard, complicated work to sort through both genomes, comparing the sequences to each other."

"Computers would help, right?" Harry said.

"Yes, computers would be invaluable, but it still takes time. We're talking three billion base pairs, Harry. It would take time to sort through them all. Then one has to double check the substitutions and make sure they're accurate. Quite a task."

"It would be, yes."

"In recent months, numerous DNA studies of ancient humans have all converged on one conclusion—Neanderthals and Homo sapiens interbred. Although to scientists this may appear unsurprising or even obvious, we must remember that until fairly recently the predominant scientific theory was that Neanderthals and Homo sapiens never came in contact with each other, let alone interbred. Science is only beginning to dispel the myth that Neanderthals were primitive cave men. But for some, the idea that up to twenty percent of Neanderthal genes are still present in the human race is still very hard to swallow. However, a new study, which utilized a more superior method of testing, leaves little room for doubt—many human beings alive today are the product of Neanderthal and Homo sapiens interbreeding."

"I am only vaguely familiar with the science behind the theory," Harry said, taking a swallow of coffee, intrigued by Dr. Rawling's story.

"The new research recently published has utilized a technique that involves partitioning genomes into short blocks to calculate the statistical likelihood of distant or recent interbreeding and tracing back the biological ties that exist between humans and Neanderthals. The method can more confidently detect the genetic signatures of interbreeding than previous approaches, and has further enabled the researchers to distinguish between two possible

scenarios—the first is that Neanderthals occasionally interbred with modern humans after they migrated out of
Africa, the second is that the humans who left Africa
evolved from the same ancestral subpopulation that had
previously given rise to Neanderthals."

"So the Yeti data may take time to unravel?" Harry
said.

"In summary, Harry, it's similar to the work done with
Neanderthal DNA and its genome, which took years to
unravel. We are still debating their relationship with
modern humans."

"Yes, I can see that it's complicated. Nothing is ever
simple when it comes to human evolution. And you know
nothing of Kesler's involvement in any of this?"

"No. Wish I could be of more help."

Harry sat silent for a long moment.

"Another area of intense research, Harry, is the field of
endogenous retroviruses, ERVs for short. And they may
play a pivotal role in shedding light on this subject."

"Endogenous what?" Harry said, leaning forward in
his chair.

"Endogenous retroviruses. Endogenous retroviruses
are endogenous viral elements in the genome that closely
resemble and can be derived from retroviruses. They are
abundant in the genomes of jawed vertebrates and they
occupy up to eight percent of the human genome. Endogenous retroviruses provide yet another example of molecular sequence evidence for universal common descent.
Endogenous retroviruses are molecular remnants of a past
parasitic viral infection. Occasionally, copies of a retrovirus genome are found in its host's genome, and these retroviral gene copies are called endogenous retroviral sequences. Retroviruses, like the AIDS virus or HTLV1,
which causes a form of leukemia, make a DNA copy of
their own viral genome and insert it into their host's ge-

nome. If this happens to a germ line cell, for example, the sperm or egg cells, the retroviral DNA will be inherited by descendants of the host. Again, this process is rare and fairly random, so finding retrogenes in identical chromosomal positions of two different species indicates common ancestry."

"Wow," Harry said. "That's amazing."

"Yes," Chloe said, smiling. "And if your scientists can show that the Yeti genome contains ERVs exactly as in humans, well…" Her voice trailed off.

"The results would be earth-shattering," Harry said.

"Revolutionary."

The two sat in silence for a while, contemplating the possibilities, then Harry rose. "Well, I won't take up any more of your time, Chloe. I know you have important work to do."

"How is married life treating you?" she said, standing, then escorting Harry to the door.

"Oh fine," he said. "Some night, Dixie and I need to have you down to dinner. It would be great fun."

"Sounds great. I'll look forward to it."

"By the way," Harry said, "how is Bernard Wickingham to work with? I know you're both collaborating on a project."

Dr. Rawlings rolled her eyes and smirked. "Thinks he's God's gift to women," she said.

҂ӭҀ

Millie Harbaum was alone in the Animal Care Unit observing the female Yeti. Among her many duties was the weekly drawing of blood samples for chemical analysis and genetic research. The many blood tests were done in order ensure that the female, whom she had named Sasha, remained in good health and free of disease. Each week her blood was taken, chemistries performed along with cultures, both bacterial and fungal. Jimmy performed the same duties on Bentu, his male Yeti.

Earlier in the day, Millie had entered Sasha's cage after Dr. Siscom tranquilized her and drew the blood sample into a large syringe. The beast had lain immobile in the cage while Millie stuck the large-bore needle into her neck vein. Afterward, Millie had sat with Sasha for a few moments, stroking her massive head. Sasha's tongue partially protruded as Millie listened to her labored, rhythmical breathing. With care, she touched the long, stained fangs, teeth she knew could rip one apart without much effort. Millie had grown accustomed to Sasha's odor, a mixture of foul body perspiration and decaying food. It no longer caused her stomach to do summersaults each time she entered the unit.

Something about Sasha drew Millie close to her. Maybe it was the daily routine, or the times spent in the cage with her, or the effect the caressing had on the graduate assistant, but Millie felt a certain communion with the great creature. Each time she entered the cage, she did so with pounding heart but soon it gave way to a longing, a feeling of desperation, of empathy for the animal confined in the small enclosure. As a young girl, Millie both loved and despised zoos, feeling sorry for the many animals confined in their small spaces.

And as strange as it seemed, Millie felt Sasha, in her own way, reciprocated those feelings. That she understood Millie had grown to love her. In fact, Millie knew that the creature knew she had a friend in the research facility. It would be hard to leave Sasha when her time at the compound was up.

Jimmy Winkleman, on the other hand, appeared to be just putting in his time. At least that was the way it appeared to Millie. Besides being curt and irritable, he was gruff with Bentu, spoke to the animal in harsh tones, handled his sedated form with crude movements, and complained daily of the unit's smell. When not tranquilized, Bentu either sat in a far corner of his cage, staring at Jimmy through glowing eyes, or paced up and down at the cage's front, never taking his eyes off the assistant. Whereas Sasha had stopped with her incessant growling and snarling, Bentu howled and snarled all day long and never calmed down after Jimmy's arrival. Millie was convinced it was the way Jimmy treated the creature.

Her mother was Italian while her father came from English stock. John Harbaum was a dentist in Baltimore and had wanted Millie to follow his career path. But spending all day in someone's mouth didn't seem much of a way to occupy one's time, even if the income was satisfactory. Seeing the Indiana Jones movies convinced her she wanted to become an archeologist so she enrolled in college with that as her plan. But a professor talked her out of it, maintaining there were no jobs and the pay was dismal. So, she got her degree in history and worked for a while for the State of California. But the dream of living an archeologist's life didn't die, and she managed a scholarship at California Pacific University, studying first under Dr. Kesler then Dr. Harry Olson. When the Yeti had been captured and returned to Nevada, it was announced that two graduate assistant fellowships were being offered to live at the Primate Research Facility for a year and help study the creatures. She applied and was accepted and soon found herself atop Cinder Mountain and face to face with the Yeti.

She'd had the usual love affairs of high school and college girls but no one boy ever made it the top of her list of requirements for a long-term relationship. Once at Cal Pacific, she devoted her time to her studies with only an occasional date, usually with an undergraduate she met in lab. Now, at the research facility, there were no eligible men, which didn't matter as she was consumed by her work.

Millie hadn't expected to bond in such a way with Sasha. Observing the way Jimmy interacted with Bentu, she couldn't understand his cold detachment that translated into his rough handling of the animal. Initially, she thought the differences in behavior was due to Bentu's male gender but the more she observed, the more she realized it was due to the way Jimmy treated him. She decided she was only responsible for her own actions and put the matter out of her mind. She had work to do.

❧❧❧

The lights were off in the Animal Care Unit. The chimps were sleeping, having been fed by the technicians several hours earlier. It was quiet in the Yeti unit as well. Sasha slept in a far corner of her cage, rolled on her side, her heavy breathing punctuating the quiet in a regular rhythm. Millie had left earlier in the evening, after watching the creature eat her evening meal.

Bentu was different story. He sat in the center of his cage, panting, nostrils flaring, his red eyes glowing like the dying embers of a campfire. His breathing, although quiet, was quick, frenetic. The creature sat and rocked his giant frame back and forth, never stopping. And those eyes, embedded in a massive skull under a furrowed brow, stared straight ahead. He glared at the front of his cage, never looking to either side, seemingly transfixed on some invisible object just beyond.

The only sound in the Animal Care Unit, other than the Yeti's breathing, was that of the air-conditioning whirring overhead. The automated thermostat had lowered the ambient temperature to a cold forty-five degrees to facilitate the animal's sleeping, but it had no effect on Bentu. He continued to sit, rock, and stare out the front of his cage.

Near midnight, Bentu stood, pulled his massive frame to his full height—which was well over eight feet—and sauntered to the front of his cage. For a long time, he stood immobile, still staring out at an invisible object beyond, his warm breath forming a cloud in the frigid temperature of the unit. His lips were pulled tight against his teeth, baring two enormous canines—long, sharp, and yellow. His long, shaggy fur was a cinnamon brown color, and its stench, along with his female companion's, filled the unit.

Bentu grabbed the bars of his cage with huge, burly hands whose fingers were tipped with needlepoint claws. Standing there, clutching the bars, he paused, as if contemplating what he would do next, then turned his head upward toward the ceiling. His eyes narrowed to slits and he began to rattle the cage. Slowly at first, he continued his rattling, becoming more forceful with each passing minute until the cage rocked and shook in a violent manner. The noise was deafening.

Bentu opened his giant maw and uttered a shattering shriek that pierced the otherwise quiet of the Animal Care Unit. The horrific noise echoed down the hallway, through the building, and finally, out into the cool night of Cinder Mountain.

Chapter 6

D r. Miles Radner strode into the Animal Care Unit dressed in sterile coveralls, hat, and mask, and nodded to Millie and Jimmy who were sitting at their desks at the far end of the unit. Each was writing in a logbook but stopped at Radner's approach.

"Well, here are my two young graduate assistants, eagerly going about their work," Radner said. "How are you both today?"

"Just fine, Dr. Radner," Jimmy said, his forehead becoming a frown.

"Peachy," Millie said, the corners of her eyes wrinkling, as if she was smiling behind her mask.

That was the problem with masks, thought Radner. Difficult to read facial expressions and catch someone being less than truthful.

"I've come to see how the scientific part of the facility is faring in preparation for Dr. Olson's visit in a few days. Any problems here?"

The Yeti were quiet in their cages, a relief to Radner, for he was uncomfortable in the creatures' presence. Something about their immense size and snarling features made him uneasy. Along with the odor. He was glad he didn't have to come here often. Happy to accept whatever honors and discoveries might accrue to him as director of the Primate Research Facility, he nonetheless limited his time in the unit to only that which was absolutely necessary.

"Nothing out of the ordinary, Dr. Radner," Millie said, closing her logbook. "Our research is progressing along."

"At the usual snail's pace," Jimmy added.

"I understand," Radner said. "When I was at Harvard, I often complained that things didn't move along faster. But such is the nature of scientific progress."

He was aware of Jimmy's hesitancy in his presence. The boy was obviously intimidated by authority, unlike his colleague, Millie, who seemed unaffected by anything. In fact, it was Radner who felt uncomfortable around the woman. She hid her thoughts well. He prided himself in his ability to read people, to look into their eyes and discern what lay behind them but Millie's eyes were different. Enigmatic. Unfathomable.

"The Yeti well behaved, Millie?" he said.

"Most of the time, Doctor," she said, the wrinkles around her eyes twitching ever so slightly.

"Yes," Jimmy added, "but mine, I call him Bentu, is a pain. I don't think he likes being confined to a cage."

"No, I suspect not," said Radner.

"He acts out a lot," Jimmy continued. "Rocking, rattling his cage, that sort of thing."

"Animal care protocols being followed? Logbooks up to date?"

Millie pushed a piece of gum into her mouth and began chewing. "We leave most of their care to the technicians," she said between chews. "But I believe they're doing everything by the book, Dr. Radner."

"Well, fine," Radner said. "By the way, there will be a small reception when Dr. Olson arrives, and all the staff are invited, including you both."

"Thank you, sir," Jimmy said.

Radner left the unit, thankful to be out of the coveralls and away from the Yeti.

⟢⟢⟢

Harry and Dixie stepped off the plane in Reno, Nevada, and walked down the jet way and into the large terminal building. The Reno-Tahoe International Airport terminal was an expansive two-story affair nestled against low rolling hills. Harry led Dixie down the escalator and past a bank of slot machines to the baggage claim area where Dr. Radner waited. After shaking hands, Radner escorted the couple to the parking structure and his parked car.

"Here, Harry," he said, "throw your bags in the back." He opened the rear hatch of his full-sized SUV, placed Dixie's bag inside, and waited for Harry to do the same with his. "I'm glad you two decided to stay overnight. It will give you a chance to see everything...shall we say?...up close."

Harry climbed in the front passenger seat while Dixie buckled herself into the one behind her husband. Radner started the car and headed toward Interstate 80.

"Really, Miles," Harry said as they were on the highway heading in a northeasterly direction. "I'm not here on an inspection tour. I don't want you or the staff to feel that I am. I'm personally interested in the progress of the Yeti research and the genome sequencing. I know you run a top-notch facility, so don't feel pressured by my coming."

"Well, I certainly wasn't apprised of the nature of your visit," Radner said. His tone had a certain disparaging quality to it. "So. We've planned a small reception and a dinner tonight. I hope you and Dixie don't mind—the staff wanted to meet you both. After all, the Yeti wouldn't be here at all if not for you." He let out a nervous laugh.

"It's fine, Miles. I would like to speak with the scientists as soon as we arrive, if that is agreeable."

"Not a problem," Radner replied.

As the SUV sped toward Elko County and Cinder Mountain, Harry relaxed in the plush seat and studied Radner. The man seemed preoccupied about something. He appeared nervous, fidgety, and kept glancing into the rearview mirror at Dixie. He was a strange little man, Harry thought. His narrow eyes and weak chin gave him a weasel-like appearance but the man wore tailor-made suits. It was an odd combination, Harry thought. Radner's wire-framed glasses had a habit of sliding down a concave shaped nose forcing him to periodically push them back.

Dixie had tried a few times to chat with Radner but the man didn't want to talk with her. He was intent on extolling the virtues and wonderful work of the Primate Research Facility, as if he were making a sales pitch to a potential big money donor.

The rocking of the vehicle caused Harry's mind to drift into a lazy fog, and he only barely listened to Radner's monotone voice. His attention snapped into focus when Radner's voice escalated.

"...the Yeti research," the facility director was saying, "is progressing steadily and the animals are in fine health. No infectious outbreaks to date. Dr. Siscom works hard to keep it that way."

They traveled on through arid desert country and, at the junction of State Highway 786, they stopped for gas and to use the restroom. Dixie purchased a soda and Harry bought a coffee. Radner didn't get anything.

The sun was on its downward arc when Radner

steered the SUV off 786 and onto a narrow unmarked asphalt road that was filled with potholes. Since leaving the Interstate the landscape had become more desolate with only an occasional Joshua tree or sagebrush seen. Mostly, Harry was reminded that the sand and rock countryside looked like the moon's surface. And there wasn't a single animal or varmint that he could see.

"From here the road gets a little rougher," Radner said, steering a weaving path to avoid the larger holes. But the smaller ones he couldn't miss, turning the ride into a gut-wrenching one.

"Can't the county do something about this road?" Dixie asked between jolts. "I think my fillings are coming loose."

Harry and Radner laughed at her joke, and Harry patted her arm that clutched the back of his headrest.

"Don't worry," Radner said, smiling. "It gets worse up ahead."

As the car bumped along a gradual curve to the northwest, they came to a sign at the side of the road.

PRIMATE RESEARCH FACILITY
CALIFORNIA PACIFIC UNIVERSITY
PRIVATE PROPERTY
NO UNAUTHORIZED ADMITTANCE

An aged gate prevented access to a narrow dirt and gravel road that took off from the sign, leading back northeast. In the near distance loomed a rugged mountain with what looked like a winding path carved in its side. Harry jumped out, opened the gate, and, after Radner drove through, closed it, and got back in the SUV.

"Here is where it gets dicey," Radner said. "Need four-wheel drive from here to the research compound. But of course, you both have been here before."

"And each time, Miles, seems like a new experience. I can't say I look forward to this part of the drive," Harry said, grabbing the dash for security.

Radner continued over the rutted road with Harry and Dixie bouncing in their seats. Harry rolled his window down and savored the fresh sage-scented breeze that wafted into the car. The air was noticeably cooler, and he remembered they had been slowly gaining altitude since leaving Reno.

"What wild country," Dixie said. "Reminds me a little of the Mongolian steppes."

"It does," Harry said. "Isn't there old Indian ruins around here somewhere? I think I remember it from a previous visit."

"Yes," Radner said. "It is over on the other side of the mountain. A group of ancient stucco ruins at its foot. They were Paiute, I believe."

"How old are the ruins?" Dixie asked.

"Not really sure, Dixie," Radner replied. "This land was part of a large reservation until the tribe auctioned it off and the government bought it. As you know, ten years ago the university acquired this property, about six hundred acres."

"I read," Dixie said, " that humans have been in this geographic region called the Great Basin for at least ten thousand years. Paleo-Indians were the first inhabitants, followed by the four contemporary tribes, the Washoe, Northern Paiute, Southern Paiute, and Western Shoshone. The cultures of these great Nations have no separation between the sacred and the ordinary in their lives. Life is spiritual and fluid, with a sense of balance, harmony, beauty, and completeness."

"It was originally going to be a faculty retreat but thanks to Professor Kesler's influence and lobbying, he convinced the board of trustees to build the primate center instead." Harry felt a sense of pride as he talked about his former teacher and friend. "Miles, how is the road up the mountain? I remember last time it was extremely primitive."

"It's not bad, unless we get a torrential rain. Then it's impassible for days. That's why we are self-sufficient up here. Got a stock of food and water in case the cistern goes dry and we can't get groceries. But, we have all the comforts of home. Don't you remember, Harry?"

"Of course, but it's always an adventure, to be sure."

"In 1859," Radner said, "only miles from the Carson Valley trail used by so many Forty-Niners a decade earlier, came the fabled Comstock Lode. The rush to the Comstock in 1859 virtually shut down the mines of California. A new era dawned, scientifically, economically, and socially. By the late 1850s, thousands of gold seekers were doubling back from California, through the Western territories. Many were professional prospectors by now, roving from one small strike to the next. Others belonged to a new wave of novices, fleeing a severe financial depression back East. But they didn't find so much gold as silver. The blasted blue stuff as they called it, was actually a fabulous silver strike, the legendary Comstock Lode, probably the greatest single mineral strike in history. During the next year, seventeen thousand people swarmed into the Washoe region of what became the state of Nevada."

The road then began an upward climb so Radner put the SUV into a lower gear. With their speed slowed to a crawl, Harry watched as the plain became smaller below them. The mountain was forested with western juniper, lodge pole pine, aspen, and white bark pine. The soil was rocky and there were large granite outcroppings close to the narrow road. Up a serpentine course they climbed, negotiating numerous switchbacks until near the top of

Cinder Mountain the road leveled out. The final approach to the facility took them over a wooden bridge that spanned a fast moving stream. Harry watched its cascading torrents tumble over rocks and boulders on its way to the plain below.

Few landscapes in the United States were lonelier than that of northern Nevada. Towns—remote outposts connected by endless, thin ribbons of highway—were named for what miners used to pull out of the ground: Coaldale, Silverpeak, Goldfield. But the mining industry in places like Elko County had largely disappeared and, with it, the towns it gave birth to. Those, that weren't ghost towns already, clung precariously to life, burned-out and abandoned structures at their margins creeping inexorably toward the center like some scabrous and fatal disease. For many, it was just a matter of time. Even those hamlets that still had a few hundred people living in them were sometimes left off state road maps.

It was this area that Cal Pacific chose to house its Primate Research Facility and, when the Cinder Mountain land came available, the university snatched it up. Dr. Kesler saw what a great location Cinder Mountain was for a center whose aim was genetic research into hominid evolution. Under his influence and guidance, the primate facility took shape, using big money donors, and now it produced exciting results. Far away from any notable population center, the scientists could carry on their work in relative peace and security.

New research directions and technologies had increased the use of new experimental species. Dr. Kesler insisted on the introduction of transgenic mice, now widely used in genomic-based research across all therapeutic areas. This, he argued, would result in higher-density housing types of caging in order to run more studies in shorter time periods, thus generating a higher level of production. He led the way with initiatives to promote the psychological wellbeing of animals of all species. Providing for such natural behaviors as exercise, opportunities for group interactions, and nesting and foraging, the primate facility was developing new ideas to replace more stressful traditional housing paradigms.

Radner stopped the SUV at a gate. A man exited a small office and ambled to the driver's window. Radner rolled his window down and produced his ID.

"Bruce, I have Dr. Olson and his wife, Dr. Olson."

Drayton limped to the passenger side of the vehicle and Harry's open window.

"Afternoon, Doctor. I remember you and your wife from a previous visit. Do you have any ID on you?"

Harry chuckled and showed the man his Cal Pacific ID. Dixie stuck hers out the window.

"Fine, Doctors. Just a minute, and I'll open the gate."

"I like the security, Miles," Harry said as they drove through the gate.

The remark produced a smile on Radner's lips.

At the entrance to the main building a woman in a white lab coat opened Harry's door, then Dixie's. Once they were both out of the SUV she held out her hand. "I'm Millie Harbaum," she said smiling, green eyes sparkling. "I'm one of your research assistants here at the facility."

"Of course, Millie," Dixie said in a gay tone. "I remember you. Glad to see you again."

Millie stepped forward and took their bags. "I'll get you settled in the dormitory. You can come over whenever you feel like it."

"Thanks, Millie," Harry said, as she toted their bags into the building.

After the formalities of meeting the staff, Harry had the scientists gather in the small conference room next to

Radner's office. Coffee and soft drinks arrived and were placed on a buffet next to the oval dark-stained table. When everyone was seated, Radner introduced Harry and Dixie then went around the table introducing the scientists.

When he was finished, he turned the meeting over to Harry.

It was a disparate group at the conference table, and Harry marveled at the differences among his staff. From two young students to an older man, the group reflected the age diversity that President Pauling had worked hard to achieve at the university. Seeing scientists like these, gathered to discuss their work, sent a wave of nostalgia through him. He missed the day-to-day work of researching a problem.

"Thank you, Dr. Radner," he began. "I look forward to a brief tour of the facility tomorrow morning, but I want you'll to know that I'm not here for an inspection. I'm here on a scientific mission. I need an update on the current state of primate research you all are doing. So, if you will humor me, I would like to go around the table and have each of you give a brief synopsis of your work and results, if any. Let's start with you, here on my left."

A man in his fifties cleared his throat then explained his research using chimpanzees. "I'm Henry Billis," he began. "In my lab, we're taking noncoding segments of the chimp's DNA and are attempting to uncover their functions. Noncoding DNA are sequences of DNA that do not encode protein sequences but can be transcribed to produce important regulatory molecules. Even though they were not coding a gene they still might provide a function in the animal's physiology. Some might provide help in RNA transcription. The amount of noncoding DNA varies greatly among species. For example, over 98% of the human genome is noncoding DNA, while only about 2% of a typical bacterial genome is noncoding DNA."

"Thank you, Henry," Harry said. "Sounds interesting." He nodded to the white-haired man next to Billis. "And you, Felix?"

"Yes," the man said. "I am Felix Chekhov. My team is working with a retrovirus that was thought to be dormant in chimpanzees. A dormant gene is one that is present but inactive. An example of this would be when a baby is conceived by a blue eyed and brown eyed parent. The child will have brown eyes. This is because the brown eyed gene is dominant and the blue eyed gene will lay dormant. We are hoping to develop a technique to change a single letter of DNA in chimp red blood cells, triggering them to produce more oxygen-carrying hemoglobin. The technique could lead to new treatments for sickle cell anemia and other life-threatening blood disorders. And the best part is, it would do so by activating a naturally occurring gene that's normally dormant after birth."

"Well, Felix, that certainly sounds like it has far-reaching implications. Next, please."

A man in a starched lab coat talked about his work to isolate a bacteria known to be carried by chimps but deadly in humans. Chimpanzees from African sanctuaries carry drug-resistant, human-associated strains of the bacteria *Staphlyococcus aureus*, a pathogen that the infected chimpanzees could spread to endangered wild ape populations if they were reintroduced to their natural habitat. "Drug-resistant strains of *S. aureus* are a major cause of deaths worldwide," he said.

Millie and Jimmy both related their work on the Yeti genome. Millie described how, two months earlier, they had successfully sequenced the entire genome using Sasha's blood. Now they were beginning the arduous task of comparing the genome to the human genome.

This was the information Harry sought. He pressed her with questions. "According to papers in Dr. Kesler's possession, he thought the Yeti genome differed from the human by a mere thirty-five substitutions. Is this correct?"

"Well, Dr. Olson," Millie said, "those numbers were based on an initial computer run and so are preliminary in nature."

"They aren't considered hard data?" Harry said.

"Preliminary, like I said," Millie responded. "Much more work must be done to confirm and validate those initial results. For all we know, Dr. Olson, the Yeti might only be a far, far, distant relative to modern humans."

"Or it could turn out to be a very close cousin, right?" Radner said, as though he was leading a witness in a courtroom drama.

"Miles, you know we can't speculate on what the data will show." Harry smiled and leaned back in his chair, providing more space between him and the facility director. "We'll just let the results take us wherever it will."

"Of course," Radner said. "Just having a little fun."

Later, after the meeting was over, Harry and Dixie showered and changed then went to the dining hall were the promised reception was in full swing. On the way Dixie was more than animated.

"'*Just having a little fun*,' he said. Can you believe it, Harry? The man is a demeaning creep. I've said it before and I'll say it again—I don't see what Professor saw in the man when he hired him."

"Yes, honey, I'm sure you're right. But let's forget it now and just enjoy ourselves. These folks have put on this reception just for us."

Dixie smiled and took her husband's arm as they entered the dining hall.

Chapter 7

Deep in the remote jungles of Peru, Rupert Lowell was up to his waist in an unnamed muddy river. He fought against the current as he struggled for the shore that seemed to get farther away with each passing minute. His legs felt as if they were shod with lead boots, making it near impossible for Lowell to put one foot in front of the other. The strong current pushed him farther away from the safety of the shoreline where his porters watched with frightened looks.

As he continued to struggle against the push of water, Lowell wondered what on earth had possessed him to come to this mountainous jungle. The hope of gold was one thing, but his quest for notoriety was quite another. For him, the remote possibility of locating the lost Inca city of Paititi had been the overwhelming consuming motivation in mounting the small expedition. Weeks earlier, he left Cusco with an ancient map and searched valley after valley for the lost city. Legend had it that Paititi was where the last of the Inca hid their vast treasure of gold and jewels before finally succumbing to the Spanish invaders.

But he was beginning to think the city was nothing more than legend, spawned by tales told down through generations. Nothing more than myth, a gossamer story of fabulous wealth. He was tired, tired down to his soul, and needed rest. During his searching, he fell ill with a shaking fever, endured serious cuts and bruises, and had to be treated for an insidious fungal skin infection. He was ready to return to the States.

Amidst much hollering and jeering, one of his porters threw him a rope but it fell short, swept away by the swift water. The porter retrieved the line while Rupert continued to battle the current, struggling to remain upright and not be hurtled downstream. After agonizing minutes, the porter threw him the rope again. This time he grabbed it, tied it around his waist. Using tremendous effort, they pulled him through the current to the shore and safety, where he collapsed at water's edge, his lungs heaving and burning. He rolled onto his back, allowing his pulse to slow, and stared up at a cloudless, azure sky while his porters gathered around him, jabbering wildly in Spanish and Quechua.

Nash Yarak, Lowell's assistant and expedition leader, helped him to a sitting position, handed him a water bottle. Lowell took a gulp and spat it onto the sand then took another longer drink. His assistant offered him a blanket that he waved away.

"Damn, boss," Yarak said, "you almost didn't make it. And you look all in."

"I was about done for, Nash. Another few minutes, and I would have been washed downriver and drowned, in all likelihood. Piranha bait. Thank god there were none of those infernal caiman around. Thanks for getting that rope to me. The men hauled me in just in time, I'm afraid."

Lowell struggled to his feet and stumbled to the nearest burro. Yarak helped him aboard the animal, and the porters pushed along a dense jungle trail to their campsite. The hot sun dried Lowell's clothes and, soon, he was perspiring freely. After collapsing in a canvas chair, he ate and refreshed himself and watched the sun sink behind a wooded ridge of the Andes. The sky was suffused with orange and magenta hues that, in time, faded to a deep purple. As the afternoon heat dissipated and the temperature began to drop, Lowell called Yarak to sit beside him.

"Nash, we're done here. We were nearing the end, anyway, so let's call it finished. We've been unable to locate anything that remotely might lead us to Paititi, and I'm beginning to think it's all a fable. So, it's back to the States for us. I miss LA."

"All right, Mr. Lowell, I'll tell the porters, and we can get an early start in the morning. Try and get a good rest tonight."

"I need a hot shower and a cold beer, my friend."

Yarak smiled. "I thought you loved these excursions, Mr. Lowell. Getting old?"

"Sometimes I wonder. No, this wretched heat and humidity saps my strength and reserve. Our next field expedition will be in more tolerable climate."

"Well, goodnight, sir," Yarak said and stood. "I need to check on the porters before hitting the sack."

Rupert Lowell sat and watched the purple sky turn black then stumbled into his tent and into a deep sleep.

ഇൗരൗ

From his office on Empire Avenue in Burbank, California, Rupert Lowell gazed out at the verdant Verdugo Mountains to the east and watched a bird soar in the warm air thermals moving up the slopes. In the month since returning from Peru, he had gained ten pounds, bought two companies, sold one, and added another

250,000 dollars to his millions. Life had been good since returning home.

Lowell's passion was making money, and the more money he made, the happier he was, for he enjoyed the finer things that money brought him—Italian silk suits, handmade ties, a luxury townhouse in Town Center Burbank, an Astin Martin D89 Coupe, and a Gulfstream G550 corporate jet with his own flight crew. Never married, Lowell preferred to play the field with what he called serial monogamy. He would date a woman for a few months then move on to another. It was a habit with him.

Rupert Lowell was a short man. His need to win, at all costs, was a character flaw he learned from a psychiatrist when he underwent analysis during his thirty-fifth year. Early in his life, he realized he fumbled at sports, so he turned his interests and energies toward other endeavors. He had dreams of becoming an NBA star but his lack of height buried that dream. After college, he found he had a knack for making money, that it came easy for him. His niche was electronics—buying companies that made computer, aviation, and military components. Over the years, his fortunes grew, first doubling, then tripling, then quadrupling, until his personal fortune ranked him as one of the richest men in America. He was on the cover of *Forbes* and *Time*, interviewed on the major networks, counseled presidents. He traveled the world, ingratiating himself with the rich and powerful movers and shakers in business and politics.

His physical stature no longer mattered to him, was no longer an issue in his business dealings. Rupert Lowell was a big man.

He possessed a pale and watery skin whose veins were visible as thin blue lines. His thin face sported numerous scars from a bad case of youthful acne, which he tried to hide with a close-cropped beard of salt and pepper gray.

A certain penchant took root in Lowell's soul since making it big, one that nearly got him killed in Peru. He was fascinated with lost, hidden treasures, and he searched ancient books and manuscripts for possible places to mount an expedition. His latest search for the Inca city of Paititi was an example of his passion. Lowell journeyed to the Amazon, searched for the Lost Dutchman Mine in the Arizona Superstition Mountains, and dove off the coast of Barbados looking for a lost Spanish galleon. His wealth allowed him to travel the world to indulge his passion, and now he turned his attention to gold in Nevada.

Impatiently, he waited for Nash Yarak to arrive for their meeting. Lowell was eager to discuss his latest idea for their next venture together. He valued the man's opinion, for they had been through many adventures, and Yarak always had his back.

Like recently in Peru.

Lowell smiled, thinking of how the two men came to be friends. Yarak was a Russian naval officer, a Russian Marine commando, the equivalent of the US Navy SEALs and Israel's Shayetet 13. He was injured in Russia's invasion of Chechnya in the late 1990s when a land mine exploded, sending shrapnel into his back. After a long convalescence, Yarak retired from the military and immigrated to the States, where he found work as a bodyguard to a popular rock singer. He married the daughter of the singer's manager and they settled in North Hollywood. Unfortunately, his wife died in a tragic car accident on Interstate 495 near Santa Monica. Devastated by her death, Yarak just drifted, taking one odd job after another, eventually flipping burgers at a Carl's Jr in Burbank.

One day Lowell ordered lunch to be delivered from

Carl's Jr, and Yarak delivered the burgers to the office. Lowell struck up a conversation with Yarak and discovered he was an ex-Russian Naval commando. Surprised and interested that the man worked at a hamburger joint, Lowell invited Yarak to his townhouse in Town Center. The man's easy-going, confident manner, a quiet calm that said *don't mess with me,* intrigued him. Lowell offered the man a job and, at first, Yarak worked on small projects, ran errands, chauffeured him to various meetings. With time, Lowell came to trust Yarak and his responsibilities increased, until his present position was one of friend and confidant.

There was a soft knock on the door.

"Come in, Nash," Lowell said, "and please, take a seat. I've got something to show you."

Yarak slouched his taut frame into a leather chair next to Lowell's hand-carved teak desk and smiled.

"May I?" he said, removing a pack of cigarettes from a shirt pocket.

"Of course," Lowell said and handed him a crystal ashtray.

Yarak lit his cigarette, inhaled, then blew the smoke toward the ceiling. "So, what's up?"

Lowell had a map of the state of Nevada spread on his desk, the part that included a topographic region of the northern portion of the state. He stood over it and pointed. "I've been reading about the Lost Coyote Creek Mine, Nash. Ever heard of it? No? It was a mine in northern Nevada that legend says is worth billions in gold. If it could ever be ever found."

Yarak rose from his chair, stood alongside his boss, and stared at the map.

"Legend has it that it is somewhere around here," Lowell continued, pointing with a long finger, "in Mule Valley near the Taber River. Over the years, a number of prospectors have tried to locate the mine but without success."

"No one knows its exact location?" Yarak said. He snuffed his cigarette in the crystal ashtray.

"Its general location is known but this area is a remote, desolate high-desert mountainous region. Getting lost here is easy without the proper navigation aids."

"You are interested in finding this mine?" Yarak asked, lighting another cigarette.

"Possibly, and here's why. According to various sources unearthed down through the years, prospectors had been in this vicinity since the late 1870s, although little gold was ever found in those early years. Then in about 1890, a prospector known as Sims made a trip into the area. He intended to prospect until winter set in and then return to more civilized climates, but in late summer, he stumbled upon some very rich gold deposits. He was still trying to locate its source when the first snow of the season began to fall, so he hurriedly stuck his pick and shovel in the ground to mark the spot.

"For some reason, which has never been determined, Sims told a man about the deposit he had been tracing all summer. He described the terrain and landmarks and even told him of the pick and shovel in the ground marking the highest reach that he had traced the ore. He also said that the man should consider the gold his if anything should happen to Sims and he did not return within the year.

"The following spring, when the snow melted off the mountain meadows, the man returned and, as rapidly as possible, he started hunting for the landmarks which would lead him to the gold. He eventually found the pick and shovel stuck in the ground, and nearby he found a human skeleton. He could never establish whether the bones were that of Sims.

"He wandered in the desert for several days with only a few provisions until he finally found a spring. Resting there, he found gold in a rich deposit of quartz and built a crude mine, vowing to return if he could ever find his way out of the desert. Heading south with a pack loaded with ore, he eventually came upon wagon tracks that he followed into Nevada's eastern Mohave Desert where Indians found him. Taking him captive, they worked him as a slave for months. Finally a Mormon wagon train came upon the Indian village and freed him with a ransom, taking him to a ranch. He was cared for by the rancher's elderly mother but, unfortunately, he died before revealing the location of his mine."

"Quite a lost treasure," Yarak said.

"Yes, it is. Now, for the current story. In 1961, a map surfaced, claiming to point the way to the Lost Coyote Creek Mine. Sadly, the man who owned the map was murdered and the map was lost. That is, lost until this year when I bought it.

Yarak inhaled deeply on his cigarette and smiled.

"You bought it?"

Lowell nodded.

"So, it's another adventure for us, eh?" Yarak said. "Aren't you tired of funding these costly adventures, Mr. Lowell?"

"Look here, Nash. I have no family, no children, no heirs. In fact, you're the closest thing I've ever had to a son, so if I want to throw my money after extravagant ventures, I think I'm entitled."

"I know. I just don't want you to throw your money away on senseless expeditions."

"You think this could be a wild goose chase, then?"

"In my humble opinion, sir, they all are. But you're the boss. Besides, it will be fun, no?"

"Hope so, my friend."

"Anything else to go on?"

"Not much. These legends all sound the same to me. It goes something like this. A miner staggers in to the saloon tent, loaded with nuggets. He is a stranger. As he gulps down his whiskey, he mumbles a tale of fabulous wealth, a veritable mountain of gold. At first, the other miners are skeptical, but the size of the stranger's poke lends certain validity to his story. The miners become convinced that the fabled El Dorado has been discovered—the source of all the flakes and nuggets revealed. Next morning most of the stranger's gold and all of the whiskey are gone. What remains is hangover, with disappointment later, as the gold cannot be located. The fabulous find is lost again.

"Take, for instance, the case of Jacob Breyfogle, a Nevada blacksmith, who set out in 1864 with a saddle horse and a pack animal. His horse strayed one night and the next morning's search led to more than a missing mount. Breyfogle claimed to have come upon a ledge of red quartz loaded with the yellow metal. But his luck was mixed. Without his animals, the prospector soon found himself in dire need of food, water, and transportation. Breyfogle was found and rescued by Paiute Indians, who had also found his horse. He returned with his life, but died years later without ever again finding the Lost Breyfogle Mine.

"Another legendary strike is the Lost Cement Gold Mine, said to lie somewhere in dense woods near the Sierra Mountain headwaters of the San Joaquin River's middle fork. In 1858, a small band of roaming placer miners found a ledge of red cement-like lava, loaded with gold. Partner trouble led to an axe murder, and Indian trouble brought on a hasty exit. The spot was never again located.

"The Lost Gunsight Mine got its name from a rifle

part fashioned by Mormons from found metal in the Panamint Mountains. They were unable to find the spot again. The Adams Diggings uncovered a sizable strike for the Mormons near San Bernardino in 1886, but Apaches, taking the lucky location with them to the grave, killed most of the miners.

"Mines were being found and then lost again long before the Gold Rush started. In 1827, horse trader Thomas Smith took a short cut and became lost west of Yuma, Arizona. He climbed a small hill and found its top covered with pebbles colored a dull bronze. Smith put a few handfuls of the strange pebbles into his saddlebags and forgets about the hill where he had found them. Years later in Yerba Buena, the future San Francisco, Smith hauled out the rocks amid the frenzy of northern California's Gold Rush. The strange rocks assayed two thousand dollars to the ton—nearly solid gold. Smith had lost a leg in the intervening years, picking up the name Peg Leg. Try as he might to find his way back to that fabulous strike, the Lost Peg Leg Smith Mine took its place in western legend. Smith died of drink in San Francisco in 1866."

"Fascinating stories," Yarak said, bending over the desk for a closer look at the map.

"That's it in a nutshell, Nash. We can start the initial planning over the weekend."

Chapter 8

The sheriff's office of Elko County, Nevada, was located, not surprisingly, in the small town of Elko, population of fifteen thousand people. Sheriff Buck Calder had his office inside the Elko County Law Enforcement Center that also housed the county jail. The brick-and-plaster building with its ribbed-metal roof was located where Highway 535 made an abrupt ninety-degree turn to the southeast before crossing the Humboldt River and heading out of town.

Founded as a railroad-promoted town site and railhead for the White Pine mines in 1869, Elko served for generations and now reigned as the provincial capital of an enormous cattle ranching empire—embracing parts of four states. Lowell Thomas once described Elko as "the last real cow town in the American West," and, until recently, that was still a good thumbnail description. But sophisticated new mining technologies permitted the harvesting of microscopic particles of the precious metal from mountains of rock and dirt hauled two hundred tons at a time to the crusher.

Half a dozen large mining operations now produced millions of ounces of gold a year in the region, and even though mining was now on the wane, their impact transformed the old cow town into a prosperous young city.

In 1870, town site lot prices had multiplied three and four times, the population had risen to two thousand, and the place began to assume its character as the leading settlement of Nevada's great northeastern cattle country.

By 1873, Elko was in such a soaring and optimistic municipal mood, largely on account of the success of the mining discoveries in the districts to the north and south, that it bid for, and won, the state university. The university opened with seven students in 1874, and closed ten years later with fifteen, to be moved unceremoniously to Reno. As a freighting center, Elko fell into decline after the mining towns it served and population fell to less than a thousand souls.

Despite the steady growth and importance of the livestock business in the high-desert valleys around Elko, the town's affairs did not brighten considerably until after 1900. In those early years of the new century, not only did the Western Pacific Railroad reach Elko, but mining revived. The price of beef and wool prices quadrupled. In 1911, Elko's population pushed three thousand. Prosperity continued until the devastating one-two failure of a large banking chain and the national depression, which followed. Caught in the machinery activated to sort out the bank failure and bled by the decline in livestock prices, many of the ranches around Elko were foreclosed. In the years after the beef and wool economies fell into chaos, gambling was legalized by the state legislature. Elko, like towns everywhere in Nevada, had a new industry. Like the fabled phoenix rising from ashes, the town reinvented itself.

This morning the sun was high in the sky and the temperature was climbing, predicted to hit 105 by noon. Calder was in the jail anteroom, helping Undersheriff Andy Hardin book a vagrant whose identity was unknown.

Calder filed the necessary paperwork while Hardin fingerprinted the man. The man was drunk, had no identification on his person, and kept singing "When the Saints Go Marching In," and doing it off key. He wouldn't or couldn't answer questions like *who are you and what are you doing in Elko?* so they had no choice but let him sober up in jail while they ran his prints. When Hardin took the man to his cell, Calder sauntered to the administrative wing of the building and his office.

He was a burly man with a tanned complexion, a striking resemblance to a stereotyped image of a small-town Nevada sheriff. His khaki shirtsleeves were rolled up to just above his elbows and his badge reflected brightly over his left breast pocket. Calder liked being a sheriff, had won the election six years earlier, and had a popular following, thereby managing to get re-elected every two years. His favorite clothing apparel was a straw cowboy hat and he wore it consistently when out of the office. His nose was crooked, the result of too many altercations while attending Elko's high school.

He dropped into his chair, picked up the phone, and dialed home. When Helen picked up he gave her a kiss.

"Hello, gorgeous," he said after smacking the receiver. "How's my girl this morning?"

He listened as his wife gave him the particulars.

"Well you can tell those boys I'll fix the bike when I get home. I should be home for lunch at the usual time. Andy and I just booked a vagrant."

"A vagrant? You know who he is?"

"No, don't know who he is. Caught him wandering around down by the river, drunk as a skunk."

Andy Hardin sauntered into the office and took a chair opposite Calder.

"Okay, honey, I'll see you in a bit," he said and hung up the phone.

"Got him bedded down, Buck. I think he passed out as soon as he lay down on the bunk."

Both men laughed. Hardin fixed two cups of coffee and handed one to the sheriff.

"Did you manage to get his fingerprint scan sent off to IAFIS?" Calder asked.

Hardin nodded. "Roger, Buck. We should know something here in a few minutes. Usually within half an hour."

"Well, I'm going home for lunch. Helen's cooking some chops. Don't ask me why but ever since she started watching that cooking show I've been eating like a king."

"You know I'm envious," Hardin said, chuckling over his coffee.

"You need to find you a squaw, Andy. An old Paiute like yourself could stand a better diet. And do your laundry more than once every couple of weeks."

Calder sprang to his feet and dove out the door in time to dodge the empty Styrofoam cup Hardin threw at him.

ℰↄℰↄ

Harry was at home when his brother Max called to say that their father had died earlier in the day. Harry slumped in a chair and swallowed hard.

"How did it happen, Max?" Harry said.

Max was in New York. Their parents lived in Chicago.

"Heart attack, I guess," Max said. "When I talked to Mom—"

"You talked to Mom?"

"Yes. She called me. She said she was going to call you but I told her I would do it."

"How is she doing?" Harry said.

"Pretty well, I guess. It was a shock. Her neighbor, Mrs. Peabody, is with her. I chatted with her for a few

minutes. A few friends are bringing in some food, later."
Max's voice sounded clipped, curt.

"He had a heart attack, you say, Max?"

"I guess so. But you know Dad. He was a heavy drinker for years. For all I know his liver could have given out. He's at the funeral home now. Mom wants him cremated."

Serves the bastard right, Harry thought, then immediately felt guilty.

"There going to be a funeral or something?" he said.

"The urn will go into the ground this Friday. There's to be a small service at the gravesite, just family and a few friends. Can you make it?"

"Sure. Dixie and I will be there, of course. You holding up, Max?"

"I'll be fine. I've already booked a flight into O'Hare for tomorrow. We can stay at the house so don't worry about that."

"I'll call Mom as soon as I hang up. See you when I get there, brother."

After hanging up, Harry called his mother and the two talked for a long time. *In a way*, he thought, *she sounds almost relieved.* The man had been an alcoholic and was verbally abusive to her, a fact that caused Harry to contemplate the man's demise many times over. But his mom seemed content to put up with the bastard, so Harry just left home and never returned except for holidays. This would be the first trip home since he and Dixie were married. Mom had never met his wife.

❧❧❧

It was a raw, blustery afternoon and the mourners, seated under a dark green canopy, were shielded from the bitter north wind by a copse of hickory trees. Earlier, a late spring arctic storm pushed into the Great Lakes region, sending temperatures plummeting. Rising out of the same wilderness as Chicago itself, Oak Woods Cemetery was located at the apex of a triangle formed by the train tracks and South Chicago Avenue to the southwest of Jackson Park. One of a few cemeteries to be organized and operated by virtue of a special legislative act, its charter guaranteed a permanent resting place for all those who would find peace for evermore among its wooded, lake-studded acres.

Harry and Dixie sat on the front row of a line of folding chairs between Harry's mother and Max. They had arrived the day before and spent the evening at the family home, reliving old memories. Harry's mother was infatuated with Dixie and chatted a long while, marveling that she had a doctorate like Harry.

There were a few other people, whom Harry didn't know, except for Mrs. Peabody who had come by the house the night before with several dishes of food. When the service was concluded, Dixie escorted her mother-in-law to the car, leaving Harry and Max alone next to the grave.

"I can't say I'm sad, Max. I hope the man got his just reward for all the misery he caused. He made Mom miserable. And me, as well."

"He wasn't all that bad, Harry. I remember—"

"No, Max, he treated you differently than he treated me. I was the kid who would never amount to anything. I remember him saying that time and time again. To you, he was a different father. To me he was just an asshole. Sorry."

"Don't let Mom hear you say those things. It'll hurt her."

"Maybe it's time to let the cat out of the bag, brother. So we can all deal with it. Might do Mom some good."

"Please, Harry, I beg you. Maybe another time. Just not now, all right?"

They strolled back to the car. Harry thought Max had aged considerably since their last visit, and it surprised him. Maybe all that Wall Street stress was taking a toll.

"All right, Max. We'll play it your way. We'll have a quiet family dinner tonight and tomorrow Dixie and I will return to Frisco. Now, let's get out of this wind."

Later that evening and alone in their bedroom, Dixie quizzed Harry about his meeting with Pauling.

"I told him everything at the facility ran according to Federal standards," Harry said. "It was the truth, our inspection didn't reveal any problems. He seemed relieved."

"I imagine he did," Dixie said, lounging in the bed. "It's beautiful up there, honey. I envy Miles. I just don't want you to upset yourself where your brother is concerned. I worry about you."

"Max and I have never seen things the same, Dixie, never. He went his way and I went mine. We live in two different worlds, but I'm the lucky one—I have you."

When Dixie smiled, her eyes sparkled. "Your Mother is the important one, honey. Don't antagonize her by causing grief with your brother. Let it rest. Now, come to bed."

❦❦❦

The morning started cloudy with fog rolling in over the bay area from the Pacific but, as the morning progressed, the sky cleared and blue peeked through large holes in the clouds. Harry liked watching the weather change from his office window as it afforded him a rest break now and then from his work.

Walking in from the parking lot earlier, he noticed the

group of animal rights protesters were still parading with their signs. Some chanted, others sang. One lone man on the street corner shouted, arms raised, as if preaching a Sunday sermon.

> "FAAR demands justice!
> Justice for animals!
> End the cruelty!"

FAAR—Federation Against Animal Research, Harry surmised. *Can't these people get more creative with their names?* Did they expect the scientific community to just stop with animal research? Did they not realize the many scientific and medical advances given the world came by using experimental animals?

He spent his morning going over the progress of the graduate students in the department. Their respective major professors filed a report on them, and he scanned them with varying degrees of interest. It appeared that he was going to have to counsel one of them for near-failing marks in two of his classes, a task he never relished. Then there was the ever-present request from Dr. Wickingham for a lab of his own. Nothing Harry said reverberated with the man. He needed to sit the new faculty member down and read him the facts of life—publish first.

All of a sudden, his secretary rushed into the office, sporting a terrified look, while the three lines on his phone began blinking at once. He could hear them ringing in the outer room. Dixie followed the secretary into the office, a stunned look etched on her face.

"Good grief," Harry said. "What's going on here? Emily, what's the matter?"

"President Pauling is on line one and he is in a panic. Something terrible has happened."

As he picked up the phone, Harry caught a glimpse of

Dixie plopping into a chair, tears streaming down her face. Good grief, he thought, has someone died? He usually didn't get a phone call from the university president.

"Yes, sir?" Harry said into the phone.

"Harry," Pauling shouted in a near-panicked voice on the other end. "There's been a catastrophe. At the Primate Research Facility. You need to get up there as fast as possible."

"Please try and calm yourself, sir. What exactly has happened?"

"How the hell should I know, Olson?" Pauling demanded becoming irate. "Just get up there quick. The report is that someone's been killed, and something terrible has happened with the Yeti. Get going, son."

Harry's heart pounded in his throat, his head throbbed. He tried to look past the president's tone, which sounded out of control. Harry had never heard the man speak like this. "Sir, please. With whom did you speak up there? What did they say happened?"

"One of the graduate assistants, I believe. A woman, I think."

"And what did she tell you?"

"I don't remember, exactly," Pauling said, sounding at the end of his rope. "Something bad has happened to the Yeti and a person is dead. That's all I can remember right now. Jessums, Harry, please!"

"All right, sir, Dixie and I will head up there right away. Maybe I can charter a helicopter to take us right to the facility. Please don't say anything to the press until I have had a chance to find out what has happened. We'll pack a quick bag, and if someone in your office can find us a flight of some kind it would save some time."

"Will do, Harry. And call me as soon as you get up there. Understand?"

The president now sounded calmer, more in control.

Harry didn't know if he could count on the man's silence where the press was concerned but he hoped so. Harry hung up, and Dixie rushed to his side.

"It's a disaster, honey," she said.

"What do you know about it?"

"Wickingham tracked me down. He was in Administration and he overheard the commotion. Someone has been killed at the facility, and something has happened with the Yeti."

"Yeah, what?" Harry said, impatient with the vague reports.

"I don't know. Wickingham didn't know or say. He was his usual arrogant self."

"I guess we should run by the house and get a few things and, hopefully, by then Pauling will have found us a flight or charter. Too bad our home is such a ways down the peninsula."

He stood, crammed papers into a soft briefcase, and led Dixie down to their car parked in the faculty lot. He screeched out onto the freeway and sped south, weaving through traffic, honking his horn at the slower cars in front of him. As he neared the airport, the traffic got a lot heavier. Harry lost his patience and began honking at everyone he passed.

"Slow down, Harry," Dixie said, "don't go and get us killed because you're in a hurry."

When he shot past a double trailer semi rig, he let off the accelerator. "You're right. It's just that I can't figure what could have gone wrong up there. Someone dead? It's unbelievable."

As Harry zoomed past San Francisco International Airport, the traffic thinned, and he was able to drive faster. He kept looking in his rearview mirror, expecting at any moment to see flashing red lights gaining on him. As he closed in on San Mateo, his cell phone rang.

"Dr. Olson, this is Jason Buchwald, President Pauling's administrative assistant."

"Yes, Jason. What's up?"

"Doctor, there is an air national guard helicopter waiting for you at the air guard hanger at International. They will fly you direct to the research facility. Their hanger is at the southern end of the airport. Understand?"

"Yes, Jason, thank you. My wife and I will be there within the hour so can you relay that information? They will have two passengers."

"Will do, Dr. Olson. And good luck."

౭ఌ౭ఌ

Harry threw several pairs of pants, shirts, shaving gear, a handheld GPS receiver, and boonie hat into a bag. Dixie did likewise and, within thirty minutes, they were back on the road, speeding toward the airport. Dixie had hurriedly made sandwiches so the couple ate on the way, sipping bottled water between bites. The sun was high overhead so Harry hoped they would be at the compound well before dark.

He mulled over what he knew. Someone had been killed, that seemed certain. And the report was that something had happened to the Yeti. Had they died? Killed? What could account for the two reports? There could have been an explosion that took out most of the facility. An epidemic of some disease that spread like wildfire through the animals then jumped into a human, causing death. Food poisoning? Doubtful. A virus? Possibly. A bacteria that infected the animal feed? Maybe. If the Yeti were dead, there would need to be a post-mortem on each of them. The veterinarian could perform that task. He realized he was getting ahead of himself so he tried to block the reeling thoughts and concentrate on his driving.

The airport exit loomed ahead as Dixie spoke.

"What?" he said, steering the car onto the off ramp.

"I said what could have happened up there? Any ideas?"

Her face was taut, her eyes mere slits. She was feeling the stress as well, Harry thought. "Other than some deadly disease or epidemic, I haven't a clue," he said. "They were isolated up there. They took protocol seriously. They did everything by the book. At least that is what we were led to believe. Is it possible they didn't? I didn't look over their shoulders very closely. Could I be at fault, honey?"

"Have they been working with a strain of virus we know nothing about?" Dixie said.

"Don't know, but I doubt it," Harry said. He passed several cars and honked at a truck until it swerved out of his way.

Harry followed the signs directing him to the air national guard hanger. Closer, he saw a UH-60 Blackhawk helicopter on the tarmac with several uniformed troops milling about it.

"I feel responsible," he said. "I'm the departmental chairman."

"That's plain silly, honey," Dixie said. "There is no way you are culpable. If anything, Dr. Radner, as director, carries the bulk of the responsibility for the facility. Not you."

"That's reassuring. I just hope Pauling and the trustees feel as you do."

At the flight operations center, Harry parked the car and carried their bags inside. A major with a funny name glanced at their IDs then escorted them onto the tarmac and the waiting chopper and introduced them to the pilot and copilot.

They climbed aboard, strapped themselves into their

seats, donned a helmet, and waited as the engine fired up and the rotors began moving.

Harry's pulse raced. He shot a weak smile at Dixie in an attempt to reassure her. She looked a fright.

Soon they were airborne, banking hard to the northeast toward Nevada. The five-hundred-mile trip, Harry estimated, would take close to three hours. The Blackhawk shot toward Cinder Mountain, and Harry attempted to relax the aching muscles in his neck. He reached out, took Dixie's hand, and gave it a gentle squeeze.

What would be waiting for them at the Primate Research Facility?

Chapter 9

In a small unpretentious office tucked away in the middle of San Francisco's Embarcadero, a group of men and women labored quietly. Several tables were stacked with markers and pasteboards. They murmured among themselves and, while they constructed their signs and banners, they waited patiently for their leader to arrive and begin the meeting. Most of the room's occupants were young, under forty, but there were several older adults who had joined the group in the past weeks. They were opposed to using animals in scientific research and called themselves the Federation Against Animal Research. Not novel but descriptive.

The office door opened, ushering in a flood of bright sunlight followed by a tall woman in her thirties who wore denim jeans and a sweatshirt. Her dirty blonde hair fell in soft curls about her oval face and a beaded necklace drooped around her neck. She made her way to the front of the crowded room and smiled. All eyes turned toward her.

"We are here," she began, "because all of us love animals. We believe in an animal's inherent worth. Supporters of animal rights believe that animals have an inherent worth—a value completely separate from their usefulness to humans. We believe that every creature with a will to live has a right to live free from pain and suffering. Animal rights is not just a philosophy, it is a social movement that challenges society's traditional view that all nonhuman animals exist solely for human use. As our founder has said, 'When it comes to pain, love, joy, loneliness, and fear, a rat is a pig is a dog is a boy. Each one values his or her life and fights the knife.'

"Only prejudice allows us to deny others the rights that we expect to have for ourselves. Whether it's based on race, gender, sexual orientation, or species, prejudice is morally unacceptable. If you wouldn't eat a dog, why eat a pig? Dogs and pigs have the same capacity to feel pain, but it is prejudice based on species that allows us to think of one animal as a companion and the other as dinner.

"FAAR has become a model for other humane organizations throughout our country. Since then, hundreds of laws have been enacted on the federal, state, and local levels, providing protections to many species of animals. Today, FAAR carries on our founder's mission to better protect animals and provide for their wellbeing by establishing public policy through the legislative process, citizen initiatives, and consumer education campaigns. We also offer advocacy training and support for citizens who wish to engage in grassroots lobbying. Stay informed and get involved—politics is not a spectator sport!"

Thunderous applause erupted at the conclusion of the woman's speech. The room's occupants nodded and whooped for a few minutes, luxuriating in the glory of the moment. When the cacophony dwindled, the woman held up a hand.

"All right, folks," she said. "I have some news."

Men and women gathered around the woman and waited.

"Our demonstrations at Cal Pacific have been well-attended and have received good media coverage. I was pleased to see the television cameras there yesterday. We made the news." She paused and allowed the resulting buzz to quiet before continuing. "Yes, I know we are all excited about that. In fact, it gained us a few new members, and so I suggest we double our efforts and organize a demonstration at Stanford. I will need some volunteers to get that underway."

More chatting.

"I am considering a demonstration at Cal Pacific's Primate Research Facility, as that is where they have housed their famed Yeti brought here from Mongolia. There is no telling what they do to those poor creatures. The sooner we get up there and begin applying pressure the better it will be for them."

A member of the group raised her hand. "Miss Treadwell," she said, "I am happy to volunteer. We can use my car to drive to the Nevada site."

"Fine, Vickie, fine," Norma Treadwell said. "Let me know when you have a group together, and we'll coordinate plans. Let's do it fairly soon, okay?"

When the meeting ended, Norma Treadwell remained behind and sat at a steel desk, alone, thinking. This local chapter of the Federation Against Animal Research was her brainchild, borne from a frustration she encountered as secretary for United Cause, a lobbying group for the humane treatment of laboratory animals. When she realized that the group solicited donations but didn't do anything of a positive nature to insure correct treatment of the animals, she decided to form her own, proactive organization and the local chapter was birthed. The only way, in her opinion, to ensure that laboratory animals were humanely treated was to eliminate animal research altogether. It was fortunate that her husband didn't care how she spent her time. In fact, he didn't care, period. The man was married to his job.

So, FAAR became her overriding passion. She labored tirelessly, organizing demonstrations and rallies, in an effort to catalyze public support and media interest. The going had been slow. The public favored animal research. There are so many universities in the state that did research. She had much work to do.

❦❧❦

Harry helped Dixie off the Blackhawk helicopter and the pair scooted under the whirling rotors to a waiting Dr. Radner and Bruce Drayton who led them into the lobby of the main building. An Elko County Sheriff's Department car was parked near its entrance. As soon as they were out of the heat and bright sun, Harry started with the questions. It looked as if a tornado had hit the lobby.

"What happened here, Miles?" Harry demanded, concern filling his mind.

"Tragedy, Doctor, a complete and utter tragedy. Follow me to the Animal Care Unit."

Harry and Dixie followed Radner through a series of hallways, and Harry watched the research facility staff scurry about, chattering in wild tones.

"We heard someone was killed," Dixie said, trailing behind Harry and Radner.

Radner acted like he hadn't heard Dixie but kept hurrying, finally stopping at the first air lock. Before pushing the button to open the door, he turned toward Harry. "Don't touch anything," he said. "The sheriff hasn't finished."

When Harry nodded, Radner opened the air lock and the three of them entered and waited for the door to slide closed behind them.

"No need to bother scrubbing," Radner said and he opened the air lock door into the Animal Care Unit. The cold air hit Harry in the face like a fast-moving cold front.

The scene inside the unit was surreal. There was splattered blood everywhere. Both cage doors stood open and the Yeti were gone. The body of a man was askew on the floor, his limbs mangled, his face a mass of gore, and he lay in a large pool of dried, dark blood. Two men in khaki sheriff's uniforms were in the unit, one bent over the body, the other took photographs. Papers and equipment were scattered in disarray throughout the unit. Harry's stomach revolted and he pushed down the urge to vomit.

"Oh my god," exclaimed Dixie in a low groan. "What in god's name happened here?"

The man bent over the dead body looked up then stood. Dr. Radner stepped around an overturned stool.

"Sheriff Calder, this is our departmental chairman, Dr. Harry Olson and his wife, also Dr. Olson."

Harry shook hands with Calder and Dixie smiled faintly at the man. Harry pointed to the body. "Who?"

"Jimmy Winkleman," Radner said, shaking his head. "So sad. I'm going to have to call his folks."

"Yes," Dixie said. "I remember him from our previous trip."

"What happened in here?" Harry asked. "The place looks like a bomb went off."

His stomach reeled. The strong smell of iron permeated the unit, making his nausea even worse. His body felt light, as if floating, his head spinning. It was like the time he was coming out from under anesthesia after his appendectomy when he was in high school. He floated on a cloud, half-conscious of this world, half not.

Now, he had trouble concentrating on the scene. Instead, he listened to the rustle of his pants as he crossed the room. He noticed a young woman huddled in a far corner.

Radner shook his head, walked over to a cage door, looked in, then turned. "As best as we can determine, Winkleman opened the cage door without the male Yeti being sedated. Don't know why he would do that. But the Yeti must have attacked him, killed him. Pretty brutal."

"But both cage doors are open," Dixie said. How—"

"Impossible to say," Sheriff Calder interjected. He stood to his full height, next to Dixie.

Harry ambled to the open door of the cage that had housed Bentu and gazed into its interior. "Why—why would he open the door without the animal being sedated?" he asked. "Isn't that against policy? And shouldn't he have known better?"

"He's dead," Radner said. "He can't tell us why."

The woman in the corner stepped forward. Harry saw she wore a lab coat and looked familiar.

"Yes, Millie?" Radner said.

"I—I—may—know why," she said, as if nervous.

"Sheriff, this is Millie Harbaum, our other graduate research assistant."

Harry tried to smile, now able to concentrate. "Millie, Dr. Olson. Remember me?"

She nodded, her eyes darting around the unit.

"Good. Now why would Jimmy open the cage door without first sedating the Yeti? Hardly normal procedure, right?"

"He knew better, of course. Jimmy—Jimmy was a jerk," Millie said, wringing her hands in front go her. "He always said Bentu wasn't aggressive, even though I tried to tell him otherwise. I'd seen Bentu stand at the front of his cage and rattle it for over an hour. I had a feeling that Bentu was unpredictable, more so than Sasha, my Yeti. These are huge wild animals. But Jimmy thought he knew best, so this morning he opened the cage himself and went in to feed Bentu, leaving the door open behind him. Usually the technicians feed the animals but this morning Jimmy was intent on feeding Bentu. I told him not to do it, sir."

"I see," Harry said.

"My God!" Radner exclaimed, slamming an open hand on a nearby counter.

"Hold it, Miles," Harry said. "Please continue, Millie."

"These Yeti aren't dumb, Dr. Olson. Bentu saw the open door. He attacked Jimmy, nearly ripping his head off, and got out of his cage. I screamed, fearing Bentu would come for me. Jimmy was dazed but he managed to get up and follow Bentu out here. The two struggled again, this time Bentu hurt Jimmy bad, and he just slumped to the floor. I was terrified so I ran out of the unit. I think Jimmy was trying to get Bentu back into his cage. Somehow Bentu must have unlocked Sasha's cage and the two of them escaped the Animal Care Unit."

"Where are they now?" Harry asked.

"Don't know, Doctor," Calder said.

"You called them Bentu and Sasha," Dixie said.

"The names Jimmy and I gave them," Millie said. "I actually thought Sasha, and I were bonding but, the way Jimmy treated Bentu, I knew it would never happen with them."

"What do you mean by that?" Radner said. He stood in the unit in his shirtsleeves, his tie loose around his neck.

Millie shot an awkward glance at Harry and Dixie before answering. "Well…" she began slowly. "Jimmy was always real gruff with Bentu, talked in a mean voice or shouted. He didn't handle the animal with gentle hands when drawing the blood specimens. He sometimes would beat on the cage, teasing Bentu, an act I thought unprofessional. In fact, I never understood why he chose this line of work. When he would pound the cage, I asked him to stop but he didn't. And Bentu acted real agitated when Jimmy did that. The Yeti would pace around his cage and rattle the bars, growling at Jimmy. Sometimes Bentu would stare through the bars, just stare. I didn't like it."

"You mean Jimmy intentionally provoked the Yeti?" Harry said.

Millie nodded. "I don't know why he was here, I mean with the way he treated Bentu. I came back here often before going to bed just to check on them."

"Why didn't you report him, Millie?" Radner asked. He was obviously dismayed to hear her story.

"Dr. Radner, Jimmy was weird, and I was somewhat afraid of him. I'm sorry."

"I understand," Harry said, reaching out and to pat her on the shoulder.

Sheriff Calder finished writing in a notebook and put it in his shirt pocket. "Doctors," he said, "we need to talk. Is there somewhere we can go? I'll want your security chief and the veterinarian present as well."

"Yes," Radner said. "We can talk in the conference room adjacent to my office. Follow me. I'll have my secretary find Drayton and Dr. Siscom."

 espes

Dr. Bernard Wickingham sat in his office and fumed. He had just come from the paleontology lab where he was forced to work in a corner that was used by students. Students! Harry, his departmental chairman, had left suddenly on some wild goose chase without hearing his case for his own laboratory space. Some crisis at the primate facility in Nevada. A death or something.

Since coming to Cal Pacific, Wickingham's office was

a small cramped affair at the end of a long hallway on the top floor of the science building. His large personal library barely fit in the meager bookshelves on one wall. A tiny window looked out over the parking lot where the animal rights demonstrators had gathered days earlier.

His faculty appointment at Cal Pacific was his first since earning his doctorate, one that he was grateful to obtain, although most of his colleagues back home felt he was unworthy. But he would show them—he would show them all. Just because his father was doing time for tax evasion was no reason for Wickingham to be treated the way he was by his fellow graduate students. He had a lot to prove.

He realized that the most cogent argument for a larger lab was his own funding. That would mean more people, which, in turn, would increase the department's overall productivity. Apart from having his own grant money, he knew such decisions weren't made on a strictly monetary basis. Productivity and scientific quality in terms of publications and student training were always a big factor. But if he had a grant, things would be different—he could sway Olson. If he had a series of publications under his belt, things would be different.

As a new faculty member, he knew he was swimming upstream.

But Wickingham wasn't a patient man. Nor was he above dirty politics if it came to that. The Anthropology Department seemed free of internal strife but that could change. Especially if he helped things along.

e/oe/o

Once the parties were all seated around Radner's conference table, Calder removed the notebook from his pocket and set it in front of him. Electric tension filled the room, and he noticed the grim, haggard faces staring back at him. No one talked. The conference room was as quiet as a morgue. The sheriff had the sense that he wasn't going to get much more information from the scientists. His best bet was going to be the veterinarian.

"Okay, folks," he began, "this is what we have. Correct me if I don't have it right." He paused, waited for a few nods, then continued. "The research assistant, Winkleman, who apparently delighted in tormenting the beast he was assigned to watch and care for, opened its cage and entered it. The beast—"

Harry eyed Calder with narrow eyes. "Sheriff, the beast to whom you refer is a Yeti, a humanoid species found in Mongolia."

"Yes, excuse me, Doctor. As I was saying, the Yeti attacked Winkleman, and the pair apparently fought for a while, eventually reaching the area outside the cage. This Yeti killed Winkleman. He then escaped the unit with the female Yeti. How she was able to get out of her cage is unknown at this time. I have sent my undersheriff out with your security chief and a number of your employees to search the grounds for these animals."

"Sheriff, may I say something?" Millie said. She had raised her hand and looked about the table with wide eyes.

"Go ahead."

"Sir, if none of the science staff unlocked the cage, and certainly there would be no reason for them to do so, then we have to assume that Bentu unlocked Sasha's cage himself."

"Why do you say that?" Calder said.

"It stands to reason. If—"

"You said yourself that you had fled the unit," Calder interrupted. "You didn't actually observe him releasing the other Yeti, correct?"

Millie ran a hand through her hair and squirmed in her seat. "That is right. But, sir, these animals are highly intelligent. They learn with incredible speed. Each of them spent the better part of a year watching everything that went on in the Animal Care Unit. They observed our coming and going. They watched as we went about our daily routine. I'm sure they saw and learned how we opened their cages."

"Dixie and I can certainly attest to their intelligence," Harry said, looking around the table at each person. "We observed how smart they are, up close, back in Mongolia. As a group they were able to strategize and mount a coordinated attack."

"And they lived in small family-like units, seemingly caring for each other," Dixie added.

"All right," Calder said, nodding, "I'll give you that these Yeti are intelligent beyond belief and that the murdering male opened the female's cage. If you rule out the Winkleman kid opening the other cage, it's the best explanation we have. The point is that the two of them escaped to parts unknown. Hopefully, they are hiding somewhere on the compound and we'll soon find them. Your veterinarian…"

"Siscom, right here," Dr. Siscom said, raising his hand.

"Yes, Doctor. Are you ready and able to tranquilize these animals when we locate them?"

"Absolutely. I've got plenty of tranquilizer darts on hand. I don't miss, either."

"Great, and thank you."

"Sheriff," Radner said, "how soon can we move the body and get the unit cleaned up?"

"Well, the Elko County Coroner is on his way so as soon as he gives you the thumbs up you'll be free to do so. My office will take care of notifying the young man's next of kin later this evening. So for now, we just sit back and wait for these animals to be found. Surely, they couldn't have gone far."

Siscom stood. "I'll get the tranquilizers ready." He left with Millie right behind him.

Calder watched the veterinarian leave the conference room and wondered about the place in which he found himself. The Primate Research Facility was as foreign to him as China, which said something, for he had never been outside the state of Nevada, except once when he went deep-sea fishing off the coast of San Diego. The scientific people spoke a language different than anything he ever heard. The place seemed more like a hospital than what he thought a research facility should look like. Having never progressed beyond high school, he felt out of place amidst all the educated people at the facility. It was always a source of embarrassment when he found himself talking to a more educated person, causing him his mouth to become dry and his bowels to loosen.

Suddenly, Millie burst into the room and everyone's heads jerked toward the door.

"What is it?" Calder said, his voice rising.

"They're gone," Millie said, tears streaming down her cheeks. "The Yeti. They're not on the compound."

Chapter 10

Bruce Drayton and Undersheriff Andy Hardin led a number of the research facility's workers on a search of the compound. Once they cleared the main building and dormitory, they searched the rest of the outbuildings. Drayton stopped at his office, grabbed his 30-30 rifle, and slung it over his shoulder. The undersheriff had his nine-millimeter Heckler and Koch pistol holstered on his hip but, from what Calder said, he knew it wouldn't stop these animals. Drayton checked his walkie-talkie, made sure the frequency was the same as the veterinarian's, and began the search.

Slogging along under a high hot sun, his leg ached, accentuating his limp, while the workers fanned out behind him and Hardin. Drayton was a recent addition to the Primate Research Facility, only coming on board less than a year ago.

Radner had seemed pleased with his credentials, being an ex-cop and all, but he always felt the director looked over his shoulder, watching everything in the facility, making mental notes.

Now this business with the assistant's killing and the Yeti getting loose was enough to make Drayton even more paranoid where Radner was concerned.

"What tribe are you?" he asked Hardin as they continued searching the buildings under a sweltering sun.

"Paiute," replied Hardin, not looking at Drayton.

"Paiute, eh? Been in this area very long, Andy?"

"My mother was descended from Chief Truckee."

"Who was that?" said Drayton after the pair looked in the building that housed the generator and found nothing.

"He was Big Chief over all Paiutes in Western Nevada at the time of the arrival of the first white man. Chief Truckee was the father of Chief Winnemucca and the Truckee River and the town of Truckee were named for him."

"I see," Drayton said. I have heard of the Pyramid Lake War. It's about the only Paiute history I know."

"Yes. In 1860, the war was a series of two battles between the Paiute and the white settlers. The settlers came to the area in search of gold and silver and, in their search, destroying the Indians' valuable natural resources. This created a great deal of tension among the Paiutes.

"The Paiutes reached their breaking point when two Paiute girls were kidnapped by white settlers. It sparked the most intense battle in Nevada's history, and the initial battle left several white traders dead and seventy-five members of the militia dead. In retaliation, the white militia attacked several weeks later and a great number of Paiute Indians died as a result. A treaty was signed to end the fighting a few months later."

"You sure know your history, Andy," Drayton said, slapping the man on his back.

Hardin smiled. "Yes," he said. "I am a good Indian."

The men laughed and continued their search. When all the outbuildings had been searched and deemed clear of the Yeti, Drayton turned the workers loose, and he and Hardin headed back to the main building.

In the lobby he saw Millie, told her that the Yeti were

nowhere to be found, and watched her run to tell Radner and the others.

❧❦❧

The conference erupted with the participants all chattering at once, shouting over one another. Harry raised his voice and rapped his knuckles on the table.

"Please, everyone," he shouted, trying to get their attention. "Please, everybody return to your seats. Let's have some order so we can discuss this calmly and objectively."

Dr. Siscom and Bruce Drayton entered and took a seat at the conference table along with Dr. Radner, Millie Harbaum, and Dixie. Radner lit a cigarette and toyed with his lighter while the talking gradually subsided.

"Where is the Sheriff?" Dixie asked.

"He and his undersheriff are out on the mountain organizing a search party," Radner said. "I believe they intend to begin searching the mountain."

"All right," Harry continued, "let's try and get to the bottom of what happened here. Mainly, how did the female Yeti, Sasha—I believe she was called—how did she get out of her cage? Millie believes Bentu let her out. Any other ideas?"

"The most obvious answer to that question," Drayton said, panting, still out of breath from hurrying to the meeting, "is that, if it wasn't the male Yeti, then someone unlocked the damned thing."

"Who might do such a thing?" Dixie said, her voice showing surprise at the security chief's suggestion.

"Either someone who had a grudge against the facility or some animal rights psycho," Drayton replied.

"I can speak to that," Radner said. "We screen and vet our employees with meticulous care. Use a microscope, as it were, and go over every minute detail of their background check."

"What are you saying?" Harry said.

"Dr. Olson, you know what lengths we go to ensure quality people work here, including the scientific staff. So I doubt if any of our facility's staff had anything to do with the Yeti's escape. I would be willing to stake my reputation on it."

"Yes, yes, Dr. Radner," Harry said. "I tend to agree with you. But I have seen the animal rights demonstrations near the campus."

"So, if none of the staff unlocked the cage how did it get opened?" Dr. Siscom drummed a pencil on the table while he spoke.

"Someone from the outside?" Dixie said.

"Nope, not possible," Drayton said. "Security here is tight as a drum. Never could happen."

"Someone couldn't have sneaked in without being seen? One of the demonstrators perhaps?" Dixie pursued her train of thought.

"Highly unlikely. A tall fence secures the perimeter and is monitored with video surveillance. If someone entered by another way, other than the front gate, I would know it."

Siscom raised his hand. "It still begs my question. If no person unlocked the cage, how did it get opened?"

Millie raised her hand and cleared her throat. "Excuse me, everyone. I realize I'm just a graduate assistant here, but I have worked with these animals for nearly a year."

"No, Millie, you're fine," Harry said. "Please tell us what you think."

"It's like I said earlier." Millie toyed nervously with the lapel of her lab coat. Her eyes darted around the table. "These Yeti are extremely smart. Their intelligence far exceeds what we have thought previously. I should know,

I work with them every day. In fact, I was about to suggest some experiments to measure their intelligence when today happened. These…" She stopped, as if unsure if she should proceed.

"Please, Millie," Dixie said, smiling at her. "Go ahead, finish what you want to say. We're here to listen."

Millie rubbed her hands together. "Well, these Yeti have watched us every day open and close their cages. In fact, they watched our every movement in the Animal Care Unit, especially Bentu, the male. In my opinion, these Yeti have the intelligence to learn and duplicate what they saw day after day. When Bentu escaped from his cage, I believe he unlocked Sasha's cage, and the two of them found their way out of the unit."

More chattering, raised voices.

"I don't believe it," Radner said. "These are animals for Christ's sake. Some kind of ape relation. No way they could learn such a maneuver. And even if they could duplicate something like Pavlov's dogs, I seriously doubt they have the reasoning ability to figure it out and know what escaping meant."

"On the contrary," Dixie interjected. She spoke directly to Radner. "I can personally attest to these animal's reasoning ability. They have cunning, possess the ability to strategize and carry out a plan of action. No, Dr. Radner, you are mistaken. "

Radner sat back in his chair, without a response to Dixie's remarks.

"All right," Harry said. "We've known for a long time that chimps can learn simple tasks. Our animals have escaped the compound. We know they are dangerous. And we need to find and subdue them as soon as possible. Chief Drayton and I will coordinate search activities with Sheriff Calder. I hope he has already begun a search of Cinder Mountain."

೧౩೧

Harry ventured outside and noticed the Blackhawk helicopter that had brought him and Dixie to the facility was no longer on the compound. Instead, a Tri-County Law Enforcement helicopter occupied the spot where the Blackhawk previously sat. Sheriff Calder and Undersheriff Hardin were standing next to the aircraft, talking to a man Harry surmised was the pilot. The sun was still high in the sky, beating down with its usual ferocity, and glinted off the chopper's rotors. Harry wiped beads of perspiration from his forehead and neck.

When he approached the pair, Hardin turned and acknowledged his approach by a small wave. "Dr. Olson," he said, "this is our pilot, and we will begin an air search of the area shortly."

Harry extended his hand and the men shook hands. The pilot's grip was firm.

"Thanks for your help," Harry said. "Sorry to get you out on such a flight as this."

The man didn't say anything but nodded. Calder took Harry by an arm and led him a safe distance from the helicopter. They watched the pilot climb aboard and the jet engine started to whine. Finally, the rotors started turning and, soon, the chopper was airborne, banking hard to the south. When it was out of sight, the two men stood in the shade under the portico of the main building. The air temperature dropped ten degrees out of the sun.

"So, Sheriff, what do we do now? Just wait? I don't think I can just sit around here waiting for that pilot to report back."

"I've ordered two deputies to bring a trailer and a number of horses up here," Calder said. "I plan to begin searching from horseback as soon as they arrive."

"When will that be?"

"They should be here sometime this evening. We'll start out at first light in the morning."

"I want to participate," Harry said. "And I know my wife will want to as well."

Calder shook his head. "I don't know about having a woman along," he said. "I can't be responsible for her safety."

"I assure you, Sheriff, Dixie is as tough as anyone I've ever known. She proved that in Mongolia. Trust me."

"Well, we'll see, Doctor. In the meantime, I want to check on the coroner. He should be finishing up."

Inside, they found the doctor sitting in a chair writing on a legal pad. He looked up when Calder walked up to him.

"Ah, Sheriff Calder," he said. "All done. The body can be removed now. I just finished my notes."

Harry noticed various sketches of the body with a number of labels attached to them. "Doctor," Harry said. "I'm Dr. Olson, in charge of this research facility. What can you tell us? Anything?"

The balding gray-haired man cleared his throat and looked at Harry with steel gray eyes.

"Not much, I'm afraid. The man's skull was crushed, which was the immediate cause of death. My tentative opinion is that death was instantaneous. All four limbs were broken in several places, with the right femoral artery completely severed. That accounted for the large amount of blood at the scene. Finally, multiple bruises and abrasions, most reflecting defensive wounds." He shook his head and put his pen into a shirt pocket. "Quite a brutal killing, actually. One of the worst I've seen in forty years. Who was the young man?"

"A graduate research assistant here," Harry said. "Simply a tragedy, a huge tragedy."

"Thank you, Doctor," Calder said. "Well, I need to inform the boy's next of kin. Where can I use the telephone?"

"Dr. Radner's office," Harry said. "I'm sure he won't mind. This way."

The two men walked through the lobby and down a hallway, leaving the coroner to find his own way off the mountain. On his way to find Dixie, Harry found the picture of Jimmy's crumpled and bloody body rattling around his brain, causing his mind to do somersaults. He didn't know Jimmy but had interviewed him for the position he came to occupy at the facility. If Millie's assessment of him was accurate, Harry didn't know him at all. He remembered the power and ferocity of a Yeti attack from his two expeditions to Mongolia when he observed them firsthand. If they weren't able to locate the Yeti soon, the massive creatures would wreak havoc on an unsuspecting public. Widespread panic would ensue.

Chapter 11

A contingent of four-wheel-drive vehicles sat perched along a small tributary of the Taber River nestled in a shallow canyon of Mule Valley. A rising sun was low on the distant horizon, and it cast long shadows over the dark waters of the nearby stream. A pale orange hue filled the eastern sky and blackbirds chirped in the pines.

Rupert Lowell paced along the shoreline, his boots crunching on the uneven surface. He held an insulated mug of coffee in one hand and a portable GPS receiver in the other. On a nearby rock sat Nash Yarak, sipping coffee while studying his boss. They had been in the mountains for over a week, searching for the Lost Coyote Creek Mine without the slightest hint of success. With them were two of Lowell's most trusted subordinates, men who had been with them on the past few expeditions and had proven their valor and loyalty. Garby and Terkel were two men that Yarak had found working the railroad line in California. Lowell had checked and rechecked their backgrounds before hiring them. The men were loyal to a fault and followed orders without complaints, a fact that elevated their positions in Lowell's estimation.

The group used Lowell's faded map, in an attempt to

locate the mine, but the landmarks didn't line up with the ones scribbled on the faded paper. Once, during the previous week, Lowell thought they were on the right track. They had followed a line of quartz outcroppings into a dead-end gorge but the rock never amounted to anything, ending in a tall bluff of limestone.

Placers could be found in almost any area where gold occurred in hard-rock deposits. Weathering forced the gold free of the rock where it was carried by gravity and hydraulic action to some favorable point of deposition and concentrated in the process. Usually the gold did not travel far from the source, so knowledge of the location of the lode deposits was useful. Gold also could be associated with copper and might form placers in the vicinity of copper deposits, although this occurred less frequently.

Geological events such as uplift and subsidence might cause prolonged and repeated cycles of erosion and concentration, and where these processes had taken place, placer deposits might be enriched. Ancient river channels and certain river bench deposits were examples of gold-bearing gravels that had been subjected to a number of such events, followed by at least partial concealment by other deposits, including volcanic materials.

Residual placer deposits formed in the immediate vicinity of source rocks were usually not the most productive, although exceptions occurred where veins supplying the gold were rich. Reworking of gold-bearing materials by stream action led to the concentrations necessary for exploitation. In desert areas, deposits might result from sudden flooding and outwash of intermittent streams.

As material gradually washed off the slopes and into streams, it became sorted or stratified, and gold concentrated in so-called pay streaks with other heavy minerals, among which magnetite, black, heavy, and magnetic were typically present. The gold might not be entirely liberated from the original rock but might still have the white-to-gray vein quartz or other rock material attached to or enclosing it. As gold moved downstream, it was gradually freed from the accompanying rock and flattened by the incessant pounding of gravel. Eventually it would become flakes and tiny particles as the flattened pieces broke up.

Pay-streaks always formed on the path that gold followed in the river. Sometimes there might be more than one gold path, because the gold might be originating in the river from several different sources. Pay-streaks were very important to miners because they were larger than single-type deposits, such as those found in a bedrock crevice along the gold path. Therefore, pay-streaks were easier to find. Because they tended to be long and wide, pay-streaks were deposits that could be worked for quite some time. Gold could be recovered from a pay-streak located on bedrock. It could also be found throughout the streambed material or on the top of a flood layer.

Most gold traveled along the bottom of the other suspended streambed material as it was washed downriver during a major flood. If the material was washed down across bedrock, then gold could become trapped in the various irregularities, cracks, and holes. Sometimes, if conditions allowed, gold might even be deposited on top of smooth bedrock to form a pay-streak in a low-pressure area of the river.

Sometimes, because the flood was not quite extreme enough to break up pre-existing hard-packed streambeds, material moving during a flood would wash over the top of already established streambed layers, rather than across the bedrock. Therefore, newly formed pay-streaks might be found on top of pre-existing streambed layers, rather than on bedrock.

Most gold-bearing rivers had some amount of gold

disbursed throughout the streambed material, so a miner could recover a small amount of gold out of each sample hole, called *traces*. This usually was not much gold; not enough to get excited about, and not enough to support a small-scale mining operation.

It generally took a few sample holes to give a prospector an idea of the average amount of gold that was disbursed in the streambed. A miner could expect to get this small amount of gold from each sample hole that he dredged or dug. If he recovered more gold from a sample hole than was showing up in the average streambed, he knew he was onto something.

"So, what now, Mr. Lowell?" Yarak said. He shot a glance upstream to where Garby and Terkel were hunched over a small campfire, warming themselves.

"I think we need to go back to that line of quartz we found last week," Lowell said. "It's been the only real clue we've seen. Maybe another line heads off in a different direction. We really haven't located anything that looks like gold or the mine itself."

"We've seen a number of caves but nothing like a mine entrance. Wouldn't it have to be near a source of water to run the sluice?"

"Yeah, it would. With all the abandoned mines in northern Nevada you'd think we'd have stumbled across something," Lowell said, frustration showing in his voice. The sun was higher and heat began to accumulate in Mule Valley.

Yarak nodded. Louis and Terkel were loading gear into a jeep.

Lowell spat the last of his coffee onto the ground. "Okay," he said. "Let's get going. We're burning daylight."

෴

Harry and Dixie sat in their dormitory room of the research facility, having just finished dressing before heading to the dining hall for breakfast. Dixie brushed her hair while Harry donned his boots.

"I didn't sleep very well last night, honey," she said, stopping for a moment with her brushing. "I kept thinking of poor Jimmy. I never knew him, did you?"

"Sure. I interviewed him for the position here as graduate assistant along with Millie. I can't believe this happened. It's not going to go well for the university if these Yeti manage to get to a town where there's more people. We've got to contain them here on the mountain. If they get off the mountain, they can go in any direction and the search area widens by an infinite amount."

"Did the sheriff talk to his parents?"

"He did late last night. They live in Waco, Texas. He said they took the news pretty hard."

"Lawsuit?" Dixie said, still brushing her hair.

"I don't even want to think of that, sweetie. We've got to find these Yeti before any more people are killed."

"I was just thinking, though. If Jimmy opened the cage as Millie says he did, the university can't be held liable for his egregious actions. Just saying."

"I hope you're right. Ready for some breakfast?"

"I'll go with you," Dixie said, "but I don't know if I can eat."

⸙⸙⸙

Millie stepped out of the shower, dried herself quickly with a towel, and dressed. There was not going to be any scientific work done today, she reasoned, so she pulled on a pair of faded jeans and a blouse.

She reflected on her relationship with the dead Jimmy Winkleman and shuddered. As bad and unprofessional as it had been, she never imagined he would be killed in the manner he was.

When they both first arrived at the Primate Research Facility, they were friendly with each other and discussed the Yeti genome project. They ate dinner together. Radner had overseen their work and seemed pleased with their progress. As the work progressed, however, Millie noticed a subtle change in Jimmy, one that she thought was due to their being isolated at the facility. Beyond the pool table and the library of DVD movies, there wasn't much else to do for relaxation. Millie enjoyed reading so it wasn't much of a problem but it seemed to put Jimmy on edge.

After an awkward attempt to take her to bed, he became increasingly withdrawn, refusing to discuss their mutual work with the Yeti, and even exhibiting aggressive behavior toward his animal, shouting at them and banging on Bentu's cage. He once tried the same with Sasha, but Millie had come down on him hard, threatening to report him to Radner if he didn't leave the animals alone. But he had only confined his actions toward Bentu, who would sit in a corner of his cage and growl for hours.

She debated whether she should go to Radner with her complaints about Jimmy and his treatment of Bentu but, after many sleepless nights, decided against doing so. The two of them had to work together so maybe she still could get him to see things her way.

Obviously, she was wrong.

Millie was worried on several fronts. She anguished over the Yeti's safety and the safety of anyone who came in contact with them. She tortured herself with thoughts that this tragedy would put an end to her research and that her doctorate dissertation was in jeopardy. If she had to start all over with another research project it would take another few years and she would be that much farther behind her peers. She longed for a teaching job at a university in the Southwest, but they might all be taken if she was forced to begin anew. Fortunately, she had the Yeti's blood samples and DNA and could always replicate the DNA at any time. She slapped on lipstick and, as she did, she studied her face. Her mother's strong Italian features were etched in her tanned face, accentuating her green eyes and strong nose. She was happy that Dixie accompanied her husband, for maybe there would be a moment the two of them could talk about her research. Millie was never close to an animal before like she was with Sasha. There was something in her penetrating red eyes, eyes that would turn soft when she was sedated and Millie stroked her massive head.

If Sasha was on the run, scared and knowing she was a hunted prey, she was liable to lash out at the first humans she encountered. And if that happened, Millie knew it would spell the great animal's demise—she would be killed without a second thought.

Millie couldn't let that happen.

She put the finishing touches on her makeup and left for the dining hall.

❡❡❡❡

Undersheriff Andy Hardin, the last of a long line of Paiute warriors, met the pair of deputies at the top of Cinder Mountain. It was just past dawn and the deputies finished parking a horse trailer that contained a half dozen horses with their tack. He hurried over to the trailer and greeted his fellow deputies.

"Good morning, Ben and Louis," he said. He ambled around the trailer, peeking inside to get a look at the horses. "Any trouble getting up the mountain with this rig?"

"Not a bit, Andy," said Ben, a tall lanky deputy. "Piece of cake."

"I'll just bet," Hardin replied. "You forget, I've driven up that winding road. Well, the boss wants to get started as soon as everyone is through with breakfast so get 'em unloaded and saddled. Should be good weather today. I'll go tell Buck you're here."

Hardin had an uneasy feeling about the upcoming search on horseback. The search by air had proved unsuccessful so, as daylight faded, the helicopter returned home. He'd never looked for a quarry quite like these animals, and he didn't know what to expect. Expect the unexpected, Calder always said. They could be hiding anywhere on the mountain, if they were still on the mountain. But Hardin didn't see how they could have gone very far. According to the sheriff, they were big lumbering animals so were probably slow afoot. It shouldn't take too long to locate them. It was the impending confrontation that had his nerves on edge.

His ancestors traced their origin to the story of Tabuts, the wise wolf who decided to carve many different people out of sticks. His plan was to scatter them evenly around the Earth so that everyone would have a good place to live, but Tabuts had a mischievous younger brother, Shinangway, the coyote. Shinangway cut open the sack and people fell out in bunches all over the world. The people were angry at this treatment and that was why other people always fought. The people left in the sack were the Southern Paiutes. Tabuts blessed them and put them in the best place.

Prior to contact with Europeans, the Paiutes' homeland spanned more than thirty million acres of present-day Southern California, Nevada, south-central Utah, and northern Arizona. Their lifestyle included moving often, according to the seasons, plant harvests, and animal migration patterns, and they lived in independent groups of three to five households. Major decisions were made in council meetings. The traditional Paiute leader, called *naive*, offered advice and suggestions at council meetings and would later work to carry out the council's decisions.

Though the mid-1800s the Southern Paiutes encountered Euro-American traders, travelers, and trappers but they did not have to deal with white settlement on their lands. In 1851, however, members of the LDS Church began colonization efforts in the area of southern Utah, and by the end of 1858, Mormons established eleven settlements in Southern Paiute territory. At first, the Paiutes welcomed the Mormon presence, as it offered them some protection against raiding Utes, Navajos, and Mexicans. However, the Mormon settlements also brought sweeping epidemics. In the decade following settlement, some Paiute groups lost more than ninety percent of their population to disease, forcing many to relocate in Nevada.

His ancestor, Chief Truckee, was a friend of the whites. He died before seeing the wrongs inflicted on his people by the pioneer whites and how they inflamed the Paiutes into the waging of a bloody war that wound up costing scores of white and Indian lives. Chief Winnemucca, at times, favored war on the whites but, at the point of conflict, he would always ride into the Humboldt River country, where his father had spent most of his life, where the grass was deep, and where the hunting was most plentiful. Within a matter of weeks of his death, the troubles broke into a massacre and the Battle of Pyramid Lake.

Hardin watched as Calder exited the main building with the two Dr. Olsons and Drayton at his side.

Chapter 12

Vickie Anderson pulled her van off the road. She was tired—no, exhausted—from traveling through the night with her companions. After leaving San Francisco, they drove through Sacramento, past Lake Tahoe, then continued into northwest Nevada until her small band of demonstrators were now gathered at the sign denoting the beginning of the Primate Research Facility's property. Cinder Mountain loomed at the end of the dirt road as a large dark shadow. Now that the sun peeked over the distant horizon, Vickie munched on an Egg McMuffin purchased in Elko. The sky was clear, the temperature cool. She hoped the television crew from Las Vegas would arrive soon so they could get the demonstration done and start the drive back home before late afternoon.

Vickie exited the van to stretch her legs and wait for the media to arrive. Her friends followed suit, including Norma Treadwell who ambled to her side, nodded.

"Well, we made it," Vickie said, finishing her Egg McMuffin. "And all in one piece."

"We all appreciate the use if your van, Vickie," Norma said.

"It was something I could do to help."

"Why are you here?" Norma said. "I'm interested."

"My mother," Vickie began, "died from breast cancer. Her treatments were developed using laboratory animals. And those treatments allowed her to live another few years. I cherish those years, Norma."

"I would think that would make you on the other side of our fight," Norma said. "It would me, I believe."

"I must admit I've been having second thoughts. Your zeal and eloquence swayed me to your cause but, lately, I've had my doubts about the ethics of our demonstrations."

"How so?" Norma asked.

"Some people believe it is not acceptable to use animals for any human purpose at all. They believe animals have moral rights to life, liberty, and other privileges that should be upheld by society and the rule of law. These are the hard-core believers in animal rights, the fundamentalists of the animal rights movement. I think that is where our group is positioned. Other people believe some animals have or should have moral or legal rights under certain circumstances. They may rescue abandoned pets, lobby for legislation against animal abuse, feed pigeons in the park, or do any number of other things on behalf of animals. These people are broadly categorized as animal welfarists. Their adherence to the idea of animal rights generally depends on the circumstances. For example, a welfarist might defend the rights of pet dogs and cats but eat chicken, steak, or pork for dinner. I am beginning to think I belong in the latter category, Norma. After all, if science cannot use animals to test and develop new treatments, what can they use? I am afraid if all animals are no longer used in medical research new and innovative treatments will no longer be possible. Maybe there is an ethical way to use research animals."

Norma shook her head. "Vickie, this is unacceptable

to us animal rights fundamentalists. FAAR argues that all animals, not just the lovable or attractive ones, have rights that apply all the time. Not just when it is convenient."

"I dunno, Norma. I am beginning to believe that the animal rights issue is blown out of proportion. Animals— or any other living thing, for that matter—do have a right to this Earth as much as we do. With that said, I have the opinion that everything on this Earth is for the utility of humanity. This in no way, shape, or form gives any one the right to abuse, destroy, become cruel, or any other form mischief. Animals should not be abused or made to suffer pain or as least pain as possible. Isn't it possible that animals can be used for medical research in a moral and ethical way? Without causing them undue pain and suffering?"

Norma walked away with slow steps then turned to face Vickie. "I think when we get back home you should reconsider your membership in our group." Her words hissed venom. "I don't need someone who's not fully committed to our cause."

Using her binoculars, she located activity at the top of the mountain, activity she surmised was from the facility. A thin haze that hung over the mountain's summit made visibility nebulous.

It was strange, she thought. Earlier, a helicopter landed and a military helicopter took off a short time afterward. What was an army chopper doing at the research facility?

There seemed to be a lot of activity so early in the morning—lights on all over the place, along with what looked like people moving about. She didn't know the usual routine on Cinder Mountain but felt fairly sure that normal activity didn't include a military helicopter.

She helped her crew unload the placards from the rear

of the van and waited in the cool morning air for the television people to arrive.

ᴄ∕ᴈᴄ∕ᴈ

"Thanks for getting the horses ready, Andy, Ben, and
Louis," Calder said when they were standing alongside
the horse trailer. He introduced Harry and Dixie to his
deputies. Harry wore a daypack and a pair of binoculars
hung around his neck. Drayton had his 30-30 slung over
his shoulder and his nine-millimeter pistol on his hip.
Harry and Dixie carried no weapons.

"No firepower, Doctor?" Hardin said.

"No. I've got a flare gun in case we spot them. You
should be able to see it from any point on the mountain."

"Okay," Calder said, "Chief Drayton and Andy will
head north from here. Ben, you and Louis search east.
Doctors Olson, you both head west, and I'll go south.
Take these walkie-talkies and sing out if you spot anything."

"Please," Harry said, "don't shoot unless it's absolutely necessary. Once we find the Yeti, we'll get Dr. Siscom
who is waiting here at the main complex to shoot them
with his tranquilizer darts."

"Doctor is right," Calder added. "These animals are
valuable scientific specimens so let's try and capture
them alive, okay? All right, let's go."

They each mounted a horse, Harry a dun gelding and
Dixie a bay mare. *Getting more used to these animals*,
Harry thought. *Mongolia was good training for horse-
manship*. As they all went in their separate directions,
Harry shot a final look at the compound, already shim-
mering in the sweltering morning sun.

He guided the gelding over a narrow trail with Dixie
right behind. The trail, made rugged by numerous rocks

and roots protruding out of the soil, wound down the western mountain slope in a gentle fashion. They had a clear unobstructed view of the desert plains below that appeared as a patchwork quilt of greens and browns. In the far distance, a blue dot interrupted the plain, signifying a lake or reservoir.

Cinder Mountain was mostly granite rock and low-lying vegetation. In the Sierra Mountain Range, it was forested by mountain evergreens. An occasional gnarled Joshua tree punctuated the arid landscape. Now and then Harry turned in his saddle to check on Dixie who gave him a repeated thumbs up as they rode.

The Sierra Nevada, a major mountain range of western North America, running along the eastern edge of California, lay between the large Central Valley depression to the west and the Basin and Range Province to the east. Extending more than two hundred fifty miles northward from the Mojave Desert to the Cascade Range of northern California and Oregon, the Sierra Nevada varied from about eighty miles wide at Lake Tahoe to about fifty miles wide in the South.

Geologists had long recognized that the Sierra Nevada was an up-faulted, tilted block of the Earth's crust. A major fault zone bounded the block on the east, and it was along this that the great mass that became the Sierra Nevada was uplifted and tilted westward. This explained the asymmetry of the range. As the block was uplifted the abrupt, east-facing escarpment was cut into by the erosive action of wind, rain, temperature change, frost, and ice, and a series of steep-gradient canyons developed. On its western flank, streams flowed more gently down the geologic dip slope, creating massive alluvial fans that encroached into the Central Valley of California. Though the massive uplift began many millions of years ago, much of it occurred during the past two million years.

In the days of the dinosaurs, a chain of volcanoes similar to the present day Cascade region coursed the Sierra. Much magma flowed out to the surface as lava through these intrusions, while even more solidified deep underground amidst immense pressures to form the characteristic ubiquitous gray-white granite common in the range. Over time, erosion scoured off much of the weaker volcanic rock above the granite, revealing domes and the widespread granite intrusion into the Earth's crust that extended the length of the range. Less than five million years ago, the Sierra Nevada began to rise as the Pacific plate pushed under the North American plate. This created a massive tilted fault along the eastern edge of the range, raising the Sierra and sinking the land to the east. This ongoing process raised the elevation of the range yet higher with each slippage of the fault.

Harry guided his horse down the trail, all the while searching the rock outcroppings and overhangs as well as the dense brush for signs of the Yeti. Not seeing any, he and Dixie continued until they reached a sheer drop off next to a narrow ledge. Harry dismounted and helped Dixie off her horse. Together they sat perched on a large flat boulder looking west into a searing sun. Harry doffed his pack, found a water bottle, and handed it to Dixie.

"Thanks," she said after a big gulp.

Harry took a drink of the water and replaced the bottle in his daypack.

"You can see forever up here, can't you?"

He nodded and put an arm around her. "It's beautiful. Can you believe, honey, that those animals that we risked our lives getting over here are now loose and somewhere out there? They could be anywhere."

He used the binocs to scan the western horizon and shook his head.

"Nothing. I don't see anything."

They remounted and continued their way down Cinder Mountain while a number of hawks sailed through the blue sky above them. As the sun began its downward course toward the horizon, a few scattered clouds formed overhead. They continued on in a spiraling switchback fashion toward the plain. Near the base of the mountain the orange ball of the sun dipped below the horizon and the temperature turned cooler. Harry hopped off his mount and stretched his legs. Dixie followed suit.

"Harry," she said, "have you ever wondered why one of our graduate assistants would turn bad, like Jimmy? I mean how did we miss something in his underlying personality that led him to do such things to his Yeti as Millie described? My god, we entrusted the animal to his care! How could he treat the thing like that? I am so ashamed for our program, I don't know what to say."

"Do you think it was a flaw in his basic character or personality or do you think he was conditioned over time by repeated dealings with the Yeti?"

"I don't know, but whatever it was, we, the faculty, missed it. We either missed it when we were selecting persons to come up here or Dr. Radner missed it in his daily dealings with Jimmy. Either way, I feel it was our responsibility to protect those animals and we failed. I'm sick about it and will be sicker still if anything happens to them."

"Honey, there's nothing we can do now but try and find them and bring them back safely to the facility. But it's starting to get dark so we need to get back up the mountain. We haven't heard from anyone today so I guess the search is a bust."

"I think in the future, if there is a future for the primate facility," Dixie said, "we need to make sure the grad assistants have the right personality for this job. This place."

That evening over dinner, the Sheriff outlined his plans for the next day. Since the Yeti were not on Cinder Mountain, the search area needed to be enlarged. He had put out an APB describing the Yeti to all county sheriff departments in the state and all police departments.

"So, first thing in the morning," he said, "we'll be moving the command post down to the base of the mountain."

Radner pushed his plate away and sat back in his chair. "I cannot believe they made it off the mountain," he said. "I just can't accept it."

"Dr. Radner," Drayton cleared his throat. "We found where they tore through the security fence, left a huge hole. The amazing thing is that it was between the visual field of two adjacent security cameras, in a blind spot, if you will. Something I never noticed before. The blind spot, I mean. They must be incredibly strong to tear a hole that size in a steel fence. Hard to believe."

"Interesting how they knew where the blind spot was located," Radner said and he took a sip of his coffee.

"I am always amazed," Harry said, "when someone who isn't familiar with the Yeti is surprised at their unbelievable strength. And intellect. I'm sure our veterinarian can speak to innate animal intelligence."

Dr. Siscom put down his fork, wiped his mouth with a napkin, and nodded. "It seems that every time we humans announce that we've discovered something that makes our species unique, we find nestled in some far corner some other species that renders our opinion obsolete. You would think we'd have learned to be more cautious over the years.

"Going further, people have always viewed some animals as more intelligent than others—in European cultures, dogs, horses, great apes, and, more recently, dolphins, and parrots are seen as intelligent in ways that other animals are not. Crows have been attributed with humanlike intelligence by almost every culture that has encountered them.

"A number of recent survey studies have demonstrated the consistency of these rankings between people in a given culture. A common image is the *scala naturae*, the ladder of nature on which animals of different species occupy successively higher rungs, with humans typically at the top. Comparative psychologists have sought in vain for ways of providing an objective underpinning for these subjective and anthropocentric judgments.

"Part of the difficulty is the lack of agreement about what we mean by intelligence even in humans. For example, it obviously makes a big difference whether language is considered as essential for intelligence or not.

"But in any case, different animals, including humans, seem to have different kinds of cognitive processes, which are better understood in terms of the ways in which they are cognitively adapted to their different ecological niches, than by positing any kind of hierarchy.

"One question that can be asked coherently is how far different species are intelligent in the same ways as humans are; in other words, are their cognitive processes similar to ours. Not surprising, our closest biological relatives, the great apes, tend to do best on such an assessment.

"It is less clear that the species traditionally held to be intelligent do well against this standard, though among them, the crows and parrots typically are found to outperform other groups, and among the carnivores, dogs generally show better performance than cats.

"Despite ambitious claims, evidence of unusually high human-like intelligence among whales and dolphins is patchy, partly because the cost and difficulty of carrying out research with marine mammals. It means that experiments suffer from small sample sizes and inadequate controls and replication."

Dixie smiled. "Dr. Siscom, I didn't realize you were such an authority."

The veterinarian blushed and looked down at his plate. He was rarely so eloquent.

"You just make my point, Dr. Siscom, that we have barely scratched the surface when it comes to understanding animal intelligence."

"I guess I have a lot to learn about the field of animal psychology," Radner said. "I have been so consumed with genetics, of late, that I have overlooked certain other fields."

"And the strength of these Yeti," Millie said. "To think that they just ripped a huge hole in our chain-link fence. Wow."

Later, in their dorm room, Harry watched as Dixie wrote in a notebook.

"What are you doing?" he asked.

"Keeping a diary," she said.

"But why?"

"Because later I want to be able to remember every detail of this experience. Who knows why? I just do, that's all."

Harry shrugged and changed into his scrubs before retiring. As he lay in the bed, he watched his wife with amusement.

Chapter 13

The following morning Harry was back in the saddle on the dun gelding. Sheriff Calder had moved his command post and horse trailer to the base of Cinder Mountain. The command post was a small travel trailer that was parked on a wide spot off the dirt road leading to the mountain and a gasoline generator provided it with electricity. Drayton drove Harry to the command post and there he saddled the dun himself and headed northward, alone, across the plains. He persuaded Dixie to remain behind and go over the research projects with Millie and Radner. She had, predictably, protested, but in the end, Harry managed to have his way.

Armed with a topographic map of the area and his GPS, he felt he was ready for any contingency and couldn't get lost. Clouds hung in low billows over the plains, blunting the sun's fury while a gentle breeze swept him and the gelding along. Dense rock formations and mesquite shrubs punctuated the plain. Only a lone Joshua tree every mile or so interrupted the monotonous landscape.

The gelding kicked up small dust devils as Harry moved north. He had a vague idea of some ancient Indian ruins farther northwest that Radner mentioned on his earlier trip. Harry didn't know why but he turned his horse in that general direction, hoping he might pick up tracks of the Yeti.

He found nothing.

Farther along, he came to a ravine, an arroyo, a dried streambed that was carved into the dried cracked earth and meandered in a northwesterly direction. Pushing his horse down into the arroyo, he followed its serpentine course for several hours, stopping periodically to drink from his water bottle. The clouds were now darker, with a line building into menacing thunderheads. In the distance, lightning sparked in dramatic bolts and thunder rolled across the plains like artillery.

In the semiarid southwestern United States, water was an important ecological factor. However, most streams in the region were ephemeral—dry for much of the year and flowed only during flash floods or spring snowmelt. Many of these streams were confined to deep, steep-walled channels entrenched into alluvial valley bottoms. These channels were called arroyos and were found in drylands throughout the world.

Most arroyos in the Southwest were cut between 1880 and 1910. Prior to this historic episode of arroyo-cutting, settlers characterized valley bottoms as marshy wetlands or grasslands with shallow channels. During arroyo-cutting, incision and subsequent widening of channels led to the loss of thousands of acres of farmland, destruction of roads, dams, and canals, and ultimately the abandonment of a number of communities.

The one in which Harry plodded was not a particularly wide arroyo, only twenty feet wide at the most, with sides extending up six or seven feet. The floor of the arroyo was soft sand, a definite change from the rock and grasses of the plain.

Harry's horse stopped.

He kicked the horse's sides with his heels but the horse didn't move. He pawed the ground, threw his head.

Suddenly, the gelding reared, throwing Harry from the saddle. He landed on his side, legs askew, against a boulder. When his right leg hit the ground, it sent a shock wave of pain through his ankle and knee and into his head, momentarily blinding him. He rubbed his eyes hoping to lessen the pain. The gelding was nowhere to be seen.

Gone.

Damn, Harry thought, what could have spooked the animal? Then he saw it. A brown snake coiled up against a rock, its flared head at the ready.

Harry lay in the arroyo and eyed the snake until, apparently bored, it slithered away.

Harry attempted to stand but the pain in his leg made him lightheaded and he fell back to the ground. Head reeling, he pulled himself against a boulder and propped himself into a sitting position, looked about.

"Shit!" he yelled into the air. His water and lunch were on the horse as were his maps and GPS. At least the day was cooler than the previous ones or he would be cooked beneath a broiling sun. He knew he was in a precarious situation—alone, on foot, in the high desert, with no food or water, no weapon, and no one who knew the exact route he took. Dixie wouldn't expect him back at the research facility until later in the day, and all Drayton knew was he headed north.

He needed to find water and some shelter.

But how? Where?

The ache in his leg made concentration difficult. But if he just sat in this place he would become dehydrated and die before help found him.

With considerable effort, he pulled himself to the top of the arroyo and peered over its rim into the vastness beyond. Nothing but sand, rocks, boulders, and mesquite for miles in every direction. Overhead, the storm clouds billowed and the wind picked up, blowing tiny grains of sand in his face. They stung like tiny needles. He gazed off to the northwest but saw nothing that looked like Indian ruins. They must be out there, somewhere, he reasoned.

A loud clap of thunder startled him. He knew, when the rains came, the arroyo would become a raging stream so he needed to climb over the rim. He pushed himself onto an elbow, dug the toes of his boots into the arroyo's crust, and inched his way over its crest. Pain racked his leg, the throbbing pounded in his temples. With each step up the arroyo wall and each time he jabbed the toe of his boor into the hardened earth, a bolt of pain seared his brain. Where was that damned horse, he cursed. When he left Dixie earlier, the thought of dying in the desert never entered his mind. Now he was fighting for his life. Using considerable effort, he pulled himself out and lay on his back, panting. The energy expended left him exhausted but he knew he had to find the ruins before dark and the storm hit. He pulled himself along using his good leg to push, slithering over the ground like the snake he had seen earlier.

It was backbreaking work and progress was slow, agonizingly slow. The desert plain, having acted as an oven, reflected its heat back into his pain-racked body, sapping his strength further. Perspiration covered his forehead, ran into his eyes—the salt stinging them. He was surprised that he was sweating. Figured he was dehydrated by now. He continued crawling at a snail's pace, trying to concentrate, not on his predicament, but on moving forward. Mind over matter. His lips were swollen, his mouth parched. He couldn't help thinking of Dixie. And how he hoped she would start worrying sooner rather than later.

He hadn't crawled more than a hundred yards when the rain began. A drizzle at first, it progressed to a frank downpour within a matter of minutes. Harry rolled over onto his back and opened his mouth, letting the large raindrops moisten his lips and tongue. It tasted like dust, but it was better than nothing. Feeling somewhat better, he continued on.

Soon, his clothes were drenched. The temperature dropped, and the wind blew out of the north. It wasn't long before he was chilled, but he kept moving, crawling, hoping that all the work involved would keep him warmed. Within an hour, however, his body shook with a violent chill. The sky continued to dump sheets of rain, punctuated by lightning strikes and booming thunder. Harry never heard thunder so loud. Out on the desert plain, with nothing to absorb, the sound his eardrums pounded with each booming rattle.

He continued crawling.

The throbbing in his leg caused his entire body to convulse. He tried putting his mind elsewhere but it was difficult—it kept returning to his leg. Had he broken something? His mind became a swirl of jumbled thoughts, a nightmare of past events in his life. He saw his mother, his abusive father, his estranged brother. His body shook again with a painful chill that brought him back to the present.

And the pain.

Still, he continued on.

The ground over which he crawled turned to mud, a thick sticky, gooey mess that made his progress difficult. The stuff clung to his clothes, creating a sucking sound with each movement of his limbs. The afternoon had turned dark, menacing, and he began to doubt his chances for survival. If he didn't find shelter soon, those chances would diminish even further. Funny how, out here on the

desert, the weather could be just fine one minute and harrowing the next. All he wanted to do was to crawl into a
ball and forget everything, but he knew that would spell
disaster. *If I don't find shelter soon*, he thought, *I'm going
to die out here*. His teeth chattered from the chill.

Ahead, he saw nothing but a continuum of rolling
hills, buttes, rock outcroppings, endless miles of sagebrush, and mesquite. Harry searched in vain for a rock
formation large enough to huddle under or a cave to
crawl into. The raindrops pelted his skin, stung his face.
With every few yards, he felt his strength ebbing.

To his right he thought he saw a ledge so he inched his
way to it but when he pulled himself there, he found it
did not provide any protection from the driving rain. He
continued on, his arms now aching.

God help me, he thought.

He moved on.

The rain was less now, down to a drizzle, but the sky
was dark, approaching black. Then up ahead he thought
he saw something through the mist—a series of vague
gray shapes. Forcing the pain away, he doubled his efforts and pushed his way toward them. Closer, he saw the
shapes were a group of mounds and low adobe walls.

The ruins.

He had found the ruins.

They were in a shallow canyon with rugged walls on
the east and west that protected the ancient village from
the elements. For about a thousand years, from about 500
CE until their dispersal around 1500, the Anasazi, whose
name was a Navajo word that means *the ancient ones*,
lived in pueblos and cliff dwellings built in the canyons
and high mesas of the Four Corners region where Colorado, New Mexico, Arizona, and Utah meet.

The ruins were those of the Anasazi that occupied the
region, originally by the Basketmaker people sometime

after the first century, and later by the Puebloans from 700 to 1150. The Paiute Indians moved into the area after 1000. The Basketmakers lived in sub-terrain pit houses that were ten to fifteen feet in diameter and approximately six feet deep. They used spears for hunting and their name was derived from their use of baskets as storage vessels. The later Puebloans lived in above ground pueblos—nothing more than houses made of sticks and adobe. They had the additional knowledge of the bow and arrow and manufactured ceramic vessels for storage and cooking.

The Anasazi farmed corn, beans, squash, and cotton on the marshy valley floor and built multi-roomed pueblos on the gravel benches along the valley margins. In addition to farming and hunting natural resources, the Anasazi mined salt and turquoise both for their own personal use and as a prized trade item.

More advanced was the pit dwelling with an encircling wall of adobe, or adobe and stone. The pit, in this case, yielded the remains of the fallen wall. In some places there were isolated pit-dwellings, in others whole groups were placed in a more or less haphazard way, while in still others, the pits were arranged in a row, side by side, with a narrow space between.

And it was from rows of pit-dwellings like this that true houses developed, when some enterprising pit-dweller conceived the brilliant idea that he might make a single party-wall answer for two adjoining pit-dwellings, simply by digging them close together and making the intervening wall straight instead of curved. However, the true rectangular room came later.

In most of the houses, the rooms remained more like ovals, cut straight across at the ends, than like rectangles—that is, the end walls only were straight, while the side walls remained curved to a greater or lesser extent, and the floors were still more or less sunken below the surface of the ground.

It all formed an exquisitely planned city, its form aligned with the canyon wall behind it and the pattern of its connected chambers as complex and finely articulated as a honeycomb.

But it was nothing more than a series of ruins now, when Harry pulled himself into the shelter of an adobe wall. The rain had let up and the wind was only a gentle breeze. He sucked the rainwater out of his shirt, and it quenched his thirst. He looked around the low, crumbling walls and noticed a few pits with collapsed sides, the bricks scattered about as if a tornado had blown through the ancient village. To the west, a soft glow indicated a setting sun, and Harry prepared himself for a cold night on the desert plain.

Exhausted from all his crawling, he allowed his body to relax. Somewhat drier, he was a little warmer. He hunkered down, wrapped his arms about himself, and tried to forget his aching leg.

❧❧❧

He was in a black cave, black as obsidian, and he was unable to see beyond his own body. He felt around and found Dixie next to him, asleep. In the darkness, he could hear something moving about with a shuffling gait. No, there was more than one. He couldn't make them out but he could hear them. By the sound they made, he knew they were large. His pulse quickened at the thought that they were readying themselves for an attack, an attack he and Dixie were ill suited to repel. He reached out and pulled Dixie closer. They didn't stand a chance against them for they were bigger, more powerful.

Evil.

Then he thought he saw something in the darkness beyond. Just an imperceptible flicker but it was surely there. A reddish glow momentarily seen then gone. He knew what the glow was. He had seen it before. It was the creature's eye. The beast or beasts that roamed the depths of the cave. A roar went up, out of the black void, sending a wave of panic through his body. He stiffened and prepared himself for the attack.

Harry jolted awake. God, it had been a dream. His entire body now ached from lying in an awkward position on the hard ground. He gazed upward and noticed that stars were out, twinkling like tiny jewels on a black velvet cloth. He shivered.

The night was not yet over.

Chapter 14

Rupert Lowell was on the track of a line of quartz that extended into a rocky gorge covered with dense brush and small trees. It had been rough going after Yarak stumbled onto the shiny crystals to one side of a small tributary of the Taber River in Mule Valley. Earlier in the week, they had followed another tributary without any luck so Yarak's find sent a wave of jubilation through Lowell.

The fact that, the Lost Coyote Creek Mine might still remain elusive and undiscoverable, occasioned a feeling of dolefulness to alter his mood.

Yarak, along with Garby and Terkel, led the way, blazing a trail for Lowell with their machetes. The quartz was difficult to follow, with many areas along its line devoid of any crystal. Most of it lay below the surface, Lowell knew, but following its surface projections, he hoped, would lead to a vein of gold.

Gold deposits formed at many different times during Earth's history. Those in the western United States were believed to have formed about 2400 million years ago, during a period of intense metamorphism and intrusion of igneous rocks. The gold-bearing quartz reefs in Nevada were significantly younger, about 400 million years, but also owed their origin to a period of intense metamorphism in the region.

As chemical weathering and erosion gradually broke down the host rocks and lowered the land surface, the quartz and gold veins were eventually exposed to the atmosphere. The veins provided far more resistance to chemical attack than the surrounding rocks, so that mechanical weathering was required to fragment the quartz, thereby releasing the gold. Because they were relatively heavy, particles of gold were more difficult to move and so became naturally concentrated in the soil or in adjacent gullies or streambeds. These concentrations were known as alluvial or placer deposits and had yielded incredible riches on some goldfields, such as those in California and Colorado.

Alluvial deposits took many forms, including sands and gravels in the beds of modern-day streams, in old river valleys buried under lava flows, or perched on hilltops due to uplift of the land surface. The terms shallow and deep leads meant gold-bearing gravels covered by younger sedimentary layers or lava flows.

Gold would filter down a mountainside or canyon, eventually coming to rest in streams and rivers where it could be panned as placer deposits. But Lowell searched for the richer lode, the source of the deposits below. It was here that the Lost Coyote Creek Mine would be found.

He continued up the side of the gorge, struggling to keep up with the men ahead. It was rugged, hard work. Lowell understood why gold was worth so much. It was hell getting to it, finding it. Sweat poured off him, necessitating a periodic pause to wipe his brow and take a sip water.

A shout from Yarak pierced the quiet.

He looked ahead and saw Yarak waving at him, beckoning him up. Lowell hurried up the side of the gorge, stumbling along the way, tripping over a root or rock that he did not see, until he stood alongside his assistant.

"What's up, Yarak?" he said, out of breath.

"Look here, boss." Yarak led Lowell to a rock overhang bordered by thick thorny brush. He pointed with a dirty finger. "There," he said. "Look there."

Lowell looked into the dark recess under the overhand and noticed a black hole, its sides braced by thick, heavy, rotting timbers.

"What is it? An old mine entrance?" he said.

Yarak, Garby, and Terkel were smiling at each other, as if proud of their achievement.

"Looks like it," Yarak said. "What else would be braced by timbers like that?"

"They're certainly old," Garby said.

"And the quartz extends right up to it," Terkel added.

Lowell looked back down the side of the gorge to the stream. They had hiked all morning, and he was hungry. "If this is a mine, it would make sense," he said. "Especially if there are placer gold deposits in that stream down there. Nash, think you can get the jeeps and equipment up to the stream? We could eat lunch then explore this mine."

"It would be rough going, Mr. Lowell, but we can try. Both vehicles have a high clearance."

"Good. Why don't you and the boys give it a go while I wait down at the stream and rest? That climb wore out my legs."

"Fine," Yarak said, and the group slogged back to the stream where Lowell sat under a short tree and rested.

Gold might occur as deposits called lodes, or veins, in fractured rock. It might also be dispersed within Earth's crust. Most lode deposits formed when heated fluids circulated through gold-bearing rocks, picked up gold, and concentrated it in new locations in the crust. Chemical differences in the fluids and the rocks, as well as physical differences in the rocks, created many different types of lode deposits.

Over millions of years, gold flakes and nuggets worn away from veins were swept into bodies of water. The heavy gold settled in streams, lakes, and riverbeds, and on the sea floor, forming placer deposits.

Several mechanisms were at work. Superheated waters emerged from spring-like vents in the seafloor. This occurred where tectonic activity forced the spreading of the oceanic crust. Metal-rich minerals, including small amounts of gold, were deposited as the heated gold-laden water mixed with the cold seawater.

Alternatively, gold-laden water heated by magma-molten rock in the Earth's shallow crust formed a variety of lode gold deposits. Hydrothermal-hot water-fluids rich in sulfur could form gold ores in rocks of active volcanoes. Gold minerals formed in hot rocks in and around volcanoes. Low sulfur, gold-bearing hydrothermal fluids formed when hot rocks heated ground water.

Finally, fractures formed in Earth's crust as mountains rose. Hydrothermal fluids flowed into these spaces and formed gold-bearing quartz veins. These fluids were created by hot, deeply buried metamorphic rocks.

Placer deposits formed at Earth's surface when weathering action exposed gold from other, older lode deposits. The gold was swept into, and settled in, streams, lakes, rivers, or the sea floor. Many placer deposits were of recent geologic age, but some were billions of years old.

Lowell looked up when he heard a rumbling from downstream and saw the two jeeps bouncing over the rough terrain. At their approach, he stood and waited. When the jeeps were alongside Lowell, they stopped and Yarak jumped out.

"Made it," he said. "It was rough going, for sure. But here we are."

Garby and Terkel exited the other jeep and dropped onto the ground while Lowell rummaged in an ice chest and found the sandwiches and water. As the men ate, they chatted about the mine's entrance.

"Are we going in that thing?" Terkel asked. "Isn't it dangerous?"

"I've heard about these abandoned mines," Garby said. "They can collapse at any moment."

"Yes," Lowell said, glancing up the gorge. "Over the years the state of Nevada has worked hard at closing the entrances to these old mines but there's a lot of them they haven't located. Looks like this is one of them."

After eating and rehydrating themselves, the men hiked back up to the mine entrance with flashlights. Once there, they stood for a moment staring into the black hole.

"I'll lead." Lowell said.

He switched on his flashlight and stepped into the mine. Immediately, he noticed a drop in air temperature, the coolness caressing his face like a refreshing wave. Garby and Terkel followed, with Yarak bringing up the rear. The lights from their flashlights cast flickering beams against the walls and down the shaft. At regular intervals heavy wooden timbers braced the walls and ceiling of the mineshaft. A strange musty odor tickled Lowell's nose.

As they advanced farther into the mine, the shaft began a slow descent and angled toward their left. The walls were sand and rock, and Lowell surmised that whoever built the mine must have used explosives for part of it. Brown lichen and cobwebs covered the walls and their lights sent spiders and other insects scurrying for the darkness.

At one point, Lowell stopped to inspect a shoring timber. He took a small knife from his pocket and pried a small part of the timber away. The clump of wood fell in a mass of splinters onto the ground.

"Rotten," he said. "These timbers could disintegrate into nothing at any time. Cause the walls to come tumbling in on us."

"Great," Garby said. "Just what I need. A nineteenth century burial plot."

The shaft angled farther down and back to the right and, as they walked, Lowell had a strange feeling come over him. He couldn't pinpoint it, just a weird sensation that sent a shiver down his back. Soon they came to a Y, where the shaft branched into two divergent tunnels, around thirty degrees from each other. The group hesitated and shined their lights down each shaft.

"I haven't seen anything that looks like a gold vein," Yarak said. "If this was the lost mine we're after, where's the gold?"

"The Lost Coyote Creek Mine supposedly is worth billions in today's dollars," Lowell said. "So, if this is indeed the mine, there should be a lode of gold a yard wide somewhere in here."

Terkel laughed. "The Mother Lode.".

"I suggest we return to the jeeps, make camp, and come back in the morning. We'd have more time and can bring the bigger lanterns and testing equipment."

"Sounds like a plan to me," Yarak said.

The men turned around and headed back to the surface.

e⁄ɔe⁄ɔ

The evening meal was finished and dusk settled over Cinder Mountain. Harry had not returned and Dixie was worried. She saw Drayton chatting with Radner in the

lobby and walked over to them. Radner smiled and sauntered, off leaving her with the security chief. Drayton
nodded as she came near.

"Dr. Olson, I missed you at dinner. Where is that husband of yours, the other Dr. Olson?" He chuckled at his
small play on words.

"Bruce, I'm worried. Harry hasn't returned from his
searching the area north of our mountain."

Drayton's eyes narrowed and he studied Dixie. "Were
you expecting him by now?"

"Yes, I was. The sheriff has been unable to reach him
on his walkie-talkie. I'm worried, I must admit."

"There was a storm out on the plains earlier today,"
Drayton said. "He probably got wet."

"Oh dear. He could catch pneumonia. I hope he's not
hurt or something."

"Dr. Olson strikes me as the sort that can take care of
himself, ma'am. I would try to not worry too much."

"But I do."

"Tell you what," Drayton said. "If he's not back by
morning, I'll contact Sheriff Calder and get him to mount
a search for him. Okay?"

"Think we should wait till morning? Why not search
now? I am worried."

Drayton took Dixie by an arm and patted her shoulder.
"Can't do anything in the dark, Dr. Olson. He'll be fine,
I'm sure. May have to spend a cold night but he won't
die. If he doesn't return tonight, we'll get an early start
tomorrow."

"Thank you, Bruce."

Later, in her dorm room, Dixie sat at a desk and made
an entry in her diary. It was short for her thoughts were
on Harry and his welfare. He was out on the desert plain,
possibly hurt, suffering through a thunderstorm, and there
was no telling what he was doing for warmth this night.

She put her pen down and closed her diary. She wished she had gone with him—at least she could be with him, share whatever he had to endure. She knew from their experiences in Mongolia that her husband was a tough customer and could handle himself, but she worried, nonetheless. God, if he was dead, she would never forgive herself. Dixie tried to quell the fears rising within her mind that he had been hurt or might be unconscious. He had been her rock, her mentor. He had saved her life several times, once when she had fallen into a deep ravine and barely clung to its side, the other when the Yeti had kidnapped her. Both times, Harry had put his life on the line in order to save her own. She was in love with him then, of course, but those brave acts cemented her feelings. When he kissed her, her life changed forever.

He had been so pleased that his ailing mother had been able to meet her at his father's funeral. Her parents were at their wedding and again when she received her doctorate. Harry placed her doctoral hood on her shoulders at the ceremony.

Dixie climbed into bed and turned off the light. But it was a long time before sleep overtook her.

Chapter 15

D r. Miles Radner stood erect in front of a group of reporters and a company of television cameras. He was about to begin the news conference announcing the tragedy at the Primate Research Facility. There was a buzz of conversation among those gathered and, between the sun and the hot television lights, small beads of sweat formed on his brow. They were collected in front of the sign indicating the research property and warning trespassers away. Behind him were parked a number of satellite trucks, and he knew what he was about to say would be beamed worldwide.

"L—ladies and gentlemen," Radner began in a halting voice. How could he get them to understand that what had transpired was a tragic accident. The person responsible, dead.

"Ladies and gentlemen," he repeated. The buzz quieted and all eyes focused on him. "I am Dr. Miles Radner, Director of the Primate Research Facility, organized by the Department of Anthropology at California Pacific University. The research facility conducts research in all sorts of primates, research that sheds light in our genetic past as wells aids in the development of new medicines and treatments. Last year, a team from Cal Pacific returned from Mongolia with two earth-shattering living specimens—Yeti. The animals' return was the subject of much notoriety at the time. The animals, whose existence heretofore was known only through legend, were brought here, to the Primate Research Facility atop Cinder Mountain, where our team of renowned scientists were able to study them. In fact, the Yeti's entire genetic genome was unraveled during that time.

"Unfortunately, two days ago a tragedy of epic proportions occurred at the facility." Radner paused and noticed the reporters scribbling in their notebooks. He swallowed hard. "A tragedy, yes," he continued. "During the morning hours, a graduate assistant entered one of the Yeti's cage without the animal being sedated, which was a violation of facility policy. The animal managed to escape, kill the assistant, and release the other Yeti from her cage.

"A search of the compound was unsuccessful in locating the animals so the search area was extended to include Cinder Mountain. The mountain was thoroughly searched yesterday, and no animals were located. It is our belief that they have managed to roam beyond Cinder Mountain and, in doing so, may be anywhere on the desert plain. We ask the surrounding public to take all due precautions. These animals are extremely dangerous. I can take a few questions now."

Questions erupted from the reporters, all of them yelling at once.

"What do these animals look like?"

"How dangerous are they?"

"Which direction were they headed?"

"Have the surrounding towns been notified?"

"Who all is involved in the search?"

"Has the boy's family been notified?"

Radner answered each question, trying to remain

calm. Finished, he turned the press conference over to Sheriff Calder who brought the reporters up to date on the particulars of the search for the Yeti and answered additional questions.

When the news conference ended and the reporters filed into their cars and the satellite trucks headed back to Elko, Radner drove back up the mountain to his office. Seated at his desk, he withdrew a sheet of paper from a drawer and began writing his resignation.

e⁄ɔe⁄ɔ

A brutal morning sun beat down on the Anasazi ruins, causing waves of shimmering heat to undulate upward. Harry lay in the shade provided by the collapsed adobe wall, mouth parched, leg still aching. His tongue felt like sandpaper on the roof of his mouth and the blowing sand had irritated his eyes. Headache, confusion, and listlessness were signs of dehydration, and he knew he needed to find water, but his heart wasn't in the effort it would require. But another day in the baking sun and he would be a shriveled up piece of jerky. He was angry that the walkie-talkie was on his horse. It would have been a lifesaving piece of equipment.

He pulled himself to his feet and noticed the pain in his leg was less. He could even bear some weight on it. He forced his brain to focus on his surroundings. Surely, he thought, the Indians would have built their village close to water so he began surveying the area. The depression that housed the ruins fell off toward the West ending beneath a high wall of rock that formed a natural barrier to the prevailing west winds.

The sky was a brilliant blue, the color of lapis lazuli, and the wind light as Harry limped out of the depression and down toward the rock wall. The farther he hobbled, the better his leg felt. Maybe it wasn't broken after all, he thought. But it was farther away than it looked and, by the time he arrived at the wall, he fell to his knees, lungs burning.

The wall was about fifty feet high and made of solid granite. As he scoured the wall looking for evidence of water, he noticed the many small holes in the rock—hiding places or homes to small critters, in all likelihood. To the north, the wall gradually approached the plain until, a quarter mile away, it was level with it.

To the south, out of the corner of his eye, he saw a flicker of light, as if something reflected a ray of sunlight. He stared in that direction and couldn't believe his eyes—a small ribbon of water flowing dark over a bed of smooth stones. Falling to his knees, Harry pulled himself to the water and collapsed, plunging his head into it, savoring its wet coolness. He gulped down a few mouthfuls then splashed the water over his head and face. Refreshed, he sat back and pondered his next move.

It was unfortunate that he had no container with which he could collect and keep water. He would have to rehydrate before starting back to Cinder Mountain. He spent the better part of an hour drinking and cooling down, hoping that the water was fairly clean. He knew Giardia, the ameba that caused a poisoning with vomiting and high fever, was ubiquitous in Nevada. Hopefully, he would be back at the facility if, and when, he got sick.

When he was ready to start out, he drenched his shirt in the stream, stood, and started limping south. He knew Cinder Mountain lay in a southerly direction and hoped that soon he would be able to see it in the distance. It was a cloudless day so it should be easy to spot.

After several miles, pain racked his leg so he sat by a mesquite bush to rest. He thought about Dixie, whether she had mounted a search for him, and where they might be. If she had left at daybreak, they should be close, within seeing distance in the next few hours. But if she wasn't on the trail by now, it might be closer to evening. He prayed it wouldn't be that long. What if she hadn't been able to convince the sheriff or Drayton to look for him? Suppose the authorities were too busy to come looking for a lone man lost in the desert?

Back on his feet, Harry continued his trek toward Cinder Mountain. The morning was heating up, and he saw nothing on the horizon.

He stumbled on, focusing his thoughts on placing one foot in front of the other. It took effort, but he was determined to see Dixie again. He knew he could survive several days without food but water was his primary concern if he needed to spend another night on the plain. It was imperative to stay hydrated for the heat was getting intense. Since leaving the stream, he had not seen anything that looked like water in the distance, only rising undulating heat waves. Overhead, a group of hawks circled, rising and swooping in the air currents produced by the sun and heat.

Were they hawks—or buzzards? Waiting for him to collapse again?

His let felt better so he decided not to rest but to make as much distance while he was able. He was glad to have found the water earlier. It had given him renewed hope.

Then, on the horizon, he saw shimmering dark specks.

Harry's heart rate quickened.

Within minutes, the specks were much larger. They looked like animals.

Horses!

There were riders on the horses.

Harry jumped up and down, waved his arms, screamed at them. As the riders approached a trot, he could see Dixie on a horse behind Sheriff Calder.

She waved.

At last, she jumped off her horse and ran into Harry's arms, tears streaming down her cheeks. He smiled and brushed them away.

"Gosh, honey, what took you so long?" he said.

"Oh, Harry," she said, sniffling, "it's so good to find you and see you're alive. Thank god."

"I need a shower and shave," he said. He rubbed his chin with his hand.

"You're fine, honey. We brought a spare horse, just in case."

"Great, my leg is about worn out. I hurt it when my horse bucked and threw me. You haven't seen a riderless horse wandering around, have you? He lit out after he bucked me off."

"No, Doctor, we haven't." Sheriff Calder stepped down from his mount and shook hands with Harry. "Glad to see you. Not too bad for wear, I see."

"I'm fine," Harry said. "Could use some breakfast and some sleep, though."

"As soon as we get you back to the facility," Dixie said. "Ready to go?"

Harry nodded and ambled to a horse. After pulling himself into the saddle, he grinned. "Better than walking, that's for sure."

On the way back to the primate facility, Dixie peppered her husband with questions about what had happened to him and his night alone.

Harry told her about finding the Indian ruins, becoming close to delirious from dehydration, and his vivid nightmare. He spoke of his fears that she might have forgotten him. He told her of the Yeti that visited his dreams.

"See anything that looked like Yeti tracks, Doctor?" Calder said, riding alongside Harry and Dixie.

"Nothing," he said. "How about with you?"

"Nothing new to report," Calder said. "We'll widen the search area, of course."

They rode on, plodding up Cinder Mountain and arriving at the primate facility around noon.

Once he was showered and had eaten a large meal, Harry retired to the room in the dormitory where he collapsed on the bed. Dixie sat in a chair across from him.

"Dr. Radner came to me and we talked for a while, Harry. He wrote out his resignation and intends to give it to you. The little weasel feels guilty and responsible for what has happened."

"We'll see about that," Harry said. "All I want to do right now is sleep."

Dixie crossed the room and kissed him. "Okay. I'll check on you in a few hours."

Later, as they were waiting for dinner, Dr. Siscom walked up and smiled at Harry. "Dr. Olson, you're up and around, that's good to see. Feeling better?"

"Yes, thanks, Gerald. The chimps all doing well? I had nearly forgotten that we have other primates still here."

"Yes, they're all present and doing just fine. As is the mouse colony. I hope this affair with the Yeti doesn't put us in the crosshairs of the animal rights activists. That's all we would need—have a group of protesters up here on the mountain, raising all kinds of havoc."

"You are so right. They are marching around the university at this very moment."

"Any word on the Yeti?" Siscom said.

"Nothing."

"Dr. Radner held a press conference earlier this morning down at the property entrance. Quite a gathering of reporters and television crews."

"Yes, I heard. Any repercussions from it, Gerald?"

"None so far. At least none that I am aware of. Drayton said he did a respectable job. Handled the many questions with his usual flair."

"Flair, Gerald? The man has no flair," Harry said. "He's a condescending snob."

"Oh," Siscom said, eyebrows raised.

Harry was immediately sorry he had uttered the derogatory remark about Radner. At least to one of Radner's associates. Dixie poked him in his ribs with an elbow.

They went into the dining hall and sat with Radner and Millie. Millie looked as if she had been crying. Sitting next to her, Dixie leaned over and inquired if she was okay. She nodded her assent and began eating without another word.

Table talk was mostly about the escaped Yeti and where they could possibly have gone. Some speculated the heat had already killed them while others thought they might be terrorizing the nearby town of Grant. Siscom allowed that his tranquilizer gun was ready to go. Drayton said Sheriff Calder went home for the night and would return early in the morning. He planned on searching the towns in the area. Millie ate her dinner in silence.

Later, as they left the dining hall, Radner stopped Harry and pulled him aside. His face looked as if his dinner disagreed with him.

"Dr. Olson," he said. "I must speak with you in the morning. It is a matter of utmost importance and urgency."

"Fine, Miles. What time?"

Radner's frown deepened. "Say nine o'clock? Would that be convenient?"

"Of course, Miles. Your office?"

Radner nodded curtly, sauntered off, and disappeared around a corner.

Chapter 16

The four men stood in front of the mine entrance, each holding a floodlight. Garby and Terkel had knapsacks hanging from their shoulders while Lowell and Yarak carried small duffle bags. The weather was cool and each man wore a sweater or fleece jacket.

"Everyone ready?" Lowell said, adjusting a strap on Terkel's knapsack.

"I believe we are," Yarak responded. He grabbed his duffle and headed toward the hole in the side of the gorge. He was followed by Garby and Terkel, with Lowell last in line.

Inside the mine, the men walked in single file, their floodlights illuminating the path ahead and creating flickering shadows on the granite walls and ceiling. The shaft was cooler than the preceding day and, the deeper into the gorge they ventured, Lowell wondered how the place could be called a desert. Deeper in the mountain, they passed lichens of various colors growing on the rock, oranges, browns, rusts.

The sounds on the surface faded into nothingness, leaving the group surrounded by the stillness of the shaft—the only sounds their breathing and talking. The floor of the mine was strewn with rocks and trash, bits and pieces of rotting timbers from the beams that supported the shaft and prevented a cave-in.

Arriving at the Y where the shaft branched, Lowell stopped and shined his floodlight down the left-hand tunnel. Nothing but darkness and rock. Inspecting the right-hand shaft revealed a narrow set of rusty iron rails, tracks used with an ore cart. The cart tracks ran deep into the shaft beyond the reaches of Lowell's floodlight. He knelt beside a rail, ran a gloved hand over the rusted metal.

"This looks promising," Yarak said and started down the tunnel. "There wouldn't be a cart unless someone hauled ore out," he called over a shoulder.

A deep groan pierced the darkness and the mountain shuddered.

"What was that?" Garby said, shining his light over the ceiling and walls.

"Just the mountain shifting," Lowell said. "Happens all the time."

"Is it gonna cave?" Terkel said. "I can't stand the dark as it is."

"I doubt it," was Lowell's answer. "Plate tectonics, my dear fellow. It's what caused these mountains and gorges to begin with. It's still occurring."

They ambled on. The thought struck Lowell about how dangerous it was inside these old mines. Every year one or two people died in Nevada's old, abandoned mines, either from a cave-in or just falling down a deep shaft and becoming trapped. But he tried to put a positive spin on it, telling his men that if they had found the Lost Coyote Creek Mine the danger would be worth it. As he trudged along, Lowell noticed that even though the shaft was braced at regular intervals with thick timbers, most of them were rotted and falling apart. It wouldn't take much for them to collapse and bring the entire mountain down on them.

Farther into the side of the mountain, the shaft narrowed, its walls not much wider than the ore cart tracks. It was downright cold at this level, and Lowell stopped, shined his light around the shaft. It was a strange, eerie place. The mountain creaked and moaned, causing Lowell's pulse to quicken. He shivered.

What kind of men were these? he thought. What kind of men risked their lives, carving a hole in the earth? At a time when there was no modern power, no electric lights, no earth moving machines. All for the yellow metal that he and his men were now searching for. It was difficult to get his mind around the super human effort it must have taken to get the rails and heavy ore carts up the almost vertical side of the gorge.

Back then, it was all packed into this wilderness on the backs of mules and would have taken months to make the slightest progress.

Deeper, the shaft angled off to their right and broadened, leaving Lowell wondering how much farther it would go. At one point, he stopped, shined his light over the ground.

"The track ends here," he said.

His light illuminated the end of the rail tracks. Beyond, it was pitch black. Dark and foreboding.

"Can't go on much farther," Terkel said, shining his light down the shaft. "If this was the limit of their rail system, the end of the tunnel is probably right down there."

"Let's continue on," Lowell said. "Once we get to the terminus, we can decide our next move."

Yarak found it first—a vein of quartz embedded in the solid rock. It appeared in the right-hand wall and ran down the shaft at shoulder height.

"Look here!" he exclaimed. "A vein of quartz with yellow flecks in it."

The men gathered around, stared at the glistening crystal.

"Is that the gold inside?" Garby said.

"We'll see," Lowell said. He retrieved a knife from his pocket. "Break off a piece of that quartz with your pick," he said to Garby.

The man complied and began hitting the vein with a rock hammer. When a small piece broke free and fell to the ground, he picked it up, handed it to Lowell.

Lowell used his knife to pry into the piece of quartz and mashed a gold fleck.

It flattened.

"Yep, it's gold all right. See it's soft, malleable. Good, this must be the vein the old miners were working on. Now we need to follow it on down and determine whether the gold gets better or fizzles out. Sometimes, it can be a solid line of pure metal embedded in the rock."

"That's what I'm hoping for," Garby said. "A vein of pure gold."

Terkel looked at the metal in Lowell's hand. "Doesn't look much like gold."

"Impurities," Lowell said. "Need to refine them out."

"I can see that it's easier to pan and sluice the streambeds than do the back-breaking work, digging a hole into solid rock," Yarak said, now moving at a brisk pace ahead of the others.

"Sure," Lowell said. "But the riches are up here. If you can find a vein of solid gold, you're way ahead of those stream-based prospectors."

"The Mother Lode," Garby said. "You'd be rich."

"Early miners used this quartz and gold combination to find most of the hard rock mines throughout North America, usually near streams. When they found pieces with rounded edges, they would work their way back upstream until the rock and mineral combination chunks got bigger. Those telltale samples occurred commonly but some had sharp unworn edges. Early prospectors used to get excited when there were only small amounts of pannable gold in the stream if those samples were present. They knew the gold hadn't had time or distance to be eroded free from the quartz so the hard rock location had to be close by."

"I hope we find solid gold," Terkel said.

"So keep an eye out for nuggets getting larger inside this quartz," Lowell said.

Farther on, they stumbled onto an old rusty ore cart sitting on the railway. It gave Lowell an eerie feeling poking around deep in the dark shaft, stumbling across relics of other men's work and dreams. Those old miners weren't so much different from himself, searching for riches. And the techniques he used weren't much different either—hand tools and back-breaking labor. But if they could locate a pay streak, it would all be worth it.

"This looks promising," Yarak said, running a hand along the rim of the cart. "At least someone was mining in here in the past."

A hundred feet beyond the cart, Yarak stopped, peered closely at the vein in the wall, and ran his fingers over it. "Boss, come here!" he said in an excited voice.

Lowell hurried to his side and the two men stared, unbelieving, at the vein of solid yellow before them. The gold glistened under their floodlights. Garby and Terkel stumbled alongside Yarak for a look.

"Damn," said Lowell. "We've found it. We have found it." He set his duffle on the shaft floor, sat beside it with his head in his hands. "I can't believe it. Can't believe it."

"All this work, boss," Yarak said, a broad grin on his face. He slapped Lowell on the back, sending a cloud of dust into the air. "You did it."

Lowell looked up at his companions. "Well, gentlemen," he said. "In the immortal words of Walter Huston, how does it feel to be men of property?"

❧❧❧

Harold Peabody ambled out the door of his vintage gas station in the tiny town of Grant, Nevada, to unlock his two pumps for the start of another business day. The street was vacant and the sun just cleared the horizon, sending golden streaks over the high-desert plain. The morning was cool and the distant peaks had a look of indigo so familiar to Harold.

After returning the pump keys to his pocket, he turned, but hesitated a moment, for he saw something out of the corner of his eye. Something he couldn't quite make out. He stood and stared, the sun at his back making long shadows across Main Street.

At first he couldn't discern what they were, thinking they were two teenagers in fur coats, but then as they lumbered closer, he thought they were bears come into town. Grant had had its share of bears that came wandering into its midst from the nearby mountains and canyons and causing panic among its citizens. Usually, the sheriff from Elko or the local police were called to run the animals back to where they came from.

Occasionally, animal control deputies were necessary to tranquilize the bears for transport back to their original habitat.

But today was different.

Closer, the forms took shape. They were animals. Harold could tell that much, but exactly what kind he couldn't say. They trudged in an upright fashion, never once falling down on all four legs.

One of the animals held something in its large hand, a

child's doll. He could hear them grunt, a strange, low, guttural sound that gave him the creeps.

When they were across from his gas station, Harold made a remarkable discovery. The animals were not bears. In fact, they were unlike anything he had ever seen. The animals were huge, over eight feet tall and possessed a massive head that sat atop thick rounded shoulders. As he watched them, fascinated by their presence in Grant, one of them shot a glance in his direction. Harold was shocked to see two red, glowing eyes fixed upon him. The large animal stopped, turned, then lumbered across the street toward the gas station and Harold. The second animal followed suit.

Harold swallowed hard, ran inside, and locked the door. He located the pistol he kept in his desk and checked to be sure it was loaded. No sense keeping an unloaded pistol around. They were useless in an emergency. He dialed nine-one-one and, when the dispatcher answered and inquired the nature of his emergency, he replied, voice shaking, "Ma'am, there are two large animal creatures going down Main Street. Not bears. They are over eight feet tall. I've never seen anything like them. Please send help. There will be people out and about very soon."

The dispatcher said she would send someone to investigate so Harold hung up. Through the window, he saw the animals sniffing the gas pumps. His pulse pounded in his head, his stomach churned. He felt like vomiting.

A *crash* echoed from outside. Harold saw that one of the creatures had overturned a gas pump and gasoline spilled out over the concrete and into the street. God, he thought, if that catches fire, it will explode.

A shadow appeared at the door window. One of the beasts peered into the small office. Their eyes locked for a moment. The creature rattled the door and tossed its huge head from side to side. Its piercing eyes were like glowing coals. Harold felt a warm, wet trickle run down his leg. The beast growled a ferocious roar and continued to rattle the door.

Both beasts were now at the gas station door. He backed toward the rear exit, keeping his eyes fixed on the front door. The rattling was more intense, and Harold thought the beasts were going to tear the door from its hinges.

An occasional car drove past the station but not one stopped for gas, and the creatures seemed oblivious to any movement behind them. Harold knew they were coming for him.

He could smell them through the door, an odor much like rancid meat assaulted his senses.

With another loud *crash,* one if the beasts stuck a giant hand through the glass, sending shards flying through the small office. Was it a hand? Harold wondered. It certainly looked exactly like a human hand, only about three times the size. And black. The beast was reaching for the lock. *My god,* he thought, *it knows exactly what it is doing. And if I stay in this office I will die.*

Harold turned and ran out the back door. But as he turned to run, one of the great beasts was upon him. He emptied his revolver into the animal but it kept coming. He threw the pistol down and turned to run but felt a large hand grab him by the neck. Twisting, Harold turned and looked into the most hideous face he had ever seen. The beast growled, bearing its long, yellow fangs, a hot, fetid breath escaping its giant maw. Harold struggled but it was no use, the massive beast had him firmly in its clutches.

Harold fought, fought for all he was worth. At first, it seemed like the beast toyed with him, torturing him for its sordid pleasure. The claws on its hands dug deep into his flesh sending waves of nauseating pain shooting though his body. His heart raced. It felt as if it would burst from his chest. He tried to scream but no sound issued from his mouth. He could hardly breath.

Harold felt its fangs close around his head and, in a searing bolt of pain, all went black.

Chapter 17

Harry sat in Dr. Radner's expansive office, settling himself into a polished leather chair. The research facility director sat at his desk, a piece of paper in his hands. Harry knew what this meeting concerned as Dixie had already prepared him. He eased back and let Radner spell it out.

"Dr. Olson," Radner began, "I realize that I am solely responsible for events of the past few days. If I had been more diligent with respect to seeing policies were followed, I doubt we would be in this mess. Mr. Winkleman's death weighs heavy on my conscience, and it wouldn't surprise me if the young man's parents instituted legal proceedings against the university. His death and the Yeti's escape are solely my fault, and it is for this reason, I am submitting my resignation." He passed the paper over to Harry and continued. "So, I hope you will accept it without further discussion and make it official immediately."

When Radner finished, he fell back into his chair and exhaled.

Harry looked over the resignation letter for a few moments then looked Radner in the eye. "Miles," he said, a smirk on his lips. "Miles, you may be the world's biggest jerk but you are not responsible for what has transpired here. Due to a young man's inexperience and hubris, a tragedy occurred. Jimmy Winkleman is solely responsible for his own death and the escape of the Yeti." He waited for his words to sink into Radner's head. Then he continued. "So you see, Miles, I cannot accept this resignation from a man whose only crime is that he is an insufferable bore." He stood and tore the paper in half. "You do good work here. I only wish you could treat the little people with more respect."

Harry threw the paper on Radner's desk and sauntered out of his office. He walked over to the security office and found Drayton. The man was cleaning his rifle and looked up when Harry entered.

"Hello Chief," Harry said, closing the door behind himself.

"I just received a call from Buck Calder in Elko," Drayton said, still rubbing a cloth over the length of the gun's barrel. "A gas station owner in Grant was viciously killed by two large animals prowling the vicinity."

"Yeti?" Harry said.

"Sure sounds like it."

"When?"

"Earlier today. The person who called nine-one-one said they were unlike anything he had ever seen—over eight feet tall."

"That's them all right. The sheriff going over there?"

"Yeah, and he wants me with him. So I'll be meeting him there in a few minutes."

"I'm coming," Harry said. "And I'll get Siscom and his tranquilizer darts."

"Okay, meet me back here in ten minutes. We'll take my jeep."

After he found Siscom, Harry located Dixie and explained the situation.

"I'm going too," she said.

"I don't think Drayton will allow that, sweetie. He's awfully preoccupied right now."

"Doesn't matter, I'm going."

"Don't blame me if he hollers at you," Harry said, smiling. "Dr. Siscom is bringing is tranquilizers."

"Oh, Harry, I'm starting to have a bad feeling about this. I pray it goes well, for the animals' sakes."

"We'll be there to see that it does. Let's go find Drayton."

∽∾∽

Dixie didn't receive much of an argument from Bruce Drayton. He did warn her of the potential danger, but she shrugged it off with her usual flair. She and Harry piled into Drayton's jeep along with Dr. Siscom and his tranquilizer gun and, together, they headed down Cinder Mountain. As Drayton pushed on the accelerator, the little jeep sped over the rocky road, bouncing from one side to the other. Dixie felt her stomach doing flip-flops but soon they came to the smoother road at the foot of the mountain, and Drayton accelerated even more.

"Like riding a roller coaster," Siscom said from the back of the jeep. "Reminds me of my childhood on Coney Island."

Everyone laughed. Drayton nodded and continued to steer a course toward the town of Grant. They sped over a sand and mesquite plain, punctuated by short gnarled Joshua trees and stubby prickly pear cactus.

"You very accurate with that rifle, Gerald?" Harry said over the roar of the jeep. "You may only get one shot at each of them."

"I usually don't miss, Dr. Olson," Siscom said. "But I admit, the pressure is on now."

"How is it used?" Dixie asked. "What drug do you use?"

Siscom held up the rifle with its walnut stock. "This is the Pneu-Dart Air Rifle," he said. "It uses compressed gas to propel a .50 caliber dart. The dart is essentially a ballistic syringe, loaded with an immobilizing drug, and a hypodermic needle. The dart is stabilized by a tailpiece, a tuft of fibrous material, making it behave somewhat like a badminton shuttlecock in flight. On impact with the animal, the momentum of a steel ball at the rear of the dart pushes the syringe plunger and injects the dose of barbiturate or other drug into the animal. Pretty simple, really."

"What drug do you use?"

"It's a combination of clonidine and ketamine. It is used for sedation, anesthesia, muscle relaxation, and analgesia in large animals. Fairly rapid onset of action."

No one spoke for a long while as Drayton pushed the jeep closer to Grant. Dixie marveled at these men who put their necks on the line every day, at least the veterinarian and the security chief. Working with large animals always carried a certain degree of risk—one never knew what might happen. The anesthetic could wear off before the work was done or not take effect at all. The wrong dose could kill or harm the animal. Dixie felt a large degree of respect for Siscom and Drayton.

Grant was a two-block town of about two hundred residents. Main Street through Grant was reminiscent of many older, rural towns containing turn-of-the-century storefronts with diagonal parking in front. It had one stoplight at its main intersection that was not necessary but was a gift of the son of Grant's founder, Horace Grant. Most of the town's residents worked in nearby Elko or eked out a living, ranching cattle.

From a distance, Grant appeared on the horizon as a

scintillating apparition through the heat waves rising off the desert floor. Dixie's heart beat faster when they reached the outskirts of town.

The middle of town looked like a disaster had struck—several cars were overturned, a gas pump looked as if it had been ripped from out of the concrete, numerous windows were broken, and a body lay to one side of the main intersection.

Drayton stopped in front of the town's only gas station, and Dixie noticed that its front door was missing. Harry, Siscom, and Drayton joined her beside the jeep and looked in awe at the destruction around them.

"Holy cow!" Dixie said. "Looks like a war zone here."

Siscom walked around to the front of the jeep. "Is this where we're to meet up with the sheriff?"

"Yes," Drayton said. "He should be arriving any minute now."

Just as he said those words, an Elko County Sheriff's jeep screeched to a halt beside them and Sheriff Calder jumped out. Undersheriff Hardin was behind him.

"Jessums Christ!" Calder said, craning his neck up and down Main Street, surveying the damage. "Is that a dead body down there?"

"We just got here, Sheriff," Drayton said. "The body hasn't moved any so I presume he's dead, but I haven't checked. Like I said, we just arrived."

"My two deputies are on their way," Calder said, walking up to the gas station door and peering inside. "Once they get here, we'll fan out and search the town for the beasts."

Dixie stepped past Calder into the station's interior. The place was in shambles. The office was all but destroyed, counters crushed and their contents strewn all over the place. Chaos was everywhere—overturned furniture, broken glassware, other items ripped apart and scattered over the floor. Several large bloody footprints dotted the floor.

"Sheriff, in here," she said and pointed Calder to the footprints.

He whistled, a low note. "Look at how large those are," he said. "They're huge. Yeti, obviously."

Dixie continued through the small office and out the back door. A grisly scene confronted her. "Sheriff! Out here!" She was panicked. Her stomach rebelled.

Calder was at her side in an instant, and the two stared at a lifeless body, lying face down in a dark pool of blood. His arms and legs had been torn from their sockets, one arm was missing entirely. Half of the man's head was missing, leaving what brain that was exposed to glisten like congealed jelly. Flies swarmed in droves around the corpse.

Dixie turned her head and wept in short spasms.

"I need to see the other body out on Main Street," Calder said, turning abruptly and hurrying through the station.

Dixie followed. She found Harry and buried her face in his shoulder while Calder crossed the street and examined the dead body. When he returned his face appeared contorted with his jaw clenched.

"Well, this does it," he said, driving a fist into his other hand. "These beasts are as good as dead. As soon as my deputies get here, we're gonna hunt these beasts down and get rid of them for good."

"No," Dixie said, pleading. "Please, Harry, don't let them do this."

"Extermination," Calder said. "It's the only answer."

"Sheriff," Harry said. "Please listen to reason. These Yeti are valuable scientific specimens. You can't just kill them. It would be an injustice to science."

"This is not a time for scientific debate, Doctor. When we locate these murdering creatures, I intend to take them out. That's final."

"But what if Dr. Siscom can tranquilize them? We can take them back to the primate facility. Killing them wouldn't be necessary. I implore you to reconsider."

"Doctor," Calder said, "this is my call. We do it my way or you can leave the area."

"No!" Dixie screamed. "I won't let you do this!"

Another Elko Sheriff's jeep pulled up with deputies Ben and Louis inside.

"Great. Now we can get started." Calder stepped over to the jeep's open window. "You boys brought your rifles? You're gonna need them today."

"Got our 30-06s in the rear, Sheriff," Ben said from the driver's side. "What's the plan?"

Dixie took Harry's arm and listened.

"Those animals have been here," Calder said. "Just look around. We have two dead bodies. They may still be roaming about town so we need to split up, fan out, and do a door-to-door search. The main roads are vacant so folks know what's going on. The sooner we take them out, the better, before they kill again."

"For all we know there may be more bodies," Drayton said. "But I agree with the doctors. Killing them would be another tragedy. If these creatures are indeed related to us, then we owe it to humanity to study them and learn as much as we possibly can. Killing them isn't the right thing to do."

"It's too hot to argue," Calder said, stepping in front of Harry and Dixie. "We do this my way, or you can go home. If I have to call the state police, I will. Now, let's get moving before these animals can do any more harm."

∽✧∽

The dirty flophouse in San Francisco's Chinatown neighborhood was dim, illuminated only by a single bare light bulb that hung by a wire from the ceiling. Its only occupants were two men who sat opposite each other over a dilapidated desk. Outside, a soft breeze rattled the room's two grimy windows while a foghorn bellowed in the distance. On the desk lay a topographic map of northern Nevada.

"So Johnson," the heavy-set man said, "exactly where is this Cinder Mountain?"

"Right here, Falco," Johnson said, pointing with a greasy finger. "The Primate Research Facility is situated on its summit."

"How close did you manage to get?"

"There's a gate that marks their property line. From there I was able to observe the facility with binoculars." Johnson pointed on the map where he stood and surveilled the facility.

"Security?" Falco rubbed an ill-kempt chin. His pale blue eyes reflected the soft light from the bulb above.

"Of course. I was able to discern a tall fence with a gate. Security cameras were everywhere. It will difficult getting in but there may be an unobtrusive corner where we can cut our way through the fence. After dark we might not be seen."

"I wish Norma were here," Falco said, glancing at the door. "Hopefully, she obtained more information about its layout."

At that moment the door opened and Norma Treadwell entered, carrying a soft valise that she dropped on the table. Both men nodded.

"Sorry I'm late," she said. "The traffic was heavy."

"Fine," Johnson said. "You got any more information?"

Norma opened the valise and removed a sheaf of papers, thumbed through them. "I got this off the facility's website. It's a layout of the compound, where all the buildings are located."

The two men studied the diagram for a moment, Johnson running a finger over the sketched road leading to the main gate.

"Looks like a guardhouse at the entrance," he said, tapping the diagram with a dirty finger.

"The whole compound has a security fence around it," Falco said. "Just as you figured."

"Any idea what size of security force it has?" Johnson asked Norma.

She shook her head. "Not a clue." She removed her coat and leaned back in her chair, eyes on Johnson. "Think it's possible?"

"Anything is possible, Norma. It's simply a matter of difficulty and whether it's worth the risk. I don't relish the idea of getting shot for nothing."

"Five thousand dollars isn't nothing," Norma said. "It all but emptied the chapter's bank account."

"You got the money?" Falco said.

Norma smiled through a smirk. "Yeah," she said, reaching into the valise and retrieving an envelope. She passed it to Johnson. "As agreed. Half now and the rest when the job is done."

Johnson took the envelope and glanced inside. Satisfied that the money was in small bills, he turned his attention back to the map and diagram.

A gentle rain began beating against the small room's window while the foghorn again sounded somewhere out on the bay.

"Have you built the device?" Norma said.

"Not yet," Johnson said, running a hand though his long dark hair. "Don't have the explosive yet."

"What will you use?" Norma said.

"Plastic, most likely, if I can get my hands on some. I have a contact," Johnson replied. "I plan to use a digital clock as a detonator."

"We don't need a big bomb, just one that will show the university that we mean business. We don't want anyone killed or injured."

Falco stared at Norma for a few moments, scratched his grizzled face. The frown in his face deepened. "Are you for real, Norma? When you engage in something like this, there are no guarantees as to the outcome. There is always the possibility of collateral damage."

"You think we can explode a bomb," Johnson interjected, "and assure that no one will be injured? Think again. If that is your expectation, you need to find someone else for this party." He began folding his map. "Let's go, Falco."

"No, wait," Norma said. "I understand the risks. I just want to take all precautions against injury, that's all."

Johnson sat back in his seat and smiled. "All right, lady," he said. "Have it your way."

Chapter 18

From their base camp in an unnamed gorge alongside an unnamed tributary of the Taber River, Rupert Lowell and his comrades made ready to remove gold ore from the mother lode just discovered. Locating the Lost Coyote Creek Mine had been a difficult undertaking, requiring much physical effort, as well as luck. The vein of pure gold was three inches wide and ran for a good hundred yards, deep into the depths of the mountain. He had followed it with Yarak until it had ended, just stopped, at a location where the railway system ended as well. Whoever had found and worked the mine in the 1800s had left before its vast treasure could be completely exploited. Now, here Lowell was, on the brink of untold wealth, if only he was able to get it out of the rock.

The four men had brought a simple sluice that they would place in the stream and let its current wash over the dirt. Yarak and Garby worked at clearing a wide path from the stream to the mine entrance allowing for easier access. They hacked their way up the side of the gorge, sweating in the hot sun, until the path was finished.

Lowell marveled at the job. "Great work, guys," he said. "Now we have to pack the dirt and ore to the stream on our backs, using the backpacks. It's gonna be hard, difficult work and I'm not looking forward to breaking my back, but we can take numerous rest breaks. After hauling the gold ore down to the stream, we'll run the finer dirt and rocks through the sluice, picking out the gold nuggets that drop to the bottom. The bigger rocks containing gold we can drive back to a processor where they'll be ground in a grinder and the gold extracted chemically."

"Are you sure this is doable, boss?" Terkel said, the sweat pouting down his neck. "Why not get a backhoe or Bobcat up here?"

"We may have to, Terk," Lowell said. He took a long drink from a water bottle. "But I want to get this started as soon as possible and see what we have. It might turn out to be easier than it looks."

"I've never seen gold in the rough like that," Garby added. His clothes were drenched from his exertion in clearing the path. "That's pure gold, right?"

"Pure gold, yes," Lowell said. He smiled. "And it's all ours unless someone finds out we're up here."

"Yeah?" Terkel said. "What could happen?"

"This is government land we're on," Yarak said. "Might have some government agent up here telling us we had no business being here—to leave. Boss is right, better keep this our secret. So don't go blabbing about it back home."

Garby and Terkel both nodded their understanding.

The sun dipped below the rim of the gorge as Lowell sat in a camping chair next to a flickering fire. He sipped his favorite Canadian whiskey and allowed the liquor's effects to relax his aching muscles. It was good to be out in nature doing physical work, something so different than being behind a desk all day, trading stocks. He could look around and see the results of his labor. He understood the lure of prospecting, the focus required to locate a gold field, and the energy necessary to pull it out of the ground. They were using picks, so getting it out of the ground would be the most difficult part.

Yarak eased into a chair next to Lowell, beer in hand. He ran a hand through his sweaty hair. "We did a lot of work today," he said. "I'm bushed."

Lowell took a sip of his whiskey. "Tomorrow, Nash, we begin in earnest."

"Using the picks? It won't be easy."

"No, it won't. But if you have an easier idea, I'd like to hear it. Once we get started, it should go well. We'll take shifts working with the picks."

"I figure two working with the picks and two dragging the ore down to the stream."

"That's the way I figure it, Nash. After we have a pile, one of us can work the sluice."

"How long you plan to stay out here?" Yarak asked.

"At least a week. Then we can go back, rest up a few days, and restock. As long as no one knows what we're doing, we can take our own sweet time with the mine."

"Sounds good to me but Garby won't be happy. The man wants action—women and dice. It's an illness with him."

"I'm counting on you, Nash, to keep him under control. I don't want any problems on this trip. Understand?"

"Sure, boss. He's mostly just talk anyway. But I'll keep him in tow."

The stars were out and a silver moon rose over the rim of the gorge. Lowell could see about as good as during day. In the distance, a pack of coyotes yipped and howled. As their din grew louder, he reflected on the mine's name. How apt.

He sat in silence in front of a dying campfire until it was a heap of glowing coals. Now, he thought, the long-lost treasure was within his grasp. Lowell didn't mind the hard work. Sure, it was rough, but the payoff in the end made it well worth it. Yarak was a good man, as close to a son as Lowell ever would have. In fact, he nearly was a father—long ago. Seemed like centuries ago. The woman who was pregnant with his child was killed in a car accident, killed by a man driving drunk and who hit her head-on. Lowell realized it had left him a bitter man with only one remaining passion—money. Someone told him once he was destroying his soul but he no longer cared about that. In his world, there was no bright line between right and wrong. It was all shades of gray. And it was in those shades of gray that Lowell lived and worked. The ethics of high finance—it was all a nebulous playing field.

But there was a small part of him that did still care about living a good life. He never went out of his way to hurt anyone, never inflicted unnecessary pain or suffering. He sipped his whiskey and looked at the moon. It had risen in an arc from near the horizon and now was overhead. Its pale light made soft shadows out of their tent and jeep.

An owl hooted in the distance.

⌀⌀⌀

Garby and Terkel sat on a rock at the far end of camp, each drinking a beer. Garby took a big mouthful and spat it on the ground.

"Terk," Garby said, "I'm getting bored, all this digging. I need some relaxation. How 'bout yourself?"

"I'm fine," Terkel said. "I rather enjoy all this outdoor work. But I'm beat, for sure."

"Some cards or dice would be welcome. Maybe some whiskey instead of this swill. A woman would be nice, too."

"If I were you, I wouldn't even think about women. Ain't healthy."

Garby snorted. "What then?"

"Me? I'm going to dream about piles of gold getting higher and higher."

"What you think's gonna be our share, Terk?"

"I dunno. Several hundred thousand at least, I would think."

"What'll you do with your share," Garby said.

"Maybe buy a ranch and raise cattle. Maybe get married."

"Married? You? That's a laugh."

"How about you, Garby?" Terkel said. "What plans have you, if any?"

"Me? Well, first I'm going to buy a fast sports car. Then I'm going to Vegas and spend my money on the tables and women. Then, just before my money runs out, I'm going to blow my brains out."

Terkel laughed and shook his head. "You're something else," he said.

"You trust Lowell?"

"Why shouldn't I? He's always shot straight with me. Us."

"That we know of. Well, if we're not goin' anywhere, I'm going to bed."

Garby stood and sauntered off to the big tent where the men had their cots. As he lay in the dark, his mind mulled over what Terkel had said. Several hundred thousand dollars. A right tidy sum. Enough money to last him a few years, maybe forever. Terkel was a different story. He enjoyed teasing the man. He might take his share and head to the South Pacific where no one would ever find him.

He heard Terkel stumble into his cot and soon was sleeping soundly. Garby's mind was fixed on the money.

As he relaxed, he decided he would stay and help Lowell for, as Terkel had said, the man had been good to him.

He jerked awake.

What was that?

A noise?

He lay on his cot and listened to the quiet breathing of Terkel, Yarak, and Lowell.

There it was again.

A twig snapped followed by walking. Was it walking? He couldn't be sure. Garby listened intently, straining to hear.

There it was again.

There was definitely someone or something walking out in the dark.

He reached under his cot and found his boots. After putting them on, he retrieved his pistol and wandered outside.

The moon was no longer visible but the stars twinkled overhead. Standing at the tent entrance he scanned the dark, pistol at the ready.

All was quiet.

Garby strolled about the camp, peering into every dark recess, listening for any sound. After circumnavigating the campsite and seeing and hearing nothing, he returned to the tent. *Must have been my imagination playing tricks*, he thought.

When he climbed onto his cot, Terkel raised up on an elbow. "What's going on?" he whispered.

"Nothing," Garby said. "I thought I heard something but it was nothing. Go back to sleep."

But as he lay in the dark, sleep would not return to Garby. He listened but there were no strange sounds the rest of the night.

ややや

Millie worked late into the night on her research data and the Yeti genome. When a cell divided and DNA needed to be replicated, the double helix was split, and enzymes called polymerases used each of the two halves as a template for a new opposing strand. The base pairing rules ensured that the copying was exact, except for rare errors. Historically, laboratory DNA sequencing had relied on the exact same process of copying DNA. In fact, the enzymes that made copies of DNA within a cell were so efficient that biologists had used a modified polymerase to perform sequencing.

Genome sequencing was figuring out the order of DNA nucleotides, or bases, in a genome—the order of As, Cs, Gs, and Ts that made up an organism's DNA. The human genome was made up of over three billion of these genetic letters.

At the Primate Research Facility high-tech machines perform sequencing. A DNA sequence that had been translated from life's chemical alphabet into scientific shorthand might look like this:

A-G-T-C-C-G-C-G-A-A-T-A-C-A-G-G-C-T

That was, in this particular piece of DNA, an adenine (A) is followed by a guanine (G), which was followed by a thymine (T), which in turn was followed by a cytosine (C), another cytosine (C), and so on.

By itself, not a whole lot. Genome sequencing was often compared to *decoding*, but a sequence was still very much in code. In a sense, a genome sequence was simply a very long string of letters in a mysterious language.

When one read a sentence, the meaning was not just in the sequence of the letters but also in the words those letters made and in the grammar of the language. Similarly, the human genome was more than just its sequence.

The genome could be compared to a book written without capitalization or punctuation, without breaks between words, sentences, or paragraphs, and with strings of nonsense letters scattered between and even within sentences. Sequencing the genome didn't immediately lay open the genetic secrets of an entire species. Even with a rough draft of an animal's genome sequence in hand, there was much work to be done. Millie still needed to translate those strings of letters into an understanding of how the genome worked—what the various genes that made up the genome did, how different genes were related, and how the various parts of the genome were coordinated. That was, she must figure out what those letters of the genome sequence meant. A scientifically complicated affair.

Sequencing the genome was an important step toward understanding it. At the very least, the genome sequence would represent a valuable shortcut, helping scientists find genes more easily and quickly. A genome sequence did contain some clues about where genes were, even though scientists were just learning to interpret these clues.

Over time, Millie hoped to study the entire Yeti genome sequence, in hopes of understanding how the genome as a whole worked, how its genes worked together to direct the growth, development, and maintenance of the entire animal. She was happy that she had chosen this endeavor to be her life's work.

The whole genome couldn't be sequenced all at once because available methods of DNA sequencing could only handle short stretches of DNA at a time. So instead, Millie had to break the genome into small pieces, sequence the pieces, and then reassemble them in the proper order to arrive at the sequence of the whole genome.

An automatic sequencing machine spit out what was

called *raw* sequence. In raw sequence, the reads or short DNA sequences were all jumbled together, like the pieces of a jigsaw puzzle in a just-opened box. Inevitably, raw sequence also contained a few gaps, mistakes, and ambiguities.

The process of polishing that raw sequence— transforming the fragmented rough draft into a long, continuous final product without breaks or errors, called finishing—involved both assembly, in which individual reads were hooked together in the proper order, and a laborious process of double-checking and refining the sequence to eliminate mistakes and close gaps. Finishing often took longer than the sequencing itself.

Genome assembly was the job of computer programs known, appropriately enough, as *assemblers*. Those programs worked by finding and analyzing overlaps, or identical DNA sequences at either end of two different reads. The task of the assembler was to compare each read to every other, then to put all the reads in the proper order, based on how they overlapped, not using the repeat overlaps. The outcome of an assembly was a collection of big stretches of the genome that were put together correctly. The process was a lot like assembling a jigsaw puzzle— methodically placing puzzle pieces next to each other to see if they fit together, then snapping the matching pieces into place.

Millie spent the better part of a year working with Radner to arrive at the Yeti's genome, an accomplishment that gave her immense pride. What did the future hold for her? Where would she go after leaving the primate facility? The world was wide and there were so many questions left unanswered. She had a few. A human and a grain of rice might not, at first glance, look like cousins. And yet they shared a quarter of their genes with each other. The genes humans shared with rice—or rhinos or reef coral—were among the most striking signs of a common heritage. All animals, plants, and fungi shared an ancestor that lived about 1.6 billion years ago. Every lineage that descended from that progenitor retained parts of its original genome, embodying one of evolution's key principles—if it's not broke, don't fix it. Since evolution had conserved so many genes, exploring the genomes of other species could shed light on genes involved in human biology and disease. Even yeast had something to tell the human race about itself.

Millie understood that, of course, humans weren't really much like yeast at all. The genes that were shared were used differently, in the same way one could use a clarinet to play the music of Mozart or Benny Goodman. And humans' catalogs of genes themselves had changed. Genes could disappear and new ones could arise from mutations in DNA that previously served some other function or no function at all. Other novel genes had been delivered into the genome by invading viruses. It was hardly surprising that modern humans shared many more genes with chimpanzees than with yeast, because most of the evolutionary journey had been shared with those apes. And, in the small portion of genes with no counterpart in chimpanzees, scientists might be able to find additional clues as to what made us uniquely human.

By comparing the human genome with the genomes of different organisms, researchers might better understand the structure and function of human genes and thereby develop new strategies in the battle against human disease. In addition, comparative genomics provides a powerful new tool for studying evolutionary changes among organisms, helping to identify the genes that were conserved among species along with the genes that give each organism its own unique characteristics.

Using computer-based analysis to zero in on the genomic features that were preserved in multiple organisms over millions of years, researchers would be able to pinpoint the signals that controlled gene function, which in turn should translate into innovative approaches for treating human disease and improving human health. In addition, the evolutionary perspective might prove uniquely helpful in understanding disease susceptibility. For example, chimpanzees did not suffer from some of the diseases that struck humans, such as malaria and AIDS. A comparison of the sequence of genes involved in disease susceptibility might reveal the reasons for this species barrier, thereby suggesting new pathways for prevention of human disease.

It was an exciting time to be alive, she knew. However, what lay in her future was unknown. When she had time, she would talk with Dixie and get her ideas. Millie worried about the Yeti, especially Sasha.

She uttered a silent prayer that the men would bring them back unharmed. Science would lose if they didn't.

Chapter 19

The team fanned out through downtown Grant. Harry and Dixie searched the alleyway across the street from the gas station where they had seen two more dead bodies. Sheriff Calder took Ben, and the two of them went behind the buildings parallel with the station while Siscom and Louis searched each office building door to door. As the group moved down the Main Street area, Harry was struck by the devastation they encountered. It seemed that the Yeti were on a murderous rampage, intent on killing or destroying anyone or anything they encountered. The street was vacant, devoid of any people. Harry surmised most of Grant's citizens knew what happened and had either fled the town or were locked in their homes.

Harry fretted over what would transpire if and when they encountered the Yeti. Calder had lost his temper, called in the state police, and a strike force was on its way. Harry didn't see how the Yeti could survive for long in the desert heat. Their natural habitat was the high mountains of the Himalayas and Mongolia. He assumed they needed water and a cool environment, neither of which they were likely to find in the surrounding area.

Harry and Dixie trampled through the weeds covering

the alley, each searching their respective side. Backyards and porches doted one side while the backs of offices the other. When they reached the end of the alley, the pair crossed Main Street and located the sheriff and Ben.

"Anything?" Calder said.

"Two dead bodies mauled pretty bad," Harry said, shielding his eyes from the sun.

They waited until joined by Siscom and Louis. Calder looked at his deputy with a deep frown.

"Nothing, Sheriff," Louis said.

"Let's scour the outlying areas around town. If we don't find them, we'll head back to the command post. I'll call the state police and let them know."

The three men and Dixie climbed into Calder's jeep while Ben and Louis took their jeep and joined the search. After two hours of driving around Grant in ever-widening circles and not locating the Yeti, they sped back to the command post at the base of Cinder Mountain.

"What about all the dead back there?" Dixie said as Calder accelerated across the desert.

"The local police are going to handle it," Calder said. "The coroner from Elko is on his way over there as well."

"Busy man," Siscom added.

"I can't believe the plan is just to annihilate them," Dixie said.

Calder's temper boiled to the surface. "Look around you, Doctor!" he said, a vein in his forehead bulging. "Several people are dead, killed by these beasts, and the town's decimated. Because of you scientists, our little corner of paradise no longer exists. No, if we or the strike force comes upon them, we're gonna take them out. Period."

"It would be easy enough to let me sedate them," Siscom said. "We can then transport them back to their cages. They wouldn't have to be killed."

"No longer an option," Calder said, a little more under control.

"So really I'm not needed," Siscom said. "I guess I'll head back to the facility."

"Well, I'm going to hang around," Harry said. "Maybe I can change their minds when we find them."

Dixie said nothing but instead stared out at the passing mesquite. Soon the two jeeps arrived at the command post. Outside the vehicles, Calder approached his deputies.

"Ben, take Dr. Siscom and whomever wishes to go along back up the mountain to the research facility. The rest of us well stay here until the strike force arrives and discuss further search plans."

Ben nodded and, with Dr. Siscom, headed back to the facility while Calder paced around his jeep. He looked at his watch. Five p.m.

As the sun neared the horizon, the temperature started to drop. A gentle breeze blew over the desert, sending a chill through Harry. He put an arm around his wife and drew her close. Together, they ambled away from Calder, Drayton, and Louis.

"Harry," Dixie said in a voice barely above a whisper, "we can't let these guys do this, can we? That sheriff is intent on killing our Yeti. Years of possible future work could be destroyed."

"I am tired of that Calder bragging about killing these animals. There ought to be someone over him to whom we could appeal."

"He's elected, Harry. He answers only to the people. He can do what he wants until election."

Harry felt a knot tighten in his stomach. "Then it's lost. If he finds them, he'll kill them."

Dixie's eyes brightened with small green flashes. "What if we find them first?" she said. "Gerald can sedate them, then we could haul them up the mountain before Calder or the strike force locates them."

Harry looked at her for several moments, thinking. "Wait a minute, honey. Do you think we could pull it off? Actually find them and get them back in their cages ourselves?"

"It would be worth a try, wouldn't it? Better than sitting around here twiddling our thumbs." Dixie's voice was animated. "Let's get up there with Drayton and chat with Siscom."

Harry grabbed Drayton by an arm, pulled him aside, and relayed their plans.

The man nodded as Harry talked. "I'm with you," he said. "We can use my jeep."

When Ben returned, the three climbed aboard his vehicle for the ride up the mountain, leaving Calder and Louis to welcome the strike force. Halfway to the primate facility, Harry heard the whirr of helicopter rotors and, upon rounding a switchback, saw a Bell Yankee helicopter circling the command post on its approach to the desert floor. The sun, now behind the distant peaks, made it unlikely that they would begin their search at night. They would remain at the command post and start early in the morning.

Once in the lobby of the main building, Harry sought out Gerald Siscom to enlist the man's support in his and Dixie's plan. He found him in his office near the Animal Care Unit. After passing through the airlock, Harry could hear the chimps screeching as he walked down the hall.

"Gerald," he said from the office doorway. "Glad I found you. Dixie had the bright idea that we should mount our own search for the Yeti. If we can find them before Calder, you can sedate them and we can return them here without them being killed."

"Sure," said Siscom.

"If we don't do something, they'll surely die."

"Count me in." He put some papers in a desk drawer and stood. "When do we start?"

"Before dawn. Drayton is going as well, and we'll use his jeep."

Siscom stood with hands on his hips. "But where do we begin?"

"I suggest we return to Grant and see if we can pick up their trail. It's the best I can come up with unless you have a better idea, Gerald."

"We can talk about it over dinner later," the veterinarian said.

"Fine," said Harry. "See you then."

❧❧❧

With the evening light fading, Sheriff Calder sat in the trailer that served as his command post at the base of Cinder Mountain and briefed members of the state police strike force that had arrived moments earlier. Seated in metal folding chairs were Sergeant Malcomb Jessup and Corporal Steve Williams.

Two remaining members of the force remained outside chatting with Ben and Louis. The men sat in the cramped space of the trailer as they talked. Jessup chewed the unlit butt of a black cigar, moving it around his mouth with his lips.

"So that's the situation," Calder said, after briefing the two on the events of the past several days.

"Where were these animals last seen?" Jessup said.

"At the town of Grant," Calder said. "About an hour drive from here. Four people were killed. They destroyed most of the downtown."

Jessup nodded. "In the morning, we can get the chopper in the air and head up that way and see if we can pick up their trail. You can follow in the jeeps. Sound acceptable to you?"

"Fine," Calder said. He was grateful that these state police officers weren't the condescending assholes he usually dealt with. "What firepower did you bring with you?"

Jessup shot a glance at his corporal, Williams, who leaned forward in his chair.

"Enough," Williams said. "Two SMAWs, a—"

"SMAW?" Calder said.

"It's a shoulder-launched rocket weapon. It fires a high explosive rocket. It's thought of as a bunker buster weapon. Also, several grenade launchers, a flamethrower, and our M16s. Should take care of them."

"I should say so, yes indeed."

"What about the scientists?" Jessup said. "I heard they were going to mount a search themselves. Is that right?"

"Possibly," Calder said.

"Will they get in our way?"

"I hope not."

"I don't want a bunch of damned civilians out running around getting in our way, Sheriff. Will you make that perfectly clear to the scientists?"

"Will do, Sergeant. You and your men are welcome to spend the night here in the command post or you can accompany us to Elko. There is a small motel there that may have a couple of available rooms."

"Fine, Sheriff. I believe we'll spend the night in town."

Ben and Louis joined Calder inside the trailer after the strike force headed to Elko for the night. They were sitting in the folding chairs as Andy Hardin sauntered in.

"What's the word, Buck?" Hardin said, still standing next to the door.

"We start searching a wider area tomorrow morning," the sheriff said. "At first light."

The three men nodded their understanding.

"Weather should be clear and hot for the next several days," Hardin said. "Those animals will be looking for water."

"Not much water north and northeast of Grant," Calder said. "So, we'll head northwest. Might get lucky."

"How was the state police sergeant?"

"The usual," Calder said.

The four men laughed and left the command post for Elko.

☙❧

Millie was happy to see Harry, Dixie, and Siscom in the dining hall, and she joined them at their table. The three all wore troubled looks and her pulse quickened as she set her dinner tray next to the veterinarian.

"You all look so sad," she said, sitting. "Any news?"

"It's not good, Millie," Dixie said, forking up a mouthful of salad.

Millie's heart skipped a beat. "What?"

"Calder has called in a state police strike force and they plan to hunt down the Yeti and exterminate them," Harry said.

Millie noticed how haggard he looked. "Oh no," she said. "Can we do anything?"

Drayton set his food tray on the table and sat next to Siscom. He nodded at Millie.

"The four of us here plan to do our own search," Harry said, between gulps of iced tea. "If we can find them first, maybe Gerald can get them sedated with his tranquilizer darts. If that can happen, we can then, if possible, transport them back here."

"How can they just kill them?" Millie said, beginning with her dinner.

"They're looking at it from a public safety viewpoint," Drayton said. "I can understand it though, in this case, I don't agree with it."

"People get scared and panicked," Siscom added. "And they demand action. I'm sure the sheriff is only reacting to public pressure."

Dr. Radner entered the dining hall, went through the line, then joined the group at their table. He sat next to Siscom.

"What about it, Miles," Harry said. "Any feedback from your news conference?"

Radner moved his plate off his tray and nodded. "Some," he said. "Mostly bad. Lots of questions about how we could let the security here lapse and allow these creatures to escape."

"But we didn't *allow* them to escape, Miles," Dixie said. The tone in her voice betrayed an irritation.

"We know that," Radner said as he began to eat. "But that is not what most of the public believes."

"Regardless of what the public believes, we need to find these animals and get them back here without further incident." Harry made his point with his fork.

"I want to go along," Millie said. "If you have room. I worked with Bentu and Sasha for a year. I need to go. I might be of help. Please."

Siscom nodded his agreement.

"What do you say, Bruce?" Harry said. "It's your jeep. Have room for one more?"

"I think we can squeeze you in, Millie," Drayton replied. "Glad to have you."

The group finished their dinner then adjourned to their respective dorm rooms for a night's rest.

Chapter 20

Johnson and Falco had formed their friendship years earlier, while in prison, when each did time for burglary. They wound up as cellmates in the Delano prison. After their release, they bumped into each other one day in a San Francisco Chinatown strip club where Johnson worked as a bouncer. He managed to get Falco hired doing janitorial duties after the place closed. Late at night, the pair would smoke weed in Johnson's tiny walkup apartment a few blocks from the club.

One brilliant day, Johnson strolled the perimeter of Union Square, waiting for his marijuana contact to arrive, when he came upon a small rally of protestors, complete with signs and placards. It was a peaceful assembly of several dozen people, mostly men and women in their twenties and thirties who were listening to a woman speaking with the aid of a bullhorn. Curious, he sat on a nearby bench and listened. Something about animals being used for scientific research. From what he could discern, the rally was intended as a protest against universities using animals for this purpose and they had one school in their sights. Cal Pacific. The woman blamed the university for housing several large and strange animals at a facility in Nevada where all sorts of bizarre experiments were perpetrated on them. With this remark, the group hissed and booed. The speaker was quite animated and forceful. Intrigued, Johnson was immediately attracted to her.

When the rally was over, he approached the woman. She shot him a curious glance as he neared. They were next to the Holiday Ice Rink.

"I was listening from over there," he said, pointing to the bench.

"Oh?" the woman said, a frown wrinkling on her forehead.

"Yeah. You seem all worked up about these animals."

"You don't see anything wrong, Mr…"

"Johnson."

"Mr. Johnson. You don't find it appalling that these animals are being abused? That Cal Pacific's doing horrible experiments on them?"

Johnson shifted his weight awkwardly and ran a hand through his greasy hair. "What kind of experiments?"

"They keep them locked up in small cages and there's no telling what they're actually doing up there."

"You said they were doing horrible experiments on them. What kind, exactly?"

"Sticking needles in them, for one thing. Taking their blood. God knows what else. Maybe shooting electricity through them."

The woman waved an arm in the air and her voice had an intense quality to it.

"What's your name, ma'am?"

"Norma."

"Glad to meet you, Norma," Johnson said and held out a dirty hand. After a brief handshake he continued. "Maybe I'll join your group. I think cruelty to animals is wrong."

"Well, Mr. Johnson," Norma said, "we can always use

more folks who care about the welfare of animals."

After the meeting in the park, Johnson and Norma became lovers, with her visiting his apartment several nights a week. One evening, he inquired about her marriage.

"Bryan doesn't know my needs," Norma said, running a hand through his hair. "He spends all of his time consumed by his work, which leaves him precious little time for me. Once, I thought about divorcing him but realized I was addicted to his money."

Johnson raised an eyebrow then frowned.

"Yes," she said, "I suppose I know what that makes me. In this world, sweetheart, not all of one's decisions can be made with moral certitude. I could never live as you, in a place such as this."

"Yet, you can lower your standards to come here?"

"Not my standards, dear. Just because I like the finer things in life doesn't mean I don't value the way you make love to me."

"I could come to value the finer things as well," Johnson said, kissing her neck as they lay on the bed.

"Well, sweetie, if all goes well at the facility, maybe I could see to that."

They laughed together. Johnson brought Norma's mouth to his.

℘℘℘

The sun just cleared the rim of the gorge when Lowell pushed the ore cart down the track into the cool dry air where he sat and watched Garby and Terkel load the packs with the ore. With morning just underway he was already bushed from the back-breaking work. They started well before dawn using lanterns to aid their labor, first with Lowell manning the pick, then Yarak. In the dark during breakfast, Garby mentioned to him the strange sounds he heard during the night and neither could figure what it was. As Lowell watched Garby and Terkel lug the gold ore down to the stream, he could hear Yarak working the pick deep inside the mine. It would to be tough, intensive labor but it was necessary if they were to exhume the fortune waiting down there. Not having mechanized equipment with which to work meant it would require sheer muscle to pluck the gold from the vein. The mountain wasn't going to give up her treasures easily.

During the morning, they worked the right hand shaft and were about fifty yards from the Y where the main tunnel divided and branched into two diverging shafts. The shaft at this level was downright cold this early in the day, in addition to being dark and forbidding. Using only the light from two lanterns to see made it all the spookier. Lowell couldn't understand how anyone did the job for very long—never seeing the light of day.

When Garby and Terkel were on their way back up the trail to the mine entrance, Lowell pushed the cart down the tunnel to where Yarak plunged the pick into the vein. Without saying a word, he began picking up the rock pieces and threw them into the cart. The two lanterns gave off a soft golden glow that produced a glistening sheen to the walls and ceiling of the shaft. Each time the pick bit into the rock, it sent showers of small chips flying, the sound ricocheting down the shaft beyond the reach of the lantern's light. When the cart was full of ore, Lowell pushed it out into the sunlight where his two assistants took the rock down to the stream. Over and over the process was repeated until by early afternoon the pile was as high as he was tall.

The men had been working like this for three days. Late each afternoon, Lowell and Yarak worked the sluice, shoveling the sand and gravel brought down from the mine into it and using the stream's current to filter out the heavier gold nuggets. The sluice box was like a long tray open at both ends with riffles, spaced evenly along the length of the sluice, every few inches, perpendicular to the length of the sluice. These riffles caused small barriers to the water flow that created eddies in the water, giving the heavier material, black sand and gold, a chance to drop to the bottom behind the riffles.

Lowell noticed that Garby had taken to grumbling as he toted the bags of ore down to the stream with Terkel. Why this was so was a mystery to Lowell for he had treated Garby well, paid him a decent wage, even provided his transportation. He hired Garby after Yarak found him working on a railroad maintenance gang in California. Garby never talked much about his past but Lowell had learned through Terkel that the man was married once and arrested after his wife disappeared under mysterious circumstances. He was released but the woman never was found. Whether Garby had anything to do with his wife's disappearance was never determined and the man certainly didn't volunteer any new information. Garby's personal habits, although no concern to Lowell, could be improved with better hygiene. The man didn't bath often enough for Lowell's tastes, and the week the men spent working the mine only made matters worse. He vowed to speak to Yarak and get Garby bathed in the stream.

Lowell pushed the cart toward the mine entrance, trudging down the track toward the growing daylight outside. While doing so, he reflected on why he was here, forcing himself to labor away in a lost canyon in desolate Nevada. It was simple, he could see the results of his effort, unlike so many business deals where success was spelled out on the bottom line of a ledger—nothing concrete. Here, he could watch the piles of gold ore get bigger, the direct consequence of his work. It filled him with a sense of accomplishment and knowing that the ever-growing pile of rock translated into money made his gratification sweeter.

His girlfriend Julie had been the only person who didn't make him feel self-conscious about his stature, and he worshiped her, showered her with expensive gifts, always over her protests. Didn't need them, she always said, just wanted his company. She was a few inches taller then he with auburn hair, delicate features, and laughed at his jokes. Together, they seemed like the perfect couple, going to dinner, plays, sporting events. He planned a long life together. When she told him about the pregnancy, he was overjoyed for he never expected a family, never thought a woman as beautiful as Julie could love a man as unsightly as he.

Then the accident happened. And it changed his life—for the worse. Julie's death turned him into an embittered man, mourning his loss, isolating himself. He tried to have the drunk driver prosecuted but instead, the man was sentenced to time served and ordered to do community service.

There was nothing Lowell's money could do to change the outcome. He bought her parents a house—in part, he knew, to assuage the guilt he felt for not dying with her and the baby. Time, however, was a great healer, at least on the surface, the face he showed the public. The scars on his psyche betrayed a deeper, hidden wound that never seemed to heal. Her parents were understanding but were mourning themselves, so it wasn't long until they had drifted apart, with Lowell seeing them less and less. Eventually, they sold the house, wrote him a cordial letter, and moved to Florida. He never heard from them after that.

With Julie gone, he threw himself into his work and

prided himself in the wealth he accumulated. He had no close friends until he met Yarak.

Yarak wanted a break and fresh air so he left Lowell in the shaft. Alone in the dimly lit tunnel, Lowell leaned against the ore cart and rested his aching back.

Something caught his attention deeper in the mine.

Beyond the reaches of the lantern light he thought he heard something, as if there was movement in the dark. He listened.

Yes, there it was—a shuffling sound as if someone or something was prowling around in the dark. It sounded like walking.

Then it stopped.

Ears and mind on alert, he listened. But there was nothing. The noise stopped.

He turned on his floodlight and it pierced the darkness of the mineshaft, its walls coming alive in brilliant relief.

Nothing.

The eerie silence in the shaft engulfed him and, without Yarak's company, Lowell felt the walls closing around him. Being somewhat claustrophobic, he felt uneasy alone. He shined his light deep into the mineshaft but again saw nothing unusual, nothing to account for the sound he heard. *Must be my imagination in the dark*, he thought.

Yarak returned and came to Lowell's side. "What is it?" he said.

"I guess nothing," Lowell said, switching off his floodlight. "I thought I heard a noise down there. Like walking. Have you heard it?"

"Nope. You can't hear much over this pick axe banging away in the rock."

"Damn imagination," Lowell said. "It gets spooky down here."

"I don't believe in ghosts or goblins, boss. But small

animals might be living in these old shafts. But I think we would have run them out by now."

Yarak returned to banging away at the vein with his pick leaving Lowell to fill the cart once more. And so it continued the rest of the day.

ℰↃℰↃ

The Bell Yankee helicopter pilot began startup procedures, the chopper's turbine engine whining in the still morning air. Sheriff Calder and Sergeant Jessup stood next to the command post, studying a map of the area that included the town of Grant. It was a cloudless day, the sun just beginning to make its appearance.

"Here's where they were last spotted," Calder said, pointing to a spot on the map. If you can get the chopper up there and begin a systematic search of the area, we'll follow in the jeeps. You can ride with me. My two deputies will take the other one."

"Fine, Sheriff. They can radio us if they see anything."

"No one kills these animals until I'm present," Calder said. "Understand?"

"Of course, Sheriff. This is your case. We're just here to help."

Calder wasn't sure he believed the sergeant and the thought struck him it might have been a mistake to call in the state police but now he had to make the best of it. Once the chopper was in the air, Calder, Jessup, Ben, and Louis climbed into their jeeps and followed in a northwest direction at a distance behind the aircraft. It disappeared into the haze created by the rising desert heat.

As they rumbled over dunes of sand and mesquite, they rolled by ridges of rock and boulder outcroppings forming a rough and lonely landscape. Besides the mesquite and Joshua trees, there were shrubs of desert peach with their pink flowers, rubber rabbitbrush, mountain mahogany, and buckwheat. When Calder pushed the jeep through the gate indicating the Primate Research Facility property line, Jessup motioned back toward Cinder Mountain.

"Has the animal facility been up there long?" he said. "I never heard of it before this crisis."

"A few years that I know of. It didn't get any notoriety until those large animals, Yeti they call them, from Mongolia, arrived. They do some sort of research on them, I don't know what. They have other animals there as well."

"It was once government land, right?"

"Yeah," Calder said. "Don't know why they sold it, though."

"You know, Sheriff, these escaped animals are going to have to be destroyed. Whether you do it or it's us, they have to go."

"I don't know, Sergeant. Maybe Dr. Olson was right. We could call the vet. He could tranquilize them and get them returned to the facility. That's beginning to sound reasonable to me."

"There's always the possibility of them escaping again. And besides, these beasts have killed people. The public demands they be exterminated. It's justice."

"Justice?" Calder said. "How can there be justice here?"

The sheriff liked to think of himself as a reasonable man and, as such, he pondered Harry's admonition against killing the Yeti when they caught up with them. Maybe the doctor was right—science would suffer if they were destroyed. If the facility beefed up its security, maybe it would be possible to return them. He was beginning to see things differently.

After leaving the research facility property, the road turned to asphalt and curved back north then northwest.

When Grant appeared on the horizon Calder heard the helicopter circling overhead some distance to the east. They pushed past the town and into thinner scrub, where plants were few and far between. The day was turning into a scorcher.

They saw nothing.

At a dry streambed, they found tracks of a large animal. They looked like tracks of a huge human. Jessup put his foot into one of them with much to spare, half again bigger than his shoe size. Calder shifted the jeep into four-wheel drive and turned off the road following the tracks, while Ben walked in front, leading the way. Calder didn't think the tracks looked like they belonged to an animal as big as the Yeti but he pushed on for a mile or so until they gave out. Then he gunned the engine and ran up the side of the arroyo heading south.

"Nothing out here but coyotes and sagebrush," Jessup complained. "Stop for a minute, Sheriff."

Calder shut the jeep down. Jessup climbed out and scanned the horizon with binoculars. Low ridges punctuated the landscape and, off to the west, distant mountains punched skyward from the desert floor.

"See anything?" Calder said.

"Naw, nothing. A few jackrabbits and a lone coyote."

"If the Yeti aren't around Grant, I don't know where they could have disappeared to. We can see for miles out here."

Jessup climbed back into the jeep as Ben and Louis drove up. He retrieved the handheld radio from the dashboard and pushed the *TALK* button.

"Chopper One, this is Able Leader. Come in, Chopper One," he said.

There was static then a *click*. "This is Chopper One. Go ahead, Able Leader."

"See anything up there, guys?"

"Nothing, Sarge. Not a damn thing."

"Chopper One, bring the bird back home to the command post. We're calling it a day."

More static.

"Roger, Able Leader. Heading home."

The static went quiet and Jessup replaced the radio on the dash.

"Okay, Sheriff," he said. "Let's head back. We can decide on tomorrow's search area."

On the way back to the command post, Calder heard the helicopter off in the distance. Its drone got louder and louder until out of nowhere it zoomed overhead. It arced skyward and turned in a graceful curve toward Cinder Mountain.

Chapter 21

The region now occupied by the Sierra Nevada Mountains once lay beneath the sea, receiving sediment from the North American continent to the east. Through the process of plate tectonics, the Pacific Plate crashed into the North American Plate and was subducted beneath it. The incredible force of the crash caused the sediment to melt, forming an enormous magma chamber that eventually cooled to form granite. In addition, these forces caused the uplift of the land, forming enormous mountains. The process of erosion had since removed the sediment layer above the granite, exposing the sierra that we see today. Continuous movement of the plates caused additional uplift, melting and folding that produced a mix of sedimentary, metamorphic, and volcanic rock.

About thirty million years ago, an era of volcanism of massive proportions began in the Sierras. During this era, the Sierra began uplifting again to form many parallel faults. The area to the west rose, while the area to the east, now Carson Valley, dropped. The Tahoe Basin, like Carson Valley, had dropped between two uplifted blocks—the Sierra Crest on the west and the Carson Range to the east. Volcanic activity occurred frequently just north of the lake, and a lava flow eventually crossed over the Carson River. This dammed the valley and formed Lake Tahoe.

The area to the east of the range was referred to as the high desert. At elevations ranging from four to six thousand feet, this flatland received little rain because the peaks of the Sierra Nevada blocked precipitation flowing from the west. Although this area was desert, it still remained cold in the winter, and snow frequently covered the area.

The Great Basin covered most of Nevada and parts of Utah, Oregon, Idaho, and California. Generally, its east boundary was the Wasatch Mountains of Utah and the western edge was formed by the Sierra Nevada and Cascade Mountains that created a rain shadow over much of the Great Basin, preventing many Pacific storms from reaching the region. Northern and southern boundaries, depending on how they were defined, ranged from the Snake River Plain in the north to the Mojave Desert in the south.

As part of the Basin and Range Province, mountains and valleys were repeated in succession across the region, like great waves cast in time. Valleys were four thousand to five thousand feet above sea level and mountain peaks ranged over ten thousand feet in elevation. Plant communities defined different portions of the Great Basin. Forest communities occurred at high elevations and included the oldest living organisms on Earth, the Great Basin bristlecone pines, which could live five thousand years. Lower in elevation were the pinion-juniper woodlands. As elevation decreased farther, plant communities were characterized by the presence of sagebrush. In the northern Great Basin, an important plant community, referred to as the sagebrush steppe, was co-dominated by big sagebrush and several perennial grasses and forbs.

The lowest elevations were at the bottoms of valley basins. These areas often had salty soils, and the only plants that could tolerate these conditions grew in salt-desert shrub communities.

Humans had long been part of the Great Basin ecosystem. Evidence of Native American habitation had been found, dating back over ten thousand years. These people lived in small bands, growing corn and squash as well as hunting and gathering pine nuts and crickets. European explorers and trappers traversed the Great Basin during the 1700s, but settlers didn't start arriving until the early 1800s.

The Homestead Act of 1862 encouraged more settlers to come, determined to endure the sometimes harsh, always unpredictable, life in the Great Basin. Mining towns flourished and faded from the 1870s to 1930s as gold, silver, and copper were prospected. With the driving of the Golden Spike in 1869, the Great Basin became the place connecting East to West in a growing nation.

დადე

Drayton parked the jeep in front of the main building. After eating an early breakfast with Harry, Dixie, Siscom, and Millie, he found them waiting under the portico. In the early morning twilight, the sun not yet up, it was still light enough to see clearly.

Once everyone was loaded, Drayton started down the mountain.

"Where to first you think?" Harry said. "Grant?"

"No, first we'll stop by a rancher friend of mine to pick up horses and a trailer. It's just beyond the facility property."

"Horses?" Dixie said. "I hate horses."

Drayton nodded. "You never know out here. Best be

prepared. If those Yeti took out over open ground, the horses will come in mighty handy."

"Yeah, the odds are slim we'll find them along improved roads," Siscom said from the back seat with Dixie.

Once on level ground Drayton pushed the jeep hard, tearing past the property gate, then bumping onto the gravel road. They pressed hard all the way to Grant where the Yeti were last seen. Along the way they talked about the animals they were hunting.

"So what's so special about these Yeti anyway?" Drayton said. "I've never understood. You brought them all the way from Mongolia to study them. Why?"

"We believe they are an early hominid," Dixie said.

"Hominids?" Drayton said.

"A family known as great apes, forming a family of primates, including chimpanzees, gorillas, orangutans, and humans," Dixie told him. "To scientists, the term is also used in the more restricted sense as hominins or humans and relatives of humans closer than chimpanzees. Used this way, all hominid species other than *Homo sapiens* are extinct."

"Anyway that was our thinking until the Yeti were discovered," Millie said.

"What about the Neanderthals?" Siscom said. "Aren't they are closely related to humans?"

Harry nodded. "As a member of the genus *Homo* they are, yes. But they are extinct. In fact, all known hominids are extinct. What a discovery it would be if there was another living hominid species besides human living in our midst. We are studying these Yeti to determine how close to modern humans they actually are. It's possible they would be classified in the genus *Homo* also."

"It might even be possible for the Yeti to have interbred with humans like the Neanderthals," Millie said.

"You serious?" Drayton said. "You serious?" His voice had a catch in it as if he was taken aback by Millie's statement.

"The genetic difference between individual humans today is minuscule, about 0.1%, on average. Study of the same aspects of the chimpanzee genome indicates a difference of about 1.2%. The bonobo, which is the close cousin of chimpanzees, differs from humans to the same degree. The DNA difference with gorillas, another of the African apes, is about 1.6%. Most importantly, chimpanzees, bonobos, and humans all show this same amount of difference from gorillas. A difference of 3.1% distinguishes us and the African apes from the Asian great ape, the orangutan. How do the monkeys stack up? All of the great apes and humans differ from rhesus monkeys, for example, by about 7% in their DNA."

"I see," Drayton said.

"And if we find parts of Yeti DNA embedded in our own, like we have the Neanderthals, then yes, it most likely happened, Millie replied.

They circled the town of Grant. Several State Police cars and a Medical Examiner van were parked along Main Street; the town was otherwise quiet. They searched a ten mile radius around the town but found nothing.

෴

Lowell and his companions headed down the mountainside to the stream and their camp. Upon reaching their tent, Lowell remembered he left his fleece jacket in the mineshaft.

"Pour me a drink, Yarak," he said. "I forgot my jacket. I'll be back in a minute"

He grabbed his flashlight and began the climb back up the hill. A few clouds hung in a dark sky, partially obscuring the sliver of moon rising above the gorge. A slight breeze had come up, and Lowell shivered as he climbed. It had been a good day with lots of gold nuggets and ore removed from the mine. His muscles ached but he felt good about what they had thus far accomplished. In spite of his grumbling and talking to himself, Garby did his share of the work along with Terkel. Garby still didn't smell very pleasant, but Lowell could overlook that fact, as long as the man continued to pull his weight.

The trudge back up the gorge to the mine gave Lowell a chance to clear his mind and allow it time to unwind. The pressures of the expedition were enormous, weighing heavily on Lowell. Keeping this disparate group of unpredictable men working together as a unit, even with Yarak at his side, was a stress Lowell had not counted on. He put those worries aside as he approached the mine. He stopped briefly at the mine entrance, shot a quick glance at the campsite where the men had a roaring fire going, then hurried inside to retrieve his jacket.

꿍꿍

Yarak sat by the campfire and wondered what was taking Lowell so long. He followed his boss's instructions and had his usual whiskey sitting on a small folding table beside his chair. The man should have been back by now. On the far side of the fire, Garby and Terkel played cards on a blanket stretched out on the ground, oblivious to Lowell's absence.

Yarak sensed they were close to the end of their mountain sojourn. He knew Lowell was near the end of his tether physically and Yarak was not far behind. The previous evening he and Lowell talked about going back home and resting for a few weeks before returning, refreshed, to work the mine again.

Yarak gazed into the fire and reflected on his boss and their relationship of many years. For the first few years the only thing they had in common was the deaths of their wives in car accidents, or in Lowell's case his girlfriend. But during the recent years they mellowed to each other, and now Yarak loved him like a father.

During the summer of 1990, Boris Yeltsin, head of the Russian Soviet Federative Socialist Republic, addressed regional leaders and told them to *Help yourself to as much sovereignty as you can swallow.* So began the parade of sovereignties and with it, the slide toward the federalization of Russia, which became an independent state the next year.

The local elites did not all want the same thing. Most of Russia's territories readily agreed to the conditions set out in the federal treaties, but some of the former autonomous republics within the Russian federation, particularly those with oil, sought to acquire a much greater degree of independence.

Chechnya was a case in point. The fighter pilot Dzhokhar Dudayev came to power after elections and issued a decree entitled, *On the state sovereignty of the Chechen republic.* The authorities in Moscow, who just survived an attempted coup d'état, didn't accord it much importance. Then the Soviet Union dissolved. Tension between Moscow and Chechnya rose exponentially during the following year. In the end, Russian Army units left Chechen territory unopposed, leaving weapons and ammunition dumps. But Dudayev, having built up his own armed forces and equipped them with the weapons left behind, continued to insist on Chechnya's secession from Russia.

In 1993, the Provisional Council of the Chechen Republic was set up to act as a counterweight to President Dudayev. A pro-Russian head of the Upper Terek region led it. He, in turn, acquired weapons and the council's leaders began training at Russian firing ranges. Then, fighting broke out sporadically between supporters and opponents of Dudayev and in the summer the opponents appealed to the Russian president Boris Yeltsin for support. Russian army units and interior troops started to mass on the border with Chechnya.

During the winter of 1994, Dudayev's opponents stormed the capital with weapons, armored vehicles and helicopters supplied by Moscow. The Federal Counterintelligence Service, later the Federal Security Service, raised volunteers from the ranks of the Russian Army and officer corps, mainly from the tank and rifle divisions. They left with their military equipment to be captured or killed on the streets of the Chechen capital.

Yarak had been one of the volunteers.

Officially, Moscow categorically denied that its military personnel, draftees, and enlistees took part in these operations, just as it denied the shelling of the capitol. But the attack stalled and later Yeltsin signed a decree to restore constitutional law and order across the territory of the Chechen republic. War had been declared and Russian troops crossed the border into Chechnya.

Yarak's close friend had been killed when he stepped on a land mine. Shrapnel from the blast hit Yarak who walked nearby. For months, he thought he wasn't going to be able to walk but, after intensive therapy, he managed to overcome his injuries. But he was no longer in the service.

In a long circuitous route, he ended up in California, working at a burger joint, and it was there that Lowell spotted him. They became friends after Yarak delivered burgers to his office and the friendship deepened over the years. Lowell was the father he longed for, a man in which he could confide.

In simple language, he loved Rupert Lowell. He glanced up the side of the gorge but did not see Lowell returning.

It shouldn't have taken him this long, Yarak thought. He stood, walked around the fire. "Garby, Terkel, get your flashlights and come with me. The boss hasn't returned from the mine."

"He was just here," Garby protested.

"He went to get his jacket fifteen minutes ago. Now, come on."

The three men slogged up the trail, their flashlights casting soft beams into the surrounding brush. Upon reaching the entrance to the mine, Yarak hesitated and shined his light into the darkness of the tunnel.

"Mr. Lowell!" he hollered. "You in there?"

No response.

"Mr. Lowell!"

Nothing.

"Okay," Yarak said, "let's get down there and have a look. He might have hurt himself."

With Yarak leading the way, they stalked deeper down the shaft, their lights flickering off the walls. The darkness engulfed them like soft velvet, their flashlights providing the only light. Nearing the Y in the mineshaft Yarak spotted something ahead—a crumpled mass in the middle of the tunnel.

It was Lowell.

At his side in an instant, Yarak rolled Lowell over onto his back. The man was breathing in shallow gasps and the front of his clothes was covered in blood. He had a nasty head wound that oozed blood. Garby and Terkel stood behind Yarak, flashing their lights about the shaft.

"What the hell happened?" Terkel said. "Is he dead?"

"No, he's alive, but just barely," Yarak said.

"This was more than a fall," Garby said, stumbling a

ways farther down the shaft. "Somebody did this to him?"

"But who?" Terkel said. "We haven't seen anyone up here for weeks."

"He needs medical attention," Yarak said. "Let's get him back to camp. Help me carry him."

At the moment Garby and Terkel were getting Lowell up, a sound erupted from deep within the mine. It was an unusual sound, more like a growl—like nothing the men had ever heard. Yarak thought the mine shifted but continued to lift Lowell onto his back.

But there it was again.

It sounded exactly like an animal's growl or snarl. Yarak wanted to get back to the camp as soon as possible, the sound was giving him the creeps. Garby had Lowell supported by his underarms—his knees buckled as he tried to walk. Lowell groaned as he attempted to put one foot in front of the other.

"Terkel, get his feet," Yarak said.

Even though Lowell was a short man, he was stout. The two men struggled to get him off the ground. As Yarak helped steady his boss, a roar filled the shaft.

Yarak looked up and what he saw horrified him.

A large beast covered in shaggy hair stood at the Y, its eyes blazing like fire. A horrid smell filled the small space, and the beast roared, revealing fangs stained with blood. It pitched its massive head toward the overhanging wall and growled.

Yarak stood frozen, unbelieving.

გადავ

"You're saying we could be related to these creatures?" Drayton said in response to Millie's assertion.

"To date there are no known human cousins to *Homo*

sapien other than *Homo neanderthalensis*," Dixie answered. "But, like Harry said, they are extinct. The specimens we uncovered in Mongolia did not fit a pattern that would allow them to belong with the Homo genus nor any known hominoid pattern. So, to what primate category these specimens belong remains a puzzle. Unfortunately, we have only a few specimens with which to work and form an hypothesis. That is, until we brought these Yeti back, in order to study them."

"We don't actually *know* if these Yeti are a member of the genus *Homo*," Harry interjected. "At least not yet, anyway."

"Not long ago, a finger bone fragment was discovered in the Denisova Cave in Siberia from a juvenile female who lived around forty-one thousand years ago." Millie leaned forward as she spoke. "Analysis of its mitochondrial DNA showed it to be distinct from Neanderthals as well as modern humans. Its nuclear genome, however, suggested that it shared a common ancestor with Neanderthals. Scientists have achieved near-complete genomic sequencing, dating it around four hundred thousand years ago. To date, it is the oldest hominid DNA sequenced. They were able to demonstrate that some living humans can trace a portion of their ancestry to the Denisovan genome. It shows that all this is a complex puzzle."

Dixie nodded. "When we discovered a skull in a Tibetan monastery," she said, "we found it was much larger than anything in the genus *Homo*. Neanderthals had larger brains than modern humans—our brains actually shrank about twenty percent. But this skull was way larger than Neanderthal. So what it was, we didn't know until we found the Yeti. We know the animals are hominids. Are they *Homo* hominids? We can't say right now. It's why this research is so important."

"If we are related in some way to the Yeti," Millie said, running a hand through her hair, "it would be by way of a common ancestor. To be a direct descendant would be highly unusual."

"Can you prove something like that? Common ancestry, I mean."

"Of course we can, Mr. Drayton," Millie said. Her face softened and her eyes got brighter as she spoke. "Are you all truly interested in this stuff or should I just keep quiet? I'm sorry but I can get excited about my work."

"No please, go on," Drayton said. "I have always wondered what you scientists actually do."

"Well, it can get rather involved so please bear with me. I'll try and make it understandable."

Dixie moved closer to Millie and sat beside Drayton.

"Let's take the example of hemoglobin," Millie said. "Hemoglobin is the substance in our blood that carries oxygen and it's made up of four parts. Those parts are called polypeptides, but we can think of them essentially as four subunits. It has two copies of a part called alpha-globin and two copies of a part called beta-globin.

"Now, what modern molecular biology has enabled us to do is to pinpoint where the instructions are that specify these. The alpha-globin instructions are specified on Chromosome Number Sixteen and the beta-globin instructions are specified on Chromosome Number Eleven. And as our genome does for many genes, we have multiple copies of these, so we have backups. We've got extra copies of the alpha-globin genes and extra copies of the beta-globin genes, and they have interesting physiological functions, these multiple copies.

"But there's something extremely interesting about these, and it enables us to test evolution right down to the level of the molecule. On Chromosome Number Eleven, each of these copies is a set of instructions for how you build this polypeptide, the beta-globin. Five of them work, but one of them doesn't. It's given the Greek letters psi, beta, and then the number one. And the psi-beta-one sequence isn't a gene. It doesn't work. It's what we call a pseudogene, and a pseudogene is recognized as a gene because it's so similar to the other five in its DNA sequence, but it has some mistakes. It's broken, and it has a series of molecular errors that render the gene nonfunctional.

"Now, there are six distinct mistakes in this gene. And the reason that this is important in evolution is, in fact, simple, and it is this: these errors appear in a gene, they have no functional purpose. And you might ask yourself, what would I do, what would you do, if we were to find another organism that didn't just have similar genes but also had a pseudogene in the same spot and had the same set of errors?

"There's no reason why evolution would produce a duplicate set of mistakes in two copies of things. It must mean that these two organisms are descended with modification from another organism that had the same set of mistakes.

"And the gorilla, the chimpanzee, and the human being share the exact same set of molecular mistakes.

"Now, why is this significant? One of the core principles of evolution is common descent. One could always argue that because the three species are all African species, that's where they all come from, they're all primates, and they all started out living in similar environments, that the functional parts of this gene locus, they might work the same. But you cannot argue that the mistakes should match.

"And the fact that all three of these species have matching mistakes leads us to just one conclusion, and that's the same conclusion that Charles Darwin predicted

a century and a half ago, and that is that these three species share a common ancestor. Matching mistakes are
evidence of common ancestry."

Drayton stood and stretched his legs.

"So," he said, "if you find matching mistakes in the
Yeti and human genome, then—"

"We can say," Millie interrupted, "that both species
descended from a common ancestor."

Chapter 22

Sheriff Calder ambled out of the command post, stretched, and glanced at the orange glow in the eastern sky. The high-pitched call of the American Kestrel, a bird common to the Nevada desert, pierced the morning stillness, while overhead, large magenta-tinged cumulus clouds hung in the thin air. Calder waited for the arrival of Jessup and Williams of the strike force when they would again team up with his deputies and Undersheriff Hardin. Earlier, Calder and Jessup decided to expand the search area to the northwest, using the state's helicopter, with the rest of the team following on the ground.

Not having located the Yeti left a sour taste in Calder's mouth and he felt the mounting pressure.

He heard the phone ring inside the command post and soon Andy Hardin stuck his head out the door.

"Buck, it's the mayor. He wants to speak with you. An update, I suppose."

Calder nodded, stepped into the trailer, and took the phone. A loud voice banged in his ear.

"Yes, Mayor? Sheriff Calder here."

The voice on the other end sounded agitated. "Buck, how is it going up there? I've got the Elko city council breathing down my neck over these escaped animals. Tell me you're making progress."

"I wish I could, sir. Unfortunately, we've had no luck in locating them. Or picking up any signs either. We plan to take the state police chopper back up this morning so maybe we'll get lucky."

"The governor's office has called twice, Buck. The man wants action and results. Don't talk about luck."

"I understand," Calder said. "Believe me, Mayor, we are doing everything conceivable to locate these creatures. When we do, they're good as dead."

"What's your best estimate as to where they have gone? I need to tell the governor something."

"North of Interstate 80 for sure. And west to northwest of Cinder Mountain. We searched all around Grant yesterday without success so we've enlarged the search area."

"I need some help, Buck. If you don't find these beasts soon, there's going to be hell to pay—for you and me. Like I said, the governor's breathing down my neck and is likely to call in the national guard if you are unable to find and destroy them in the next forty-eight hours."

"Understand, Mayor. Rest assured, we'll locate them."

"You've got state police help?"

"Yes, sir. There's a strike force here with a helicopter. I think we'll find them fairly soon."

"Keep me posted then, Buck."

After hanging up, Calder went back outside, tried to calm his churning stomach. *I'm getting it from all sides*, he thought. The mayor's problems were none of his concern but he and the man both held elected offices so if this crisis didn't end soon, there could be serious repercussions. Like him being out of a job. And he enjoyed his job. His second thoughts about killing the animals were going out the window. He heard the *whoop whoop* of the chopper's rotors and watched aircraft circle then touch down near the command post. Shortly thereafter, Jessup and Williams arrived in their state vehicle and everyone gathered around Calder's jeep. The sheriff ran a finger over the map laid out on the hood.

"Up here," he said, "the terrain gets much rougher. Only a few trails for roads amid the buttes and arroyos."

"Any water?" Jessup asked.

"There used to be a small stream near here," Calder said, pointing. "And there's a couple of hot springs in this region as well. Mostly sand, rocks, and sagebrush."

"And a lot of snakes," Hardin said with a grin.

"Fine," Jessup said. He turned to the helicopter pilot who was leaning against the trailer. "Okay, fire up it up, and let's get going. We're burning daylight."

Once the chopper was airborne and on its way northward, Jessup climbed in beside Calder while Hardin drove Williams, Ben, and Louis. Beyond the town of Grant, they turned northwest and headed into desolate country. A single rutted dirt road meandered through the desert while Calder did his best to avoid the deeper ruts.

The landscape now turned more remote, more desolate. Vegetation was much sparser, only an occasional sagebrush or mesquite bush lined the road. The clouds, earlier tinged with a magenta hue, were now large white puffs of cotton.

They arrived at a wooden bridge that spanned a deep dry streambed. The bridge's floor had all but crumbled away leaving only the support structure baking in the morning heat. Calder got out to survey the situation. Hardin stood beside him, and they surveyed the desert beyond the dilapidated impassable bridge.

"Now what, Buck?" Hardin said.

"No choice but to try and make it across and up the other side," Calder said.

"The other side is rather steep," Hardin said.

"Any suggestions, then?"

"Nope, I guess not. Just hope we can make it up."

Jessup and Hardin got out and Calder put the jeep into four-wheel drive. The bottom of the dry streambed was lined with rounded river rock of different sizes that caused the jeep to lurch violently from side to side. Calder's insides got a good shaking. *Good thing there's Kevlar tires on this baby*, he thought.

When he approached the far bank, Calder gunned the engine and tried to accelerate up its side. Halfway up, the jeep struggled, wheels spinning, then stopped its forward progress. The sheriff backed down into the streambed for another go at the bank but it was no use. No matter what he did, he could not make it up the steep bank of the streambed. The rear wheels only sank deeper into the sand, spinning.

"Hold up," Jessup said. "Should we just follow the streambed then?" he said.

"It'll be easier on the road," Calder said, pointing to the road beyond the bridge.

"Then we'll push."

Williams waited with Ben and Louis in the second jeep while the men got behind Calder's jeep. When Calder gunned the accelerator again, Jessup and Hardin pushed from the rear. The jeep lurched forward and scrambled up the side of the bank, spewing sand from its rear wheels. Then Hardin got behind the wheel of his jeep and they repeated the effort. Once both jeeps were across the streambed, Calder continued on.

ༀༀༀ

Yarak stared into the red, glowing eyes of a ten foot tall animal. The beast had long brown hair, smelled like rotting flesh, and hissed at him. It took three steps toward Yarak, raised its eyes toward the tunnel's ceiling, and let out a loud, long growl, a penetrating, otherworldly sound that caused Garby and Terkel to drop Lowell on the ground. The three men began backing out of the shaft but stopped short when another shriek sounded behind them. Yarak wheeled on his heels only to be confronted with another beast, exactly like the first, who blocked their exit from the mine. Both creatures stood on their hind legs and the stench from their putrid breath caused Yarak's stomach to roll. The second beast was smaller than the first, but its massive head contained similar eyes, burning red like the coals in their campfires.

Yarak felt his legs go weak, his head swoon. A creature blocked their escape to the outside while the other stood between them and going deeper into the tunnel. Their weapons were at the campsite.

"Yarak!" Terkel screamed. "What do we do?"

"Fight! We either fight or we die!"

A panicked Garby attempted to run past the beast that blocked the way to the mine entrance but it grabbed him by his arm and hurled him onto his back. He screamed as the beast pounced on him and ripped an arm out of its socket. Blood spewed onto the ground and Garby shrieked in pain. While he screamed, Terkel made a dash for it. The beast caught Terkel by the throat and in one swift motion, tore his head off his shoulders. He dropped like a limp doll. And didn't move.

Turning its attention back to Garby the beast reached down with a huge hand tipped with long claws and slashed open the man's torso, spilling out his internal organs. Garby's last scream was a garbled one, blood having filled his throat.

In the meantime, Yarak picked up a rock and threw it at the beast. Strange, he thought, but the second animal deeper in the tunnel didn't move on him. It just watched its partner. The rock hit the creature squarely in the chest but the animal didn't notice. It roared and ambled toward Yarak. He felt the animal as it wrapped its strong arms about him then sank its fangs into his neck. Pain shot through his body like a missile. He struggled but it was no use, for the beast had him firmly in its grasp. His head swooned and felt his bowels loosen. The animal's hot breath engulfed his face.

Then, as if by a miracle, the creature dropped him but stood over him for a long moment. The larger animal stepped over him, joined its partner, then the pair headed for the exit. When they disappeared into the darkness, Yarak heard one of the beasts let out a growl that echoed down the mineshaft.

Then all was quiet.

For a long while Yarak lay on the ground, not daring to move. His neck hurt like hell. When he touched the wound he was surprised to find that it was smaller than he anticipated. His right arm was broken, he was sure of that, and something wasn't right about his right leg. Garby hadn't moved in a long while and must be dead, thank the lord. At the smell of his blood and internal organs, Yarak puked up bitter bile that burned his throat.

He could tell that Lowell was still breathing but his breaths were erratic and shallow. Yarak rolled onto his back and lay in the silent darkness, until he found himself floating in a murky haze devoid of light and sound.

He was in Chechnya, the late 90s. Perched inside a tank along the Terek River, he waited for the signal to advance and cross the river. Beyond lay Grozny, the object of their two-pronged pincer movement. Two school busses filled with Chechnyan children rambled down the road on the opposite side. *Must be coming home from school.* Suddenly, out of the clouds, Russian Su-24 fighter bombers dropped cluster bombs, destroying the school busses in a huge fireball. The concussion rattled Yarak's tank. From its porthole he watched until the flames dwindled, leaving behind only a mass of charred, molten metal.

Yarak twitched and realized he was still in the mine. Beside him Lowell was still breathing. When he propped himself on his left elbow a knifing pain shot through his body.

Lowell stirred and looked about.

"Yarak," he said, voice failing. "Is that you?"

"Right, boss."

"How bad are you hurt?" Lowell rolled onto his side and stared at him.

"Can't tell. My arm and leg hurt but I'm alive. What were those creatures?"

"They weren't bears, I know that," Lowell said, his voice still a whisper.

"I've never seen anything like them. Think we can get out of this mine, Mr. Lowell?"

"I'm going to start crawling, Yarak. Think you can follow?"

"I'll try. I'm certainly not going to let you leave me here alone. Those damned beasts might decide to return."

Lowell started crawling toward the mine entrance, pulling himself along using his arms while Yarak followed. His arm and leg ached, which made for slow progress. He knew he had a gaping wound in his neck for his blood had dried into a crust on his shirt and jacket.

The two men inched toward the entrance—they were a good hundred yards from it. Frequently, Lowell had to stop and rest and Yarak heard him wheezing in the dark. Yarak felt his leg—it felt wet and sticky—and he worried that he had started bleeding again.

Garby and Terkel lay dead, their bodies torn asunder

by the two beasts. While Yarak crawled, the thought of leaving them in the mine caused him to wonder if either man had a family. Neither had talked about loved ones since joining Lowell. Yarak wondered also what it must be like to die alone somewhere and know that there was no one to mourn your passing. He shuddered and moved on.

When they reached the mine opening, Yarak rolled onto his back and gulped large swallows of cool fresh air while Lowell lay on his side and moaned. Gathering strength, Yarak pushed himself to his hands and knees, crawled to Lowell's side, and touched his face. It was matted with blood.

"Sir," he said. "Can you hear me? It's Nash."

"Na—Na—Nash," Lowell said through a spasm of coughing. A wave of pain bolted through his body. "What—happened? Where are—we?"

"We were attacked by two large beasts. We made it outside the mine."

"Ye—yes, I remember. Have they left?"

Yarak patted his boss on the shoulder. Lowell moaned.

"Can you crawl back to camp, Mr. Lowell? I'll help you."

"Thanks, Nash. I'll try. I think I can make it."

Chapter 23

D r. Miles Radner sat in his office, eyeing the man across from him. Dr. Bernard Wickingham nervously adjusted his tie while Radner studied him. The research director was a man of meticulous habits, one of them being to keep a precise and well-defined schedule to his daily activities. The young doctor from the university arrived without an appointment, requesting an audience, and seemed intent on getting one. Radner, with larger issues on his mind, was irritated with Wickingham's arrival.

Radner reclined in his leather chair, a fountain pen in his hand. "Dr. Wickingham, to what do I owe the honor of this unexpected visit?"

"Dr. Radner, I appreciate you seeing me on such short notice. When I saw you on the news, I decided to take a break from my duties at the university and offer any help I could. Have they found the Yeti?"

"Not as yet. The sheriff has mounted a large search team that includes the state police. Dr. Olson and our security chief are out looking as well."

"Any victims?"

"Four. In the town of Grant, not far from here. Where the Yeti went from there is anybody's guess. Doctor, I really don't see anything that you can add at this point. I'm sorry but I believe you wasted a trip."

Wickingham's eyes narrowed and his forehead wrinkled in deep furrows. The look on his face turned sinister. "Dr. Radner, do you believe Dr. Olson is qualified to lead the department? Given the events of the past few days?"

Radner leaned forward and set the fountain pen on his desk. "I don't understand, Doctor."

"As chairman of the Anthropology Department at Cal Pacific, isn't Harry—er—Dr. Olson, responsible for the Primate Research Facility?"

"Dr. Wickingham, I am responsible for the daily operation of the facility. I am the director."

"And Dr. Olson?"

Radner shifted in his chair, uncomfortable with Wickingham's line of questioning and where it was going. "Dr. Olson is ultimately responsible for all activities of the department."

"Including this research facility?"

Radner was becoming irritated with the young doctor. "Of course. Your point, Doctor?"

"My point is that, under Dr. Olson's leadership, two valuable and dangerous animals have escaped and are now terrorizing the public. He is responsible for this fiasco—it should never have happened."

"I know Dr. Olson is extremely disheartened over these events and his responsibility weighs heavy on his shoulders. But this incident was an unfortunate accident caused by an irresponsible graduate assistant."

"That's it? You plan to do nothing?"

Radner's skin prickled under Wickingham's accusation. The young faculty member's demeanor irritated Radner and he didn't like it. The man was leading up to something. But what? "Dr. Wickingham, what is on your mind? Spill it, please."

Wickingham loosened his tie and smiled. "You and I ought to go to Dr. Pauling and seek Harry's dismissal. It is only right that a blunder of this magnitude should have consequences."

Radner studied the man for a moment without commenting.

"In short, I believe Dr. Olson must go," Wickingham continued.

Radner's pulse quickened and a pain shot through his temple. He couldn't believe what he had heard. He remembered meeting the new faculty member at a social function at the beginning of the academic year and recognized him as a climber, an opportunist. "You propose that you and I waltz into the president's office and demand that he fire Harry?"

"I wouldn't put it quite that way, sir," Wickingham said.

"How else would you put it, Doctor? You just said the man had to go."

"Well—"

"You underestimate Dr. Olson's new-found status since finding and bringing the Yeti to Cal Pacific's facility. He is the new golden boy and, as such, has raised a lot of money for the university. Reginald Pauling won't hear of it. What you ask is a nonstarter. And I suggest you allow the university president to deal with this crisis as he sees fit."

"Well, Dr. Radner," Wickingham said, "I had hoped for your assistance but, if it will not be forthcoming, I will try a different approach. I'm sorry if I have wasted your time."

"Dr. Wickingham, I'll have you know that the other day I offered Dr. Olson my resignation. He refused to accept it. I admit that before this crisis I didn't necessarily care for the man, but he has risen a lot in my estimation. I will not participate in this subterfuge and, again, I suggest, if you value your career, that you put it aside. You are quite new to the university faculty, young man. And if memory serves me, Harry hired you. Surely, you are not so ambitious as to betray him."

Wickingham stood. "I'll be off, Dr. Radner. I appreciate your time. I do hope this all ends in the university's favor. Good day, sir."

Radner watched the man leave his office. *What an unmitigated fool.* If he thought Reginald Pauling would dismiss Harry before this thing was resolved, he was skidding himself. Pauling was no naive newcomer to university politics or press management and, as such, was capable of dealing with the crisis without Wickingham's interference. The man recruited Julius Kesler and other notable scientists and academicians to the university and paid them well. As a novice to Cal Pacific's faculty, the young man had a lot to learn regarding tenure and promotions. As a tenured professor, Harry could not be terminated without cause and this crisis, precipitated by an unfortunate accident, did not rise to that level.

When Harry married Dixie, his former graduate student, Radner was heartbroken. He was a junior faculty member at the time and one of Dixie's professors— taught a field techniques class. She was the rising star of the crop of graduate students, and he soon became infatuated with her easy charm and quick mind. But it was obvious Harry had caught her eye, and after he chose her for the Mongolia expedition, Radner went into a depression that lasted until well after their marriage.

So, when the position of Director of the Primate Research Facility was open, due to the previous director's moving, Radner happily applied. When he was accepted, he said goodbye to San Francisco, moved to the Nevada desert facility, and threw himself into his work with renewed strength. Jimmy Winkleman caused him some grief but overall he enjoyed being the director.

⌒⌒

Johnson and Falco labored over the desk in Johnson's apartment. Johnson's contact provided five pounds of C-4 explosive and Falco had purchased a number of model rocket ignitors form a local hobby shop.

"Think this will do the job?" Falco said. He watched with intent interest as Johnson wired the necessary connections.

"Five pounds? I should think so. It'll blow that gate to kingdom come."

"I can't wait to see it."

"Hopefully, we'll be far away when it goes," Johnson said, working with pliers on the two wires.

"But we'll hear it, right?"

"Without a doubt, my friend. It's gonna make a very loud *bang*."

"The Treadwell lady hopes there are no injuries."

"I told her what she wanted to hear, Falco. But the truth is there are no guarantees. Anything can happen."

"She any good in bed?" Falco's eyes widened at the question.

"She's all right. She's got money, that's her main attraction. And it may work in our favor." Finished with the wiring, Johnson put the device in a shoebox, set it aside. He looked at Falco. "How about a toke?" he said.

⌒⌒

Drayton pulled the horse trailer into the desert in an ever-enlarging circle surrounding Grant. Not knowing the direction the Yeti went after leaving the town put them at a disadvantage, so driving in circles was their only option. Soon, however, they would run out of road, necessitating a journey on horseback. Harry sat in the front passenger seat and scanned the passing landscape with binoculars. In the rear were Dixie and Siscom with Millie in the far rear seat. The sun was up, a scorching heat well underway, while small puffs of cumulus clouds hung in the air. The dirt on the road was still packed from the rain days earlier.

They were skirting the edge of the Black Rock Desert area. A huge area of water once covered this part of the state, but most of its former area was now just a series of dry, alkaline flats, of which the Black Rock Desert was the largest example. The most level and uniform section was the Black Rock Playa, which stretched for thirty-five miles—a region completely dry much of the year, though partially flooded and frozen during winter. After the last major ice age some fifteen thousand years ago, the great inland Lake Lahontan, sprawling across northern Nevada for thousands of years, finally began to dry up, leaving vast alkaline silt basins known as playa. The hills and mountains around the area revealed the shorelines etched into their sides more than five hundred feet higher than the basin floor. The bones of wooly mammoth, camel and saber-tooth tigers were found all around this locale. Man ventured into the area as evidenced from cave markings, and the Northern Paiute took up residence some two thousand years ago.

At a small pond, Drayton stopped to water the horses. While Siscom unloaded the animals one by one, Drayton filled a water bucket and allowed the horses to drink their fill. Harry got out and paced around the jeep with Dixie.

"I'm worried, honey," she said. "We have driven at least several hundred miles and haven't seen them or even seen any signs. No tracks or anything."

"It's as if they just up and disappeared," Harry said, who took a drink of water from a bottle and passed it to Dixie.

"Not a good sign, I'm sure. In this heat, they can't last long, can they?"

"I wouldn't think so, Dixie. But we're not giving up till we find them. One way or the other."

Back on the road they continued to skirt the Black Rock Desert.

෧ඁ෨

Lowell and Yarak crawled into their campsite, aching, thirsty, and hungry. Dawn was a faint magenta glow, the air cool and dry. Lowell pulled himself into a camp chair while Yarak stirred the ashes of the cold campfire until a flame flickered. Once he had a fire going, he collapsed into a chair next to his boss.

He handed a water bottle to Lowell. "Mr. Lowell, as soon as we have some coffee and water, we need to take the jeep down to the main road. We both need medical care."

"I'm feeling somewhat better, Nash. I think I can make it." He took several huge gulps of the water and returned the bottle to Yarak.

Yarak made coffee and they drank the steaming liquid in large mugs. Lowell massaged his aching neck. "How are you doing, my friend?" he said. "That arm doesn't look so good."

"Broken, I think," Yarak said. "I don't know about my leg. They both hurt like hell."

"What was that back there in the mine, Nash?" I've never seen anything like those animals."

"Beasts from hell, I'd say. They weren't bears, that much I know."

"Their eyes," Lowell said. "Their eyes. I'll never forget those eyes. They burned right through me."

"Nothing on this earth can be that big," Yarak said. "And their jaws were massive."

"I'm ready to get back home, Nash. We can stop by an emergency room along the way."

Before leaving, Lowell cut strips from a blanket and used them to wrap Yarak's arm, constructing a splint of sorts. Not as good as a wooden one but he said it might keep the bones somewhat aligned. Then he fashioned a sling, gingerly placing Yarak's arm in it.

Lowell helped Yarak into the jeep and together they rumbled along the edge of the stream, rolling over rocks and small logs. Bouncing down the side of the gorge shot waves of pain and nausea through his already throbbing body. With each bump, Yarak grunted in obvious pain. Lowell veered around boulders, dipping the wheels into deep ruts that rocked the jeep from side to side. They followed the stream as it descended in convoluted fashion, following the contour of the mountainside. When it reached the level plain, it slowed, running as a placid river.

On level ground, Lowell breathed a sigh of relief, steered onto the dirt road, and headed southeast. He shot a glance over at Yarak. The man had reclined his seat and his eyes were closed, no longer wincing with each little bump.

Beasts from hell, that was Yarak's description. It brought visions of hellhounds from his readings as a young boy. Cerberus was the terrifying hellhound that guarded the gates of Hades. Cerberus's job was to ensure that no living person could enter the underworld, and likewise, no spirit escape. Cerberus was described in several ancient works of Homer and Hesiod, in the eighth century BC. Cerberus was uniformly described as immensely huge and fierce, and originally described as having fifty heads. Later texts described him as having three heads, the tail of a serpent, and manes of snakes.

In every county throughout England, there were legends of the Phantom Black Dogs. There were, of course, regional variations, but most were described as being as large as a calf, red eyes a big as saucers, and a shaggy coat. They haunted ancient paths, crossroads, churchyards and old gallows sites—all places associated with bad luck, superstition, or unexplainable events. In other places throughout England, the black dogs were believed to be portents of death. It was believed that anyone who saw this creature would die shortly after.

Then there were the beasts that were written in the *Book of Revelation of Saint John*. Three beasts were described. The first came from the oceans and had the body of a leopard with seven heads like a Hydra, and bear's paws. On each head there were ten horns each with a crown. The second had a similar appearance as the first but it was born from the ground and had only one head. The third, also known as the Scarlet Beast looked the same as the first beast but was red in color.

Finally, there was the Antichrist, the demonic being from Biblical scriptures that was said to be eighteen feet tall who would come on the Day of Judgment to bring terror to people. He was the enemy of God and Christ. The Antichrist was depicted in a dual form—the first was a monster, a chimera with seven dragonheads, the first half of a lion, and the last half of a ram. He was called the Beast from the Sea. It was also told that the Antichrist was indeed a human being, chosen by Satan himself to receive supernatural powers to enslave the whole world.

Of course, what Lowell saw in the mineshaft wasn't any of these monsters. What he had encountered and nearly killed him and Yarak was an animal—like nothing he had ever seen, to be sure. Now they were running loose somewhere in northern Nevada, possibly on a killing rampage. As soon as they had their wounds attended they would have to report the attack to the authorities.

Chapter 24

D r. Bernard Wickingham waited to see Dr. Reginald Pauling in the president's outer office. The blonde secretary pecked away on her keyboard and answered the phone while Wickingham fidgeted and gazed out the window. His stomach was in knots. On the way back from the primate facility and his meeting with Radner, Wickingham went over in his mind what he planned to say to Pauling and hoped it sounded professional. Now and then, the blonde looked up from her work and smiled. Wickingham noticed she had a gap in her front teeth. When she finally signaled that Pauling was ready for him, he nearly choked.

Inside the president's office, Pauling offered him a chair and took a seat behind his desk. He smiled and folded his hands in front of himself. "Well, Dr. Wickingham, what can I do for you? Everything going well with your class and research?"

"Yes, everything in those areas is perfectly fine. It's something else I wish to chat with you about."

"Yes, Bernard. What is it?"

Pauling was dressed in a navy blue suit with a white shirt and dark striped tie. Wickingham noticed his immaculately manicured fingernails. He shifted in his seat, clasped his sweaty palms together, and began. "As you know, Dr. Pauling, the two Yeti have escaped from the university's Primate Research Facility."

The president nodded but didn't say anything.

"The ultimate responsibility for that facility resides with Dr. Harry Olson, right?" Wickingham continued.

"Actually, Bernard," Pauling said, frowning, "the ultimate responsibility is mine."

Wickingham swallowed hard and smiled weakly. He felt his stomach churn. "Yes, sir. I meant below you, of course. Dr. Olson?"

"Yes. Dr. Olson assumes overall responsibility of the primate facility while Dr. Radner is the day-to-day director. Is this line of questioning going somewhere, Doctor?"

"To be perfectly blunt, sir, it is my feeling that the Yeti's escape proves Dr. Olson is not fit to be the chairman of our department and have the overall responsibility of the primate facility. I feel he should be demoted or dismissed for this egregious dereliction."

"I'm sorry, Bernard. I don't quite follow you," Pauling said.

"He needs to be fired, sir. He screwed up."

"Am I actually hearing you say this, Dr. Wickingham? You, a relative newcomer to the university? A junior faculty member? Are you serious?"

"Well…uh…er…"

"You wish to bring formal charges against Dr. Olson?"

Wickingham squirmed in his chair. "Like I said. The man screwed up big time. He should suffer the consequences."

"What evidence do you possess of his dereliction of duty, young man?"

"Well, sir, the obvious. The fact that these Yeti have

escaped and killed a number of people. Surely—"

Pauling held up a hand stopping Wickingham in mid-sentence. He sat for a moment and stared at the young scientist. The air was full of electricity. Wickingham's stomach was a jumble of knots.

Finally, after what seemed an eternity, Pauling spoke. "Son, I think everyone involved agrees what has happened at the facility was a tragedy. Whose fault it was and where the responsibility lies has yet to be determined."

"Sir, with all due respect—"

Pauling held up a hand again. "Son, let me give you a piece of simple advice—get out of here, now. And don't grace my office again until you have won the Nobel Prize. Good day."

Stunned, Wickingham sulked out of Pauling's office like a whipped pup. It was hard to believe the man had summarily dismissed him. He left Administration and sauntered to his small office in the Science Complex at the far western edge of campus. Alone in the dim room, he let his anger build until he developed a pounding headache. He replayed the discussion over in his mind. Had he been too direct? What had Pauling meant by him being *a relative newcomer*? In his eagerness to rise up the academic ladder, had he seized upon an issue whose roots ran deeper than he realized?

He removed his tie and slouched in his chair, feet on the desk. Well, he thought, if he couldn't get Olson fired through channels, he would try another way. There was always more than one way to skin a cat.

එංඑං

Dixie bounced along in a relative haze, the landscape outside the jeep passing without her paying much attention. Her thoughts were elsewhere. She was worried—worried about what this Yeti crisis would do to the Primate Research Facility. When she saw Dr. Radner's press conference replayed on television and listened to all the reporter's questions, she realized the escape of these killers would have a profound impact on the facility's future. Whether it was closed or merely allowed to remain open with a few chimps would be the result of public opinion and pressure. And that was unfortunate. The Yeti were one-of-a-kind specimens, a landmark opportunity to study mankind's ancestry in the living flesh.

But she feared it was not to be. Deep inside, she knew that this crisis was not going to end to everyone's satisfaction. The strike force was intent on destroying her Yeti. Yes, they were *her* Yeti. Strange as it seemed, she had forged a personal attachment with the animals, borne in Mongolia when she had been carried off by one of them. Not one of these particular Yeti but still, having Bentu and Sasha at the facility where she could visit them, had deepened her feeling for the animals. If they turned out to be a distant human relative, how wonderful to have been a part of the scientific discovery.

Dixie realized she was a worrier. She worried about a lot of things, mostly inconsequential fears that never materialized. If there weren't anything to fret over, she would worry about that. In addition to her deep concern over the Yeti, her overarching concern was what the crisis might do to her husband's career and reputation. Harry had burst onto the international stage and garnered worldwide acclaim with the discovery and later capture of the Yeti. His promotion to departmental chairman succeeding Dr. Kesler was, in large part, a result of this newfound recognition.

She knew Harry and the Graduate Committee had screened the assistants with undue care to select the two that were ultimately chosen to spend a year or two at the primate facility. And Dixie knew both of them. Jimmy was a flaky but brilliant student while Millie had shown her promise by diligent work and intuitive thinking. Jimmy was the classic nerd, pocket protector and all, but had an arrogant streak she didn't like.

Millie was quiet and shy, most of her time was spent with her head in a book. But Dixie never would have guessed that Jimmy would so blatantly disregard policy and open the Yeti's cage without the animal being sedated.

Drayton stopped for a quick lunch at the edge of Black Rock Desert Wilderness Area. He pulled the jeep next to a small copse of trees, and the group ate sandwiches in the shade. As they finished eating, Dixie noticed a small dot in the far distance getting larger with each passing second. She watched the dot get bigger, small tufts of dust billing out behind it until she realized it was a vehicle traveling fast. In another minute she saw that it was a jeep and it was heading in their direction.

"Someone's coming, Bruce," she said, pointing in the direction of the jeep.

Everyone looked up and followed the jeep as it approached the dirt road where they were parked. Drayton waved at the jeep and it rolled to a stop in a cloud of dust.

"You fellas been up in the gorge back there?" Drayton asked as he went to the driver's window. Dixie followed with Harry at her side.

"We need help," the driver said. Dixie noticed his blood stained jacket and head wound.

"What happened?" Dixie said. She shot a glance at the man's passenger who looked as if he had been in a fight as well.

"We were attacked by two large animals," the man said.

"Really?" Harry said, moving to the window. "What did they look like?"

"Large. Hairy. Not bears. Walked on their hind legs. Real scary."

"Our Yeti," Harry said, turning to Drayton.

"Your what?" the driver said.

"Large animals from Mongolia. Escaped from a research facility near Grant," Harry said.

"We need medical help, bad."

"Sure." Drayton moved to the window. "Which way were they headed?"

Dixie noticed that the man's passenger was slumped in his seat.

"Is he okay?" she said, pointing the other man.

"He's hurt pretty bad. Needs a doctor."

"Direction," Drayton pressed. "Which direction?"

"Northwest from the gorge entrance. About ten miles from here."

"Thanks," Drayton said. "You'll find a doctor in Elko. An hour's drive if you step on it."

"Fine," said the driver, and he sped off toward the town.

Dixie's heart pounded.

"We'll go as far as we can in the jeep," Drayton said, "then take the horses. Hopefully, we can pick up their trail. Dr. Siscom, get your tranquilizer gun ready just in case."

"What do we do with them once we find them and they're sedated?" Millie asked.

"We'll have to load them in the horse trailer in order to get them back to the facility," Siscom said. "They weigh a ton so it will take all us."

"This is a large area," Harry said. "Damn, they could be anywhere."

"I'll pray we get lucky," Millie said as she climbed into the rear of the jeep.

Drayton pushed the jeep with the horse trailer into the wilderness area. The region had been set aside for use without motorized vehicles but this was an emergency. There were no roads, only small trails that, to Dixie, appeared to lead nowhere.

They sped northwest as the sun headed toward the horizon, creating rays of gold, yellow, magenta, and purple over the desert floor, lengthening shadows, sending the temperature dropping.

Harry retrieved a map from the glove box and studied it. "Looks like there's an abandoned mining operation up here a ways," he said. "Rabbithole Mine."

"Might be a good place to bed down for the night," Drayton said. "It's a place to get out of the weather in case it rains."

"Good idea," Harry replied. "When I was out in the rain I got chilled to the core. I was close to being hypothermic."

When the dilapidated mining structure came into view, Drayton pulled the jeep into the shade and killed the engine. The group piled out and stretched their legs. Drayton and Harry pulled the sleeping bags and other gear from the compartment in the trailer while Siscom unloaded and hobbled the horses. They whinnied at being out of the trailer.

The abandoned mine was a series of ramshackle wooden structures, half standing, half nothing more than a pile of rubble. A group of rusted machinery stood idle, remnants of an earlier time when gold and silver reigned supreme.

A broken-down sluice stood to one side of what was once a two-story building.

Dixie and Millie grabbed the water bottles, trail mix,

and jerky, and the entire group sat and washed the desert grit from their mouths.

"Is it possible they can survive out here in this heat?" Millie said. "It's not their natural habitat nor the temperature we kept at the Animal Care Unit."

"We are in uncharted territory," Siscom said, shaking his head, and turned toward Harry. "No one knows what their tolerances are, do we, Harry?"

"You're absolutely right, Gerald," Harry said. "In Mongolia, the Yeti lived at altitude deep in caves where the temperatures rarely got above forty or fifty degrees. Here, it's well over a hundred. So I don't think we know how much they can endure. This heat may be too much of a stress for them to survive for long."

"But they have, so far," Dixie interjected. "And I think that bodes well for their endurance and survivability."

Siscom nodded. "From what we have seen at the facility, they have an amazing ability to adapt to their surroundings. So far, they have shown that out here on the desert. There is a potential problem, however."

"What is that, Dr. Siscom?" Millie said.

"In 1847, the German biologist Carl Bergmann observed that within the same species of warm-blooded animals, populations having less massive individuals were more often found in warm climates near the equator, while those with greater bulk, or mass, were found further from the equator in colder regions. This is due to the fact that big animals generally have larger body masses that result in more heat being produced. The greater amount of heat results from there being more cells. A normal byproduct of metabolism in cells is heat production. Subsequently, the more cells an animal has, the more internal heat it will produce.

"In addition, larger animals usually have a smaller surface area relative to their body mass and, therefore, are comparatively inefficient at radiating their body heat off into the surrounding environment. Galileo described the relationship between surface area and volume of objects interestingly. The volume increases twice as fast as the surface area. This is the reason that relatively less surface area results in relatively less heat being lost from animals."

"Like in bears, for example," Millie said.

"Exactly. Polar bears are a good example of this phenomenon. They have large, compact bodies with relatively small surface areas from which they can lose their internally produced heat. This is an important asset in cold climates. In addition, they have heavy fur and fat insulation that help retain body heat.

"Then in 1877, the American biologist Joel Allen went further than Bergmann in observing that the length of arms, legs, and other appendages also has an effect on the amount of heat lost to the surrounding environment. He noted that among warm-blooded animals, individuals in populations of the same species living in warm climates near the equator tend to have longer limbs than do populations living farther away from the equator in colder environments. This is due to the fact that a body with relatively long appendages is less compact and subsequently has more surface area. The greater the surface area, the faster body heat will be lost to the environment."

"What this all adds up to is that we need to find these Yeti sooner than later. The longer they're out here, the greater the risk of them dying." Harry's tone was emphatic.

"And while evaporative cooling is extremely effective in dry climates, there is a major drawback. That is the rapid loss of water and salts from the body through sweat. This can be fatal in less than a day if they are not replaced. It is common to lose a quart or more of water through sweating each hour in harsh summer desert conditions," added Siscom. "So let's get a good night's rest and get after it early in the morning," Drayton said.

Everyone nodded their agreement.

✌︎✌︎✌︎

A soft rain buffeted the dirty windows of Johnson's walkup Chinatown apartment ringing out make-believe staccato messages. He and Falco were huddled over a small kitchen table, their attention fixed on the lunch pail before them. A digital alarm clock with several wires ran to a model rocket ignitor that Johnson connected to a lump of plastic explosive. Finished working, Falco lit a cigarette and blew the acrid smoke from his nostrils.

"Johnson, where did you say you got all this stuff?" he said.

"I got friends, man," Johnson said, his right eye twitching as he looked at the man seated next to him. "You don't think I got friends?"

"Hey, I didn't say such. Frankly, I don't give a damn where you got this shit. All I care about is the money. How much you say?"

Johnson closed the lunch pail and latched it. Pushed it to the center of the table.

"Five thousand. Half now and half when the job is done. I told you that earlier."

"I know, I know. That's 2500 apiece, ain't it? Yeah, it is. Several months of feeling good. When?"

"When Norma says it's time. We're waiting on Norma's word."

Johnson rose, sauntered to the window, and gazed into the darkness beyond the dingy glass. The rain still fell in sheets. Sometimes he wondered how wise it was to keep his friend around—the man wasn't the brightest bulb on

the shelf. But Falco was loyal, if he was anything. Johnson thought back to when they were cellies in Delano
prison and a group of *La Eme* or the Mexican Mafia had
him cornered in a shower. Falco had stumbled on their
planned beating. He could have backed away but, instead,
chose to stay and fight. Turned out to be nothing more
than a scuffle when his friend unarmed one of his attack-
ers—a lock attached to the end of a belt. The four Mexican inmates scattered.

Johnson ambled back to the table as Falco snubbed out
his cigarette. The man's pale watery eyes betrayed a lonely, detached nature.

"What you thinking, Falco?" he said.

"I was just thinking about my mother, God rest her
soul. After Pa lit out, she took care of me and Bobby."

"Bobby?"

"Yeah. My brother, Bobby."

"I didn't know you had a brother. You never mentioned him."

"I know. A marine. He was killed in Iraq. Roadside
bomb went off when his Humvee ran over it."

"Sorry, friend."

"It's fine. I was just thinking it was always on nights
like this that Mom would pop popcorn for Bobby and me.
We'd sit with the window open, listen to the rain, and eat
popcorn."

"Did she work?"

"Yeah. Took in ironing during the week and cleaned
offices on the weekend. She always worked day and
night. We lived in a two-room apartment in the Bronx. It
wasn't much. Bobby and I played baseball in the vacant
lot next door." Falco chuckled at his remembering.

"Your mom still alive?" Johnson said. He poured two
glasses of whiskey from a half-full bottle.

"Naw, she died while I was in jail. Couldn't even go

to her funeral." Falco's eyes drifted toward the window and the rain. "I loved that old woman."

Chapter 25

Sheriff Calder slowed the jeep to a crawl and listened while Jessup spoke with the helicopter pilot who circled overhead.

"Nothing from up here," the pilot's voice crackled over the radio. "Any sightings down there?"

"None," Jessup responded. "Move farther north. We'll catch up."

"We're low on fuel, sir," the pilot said. "We need to set down and gas up first."

"Okay. We'll go on. You can let me know when you're airborne again. Out."

Once Jessup was off the radio, Calder accelerated over the rough terrain, heading toward the Idaho line. At the small ghost town of Sulphur, Calder stopped. Sulphur had been a stop on the Feather River Route of the Western Pacific Railroad until it was abandoned in the early forties. All that was left were several ancient, rusty mining machines aging in the desert sun while Pulpit Rock stood as a lone sentinel.

"We can bed down here for the night," Calder said. "Once the chopper has fueled, he'll join us here."

"There's still a few hours of daylight left, Sheriff," Williams said.

"When it gets dark in the desert," Calder said, "it's easy to get lost. Real easy. It's best to wait until morning."

"Any animals out here?" Jessup said.

"Coyotes are everywhere," Hardin said. He pulled a number of sleeping bags from the jeep. "Also, there's desert bighorn sheep, mule deer. Antelope, of course."

"How 'bout snakes?" Williams said. "I can't stand snakes."

"Ah," Calder said. "Yes, the dreaded rattlesnake. Be wary of where you step or put your hands, especially when you're in the shade. They love the cooler places and will strike without warning if threatened."

"Great," Williams said, moving away from the jeep.

"I knew a guy," Hardin said, smiling, "who slept on the ground and a damned rattler crawled into his sleeping bag with him. Stayed there most of the night until the man got up the use the bathroom. With all that moving around the snake bit him eleven times. Even on his pecker."

"Yeah, what happened to him?" Williams wanted to know.

"He died before he got to the hospital. They found him in his jeep down in an arroyo. His leg and pecker were swollen black purple and his eyes had sunk deep in their sockets."

Williams gulped. "I'm sleeping in the jeep," he said.

"They've been known to find their way into vehicles," Hardin added. "If I were you, Steve, I'd sleep with one eye open." Hardin shot a glance at Calder and winked.

"I'll shoot the first sonofabitchin snake I see," Williams said, putting a hand on his pistol. "Blast the bastards to kingdom come."

The group, including Calder, snickered at Williams' threat then settled down for the evening.

e/ɔe/ɔ

From a third floor office in the Chronicle Building, Dr. Wickingham looked down upon Mission Street and waited for the reporter to arrive. He'd telephoned the reporter of the *San Francisco Chronicle,* and the man seemed receptive to his idea of a newsworthy story, so Wickingham waited.

The man arrived, dressed in a rumpled shirt and tie, the stub of an unlit cigar in his mouth. "Mr. Wickingham?" he said, crossing the office and sitting at his polished desk. The reporter had a hawkish nose and narrow eyes.

"It's Dr. Wickingham," he said with added emphasis on his title.

"Yes, of course. You mentioned on the phone you had information regarding the Yeti escape in Nevada. Information that I might find interesting."

"That's correct."

"Tell me again exactly who you are, Doctor. What kind of doctor are you?"

"I am a professor at California Pacific University," Wickingham said.

"That's the university responsible for these Yeti?"

Wickingham nodded. "Dr. Harry Olson who is the chairman of the anthropology department was derelict in his duties, regarding the security of the Primate Research Facility in Nevada. My own investigation led me to this conclusion. This dereliction was the direct cause of there being no policies in place to prevent such a remote occurrence, no training in containment, no safety measures such as alarms or self-locking doors. And because Dr. Olson has become a celebrity in anthropological circles, our university president refuses to deal with him."

The reporter took notes, occasionally looking at Wickingham through narrow eyes. "Isn't this something that should be dealt with through an internal investigation, Doctor? Yours notwithstanding. I mean, what good will can follow by making this public?"

"Because, only by making Dr. Olson's blunders public will anything change. The public is in danger. Not until there is a public outcry will Dr. Olson be replaced and measures instituted to ensure this sort of thing never happens again."

"Are you sure that you are not reacting out of jealousy or a desire for advancement or promotion?"

Wickingham bristled at the suggestion. "Not at all."

"Doctor, are you familiar with the phrase, 'no good deed goes unpunished'? Well, that is usually what happens when employees report wrongdoing." The reporter put away his notebook and looked at Wickingham.

"So?" Wickingham said.

"Why would people who have positive feelings about their jobs, who have good performance records, risk the potential negative consequences—physical harm, online harassment, harassment at home, a demotion, a pay cut, and/or a job transfer—by reporting misconduct? It is simply because whistle blowing is not an act of disloyalty, but the ultimate manifestation of employee loyalty to the organization. But whistleblowers, Doctor, are not always welcomed back with open arms in the organization they outed. Are you prepared for what might follow? The fallout, I mean?"

"Look," Wickingham said, irritation showing in his voice, "Dr. Olson needs to be held accountable. If I must leave Cal Pacific, then so be it. I can always find another faculty appointment."

"Are you so sure, Doctor? Listen, I only want to make sure you have thought all this through. You wouldn't become an academic pariah? I've heard of that happening."

"It would be worth it," Wickingham said.

The reporter said he would return to his office and write an outline of Wickingham's accusations. He promised a story in the near future.

ೕೕೕ

Millie sat with Dixie around the campfire but apart from the men. She had begun her graduate studies as Dixie finished her dissertation so the two women knew each other as graduate students. She was happy when Dixie married Dr. Olson and remained on the faculty after earning her doctorate. They had formed a friendship, resulting in Dixie becoming Millie's major professor, overseeing her research activities.

Now, huddled around the dwindling fire, Millie relived her worries about the animals whom she had become deeply attached. "Sasha was so...so...I don't quite know how to out it into words," she said.

"Human?" Dixie said, finishing her sentence.

"That's it, almost human. Sure, she was a wild creature, but there was a certain quality about her, a softness that I felt when she was sedated and I was in the cage with her. I would stroke her head and muzzle, and she made a sort of contented sound. She would look at me at other times like she recognized me. The way Jimmy treated Bentu was unforgivable."

"Why didn't you report him, Millie?"

"I was afraid of him. He was weird, different."

"Dr. Radner weird?"

Millie laughed and looked up at the heavens. The stars seemed close, close enough to touch. "Oh no. Dr. Radner is just flaky. Jimmy was scary. I didn't like him. He did his work and I did mine."

"It's a tragedy to be sure, Millie. It's unfortunate but

Dr. Olson will have to do a lot of explaining when we get back. The board of trustees will have a lot of questions."

"Oh, Dixie, I'm so sorry. I feel so responsible."

"This crisis wasn't your doing, honey. Dr. Olson is responsible for the overall running of the primate facility, so he's the one who will have to answer the inevitable questions."

"I don't think I'd want his job," Millie said. She threw a small log onto the campfire and watched the flames spark and flicker.

"It goes with the territory. We'll face whatever comes together."

"You have such a perfect marriage, Dixie. I envy you."

"I've been blessed, no doubt about it. Harry is a good man."

"When did you fall in love with him?" Millie shook her head and raised a hand. "I'm sorry, I shouldn't pry."

"No, it's okay. To be completely truthful, I was infatuated with him while I was a grad student but he never gave me a second look. Mostly acted aloof. I thought he was arrogant, in fact. Then, during our first trip to Mongolia, something happened between us. I can't say what it was but we saw each other differently, and the rest is history. Like a spark or something. As I said, I'm a lucky woman."

"I hope it happens that way with me," Millie said. "Falling in love sounds so exciting."

"There's no one in your life? No special someone?"

"Not really. My research is what is important to me— the most important thing right now. Dr. Wickingham and I have had a few dates but nothing serious. He seems caught up with himself."

"Bernard Wickingham, Millie? Seriously?"

"That's him. What do you think of him, Dixie?"

"Well…"

"No, Dixie, I want the truth. I'm not serious about him but I suppose I could."

"He's new to the faculty. I don't know him well enough to advise you. But I would be careful of becoming involved with a faculty member. Just because it worked out for me doesn't mean it will for you. But I tend to agree with you—the man seems full if himself."

"Mostly, he's been a diversion from my studies, Dixie. However, one day I hope to have a family. And a man like your husband."

Later, when everyone was asleep, Millie thought back over previous conversations she had with Bernard Wickingham. He had asked her to call him by his first name, something unusual for a faculty member to do. He talked at length about his desire to become a well-known anthropologist and departmental chairman and how he hoped to find a quick way to the top. He couldn't wait forever. His research was a closely guarded secret among the graduate students, as he seemed to need no help other than his own in working in the cramped paleontology lab. He had complained repeatedly about wanting his own space and how Dr. Olson had denied it to him, always citing monetary concerns. There was something about Wickingham that was nebulous, difficult to analyze. He was smart, handsome, definitely aloof, having a cool, calculating exterior. The thought of a relationship with him was a daunting one, producing an anxiety that caused her heart to flutter.

Millie awoke and noticed Drayton sitting next to the fire, staring into its flames. She unzipped her sleeping bag and joined him.

"Couldn't sleep?" he said, smiling as she sat next to him.

"I guess I was dreaming," she said. "What time is it?"

Drayton looked at his watch. "Four-thirty. It'll be getting light soon. Care for some coffee?"

Millie nodded. Drayton poured her a mugful and handed it over.

"Think we'll find them today, Mr. Drayton?" she said.

"Don't know. Anything is possible."

"Mr. Drayton, were we at the facility derelict in our duties to allow this to happen? Dixie says Dr. Olson will have to answer some serious questions when this is all over and done."

"Millie, the Primate Research Facility followed every guideline and regulation required by the feds. They even inspected us on two occasions—we had no issues. So, the short answer to your question is no, we weren't irresponsible. Now, Dr. Olson will, most certainly, be required to give a full report on the incident but I think, once all the facts come out, we'll be fine. And Dr. Olson as well."

"That's good. I was worried. And for Dixie, too."

The eastern sky belied a faint glow, the starlight diminishing. Other members of their search team were rousing and gathering around the campfire, drinking coffee. The cool breeze that had blown up during the night had quieted, and it promised to be another hot day. Millie threw the dregs of her coffee on the ground and joined Dixie and Harry, who were sitting together.

"I hope we find them today," she said. "I don't think they can survive very long in this heat."

"Me too," Harry said. "I'm not used to sleeping on the ground." He rubbed his back and stretched.

Dr. Siscom joined the group and pointed toward a small butte.

"I found some large tracks back that way," he said. "Looks like they might belong to our animals."

Harry, Dixie, and Drayton jumped to their feet and rushed to where Siscom led them. There, on the ground and imprinted in the loose soil, were a number of large, human-like footprints.

"That's them!" Harry exclaimed. "We found them!"

"They've been here, that's for certain," Dixie said. "How much earlier it's hard to say."

Siscom knelt and felt the tracks. "These have edges that have hardened," he said. "A day old, at least."

Millie followed the tracks a short distance and noticed they headed into a shallow gorge. She was unable see much beyond the immediate area.

"Okay, folks," Drayton said, "from here we're on horseback. So we need to get the horses saddled. Dr. Siscom, can you and Harry see to that, while the women and I get the gear packed and the fire extinguished?"

The veterinarian nodded and set about his work.

Millie caught Dixie's eye.

"Horses," she said. "Just great."

Chapter 26

D r. Reginald Pauling couldn't believe the headline on page three of the *San Francisco Chronicle*. He sat at his desk and slurped his coffee, wondering how the article had made it into the paper. The headline and article read

CAL PACIFIC IRRESPONSIBLE IN YETI ESCAPE

Indifference to security concerns, a desire for national notoriety, and academic hubris led to the escape of two animals housed by California Pacific University in Nevada. The resulting carnage, which left a number of people dead, was the direct result of omissions that were the responsibility of university president, Dr. Reginald Pauling, departmental chairman, Dr. Harry Olson, and the research facility director, Dr. Miles Radner. So says a member of the faculty who is in a position to know the facts. The person wishes to remain anonymous for the present.

The anonymous faculty member named Dr. Olson and Dr. Radner as having direct supervisory functions for the safety of the animals and

employees of the Animal Research Facility in Northern Nevada. Their dereliction led ultimately to mass destruction of property and man people killed. State and local law enforcement are currently searching for the animals, known as Yeti.

The article went on to outline how California Pacific University did not follow federal regulations in its security surrounding the Primate Research Facility.

Pauling collapsed in his chair, stunned by the article. He knew immediately that the press would be at his door, demanding answers. He called Radner at the primate facility.

"Miles, have you seen today's *Chronicle*?" he said, his tone conveying a stress and anger.

"I saw the article some time ago, Dr. Pauling," Radner said in a weak voice. "Shameful is what it is."

"More than shameful, Miles, it's libelous, that's what it is." Pauling allowed his remark to sink in then continued. "Any idea how something like that got in the paper?"

"No, sir, I don't. I thought my news conference the other day went extremely well. You saw it?"

"I did, Miles, yes. I'll tell you how it got into the paper. Dr. Wickingham."

"Yes. He came to see me."

"He did? When, Miles?"

"A few days ago. He wanted me to assist him in getting Harry fired. I threw him out. What impudence."

"Bernard Wickingham," Pauling said in a tone that skewed venom. "He's responsible for that article, I'm sure of it. He came to me as well, trying to get me to discipline Dr. Olson, to demote or fire him on account of the Yeti escaping the primate facility."

"Really? Does Harry know this?"

"I haven't told him. Where is he?"

"He's out searching for the Yeti as we speak. I don't know when he's expected back."

"Well," Pauling said, his irritation growing, "when he does, have him call me. In the meantime, I'm going to meet with our lawyers to determine what our course of action should be. Harry assured me that all federal regulations were being followed up there. That makes the article's assertion libel."

"They certainly were followed. Want me to hold another news conference? I will if it will help?"

"Thanks, Miles, but let's wait until after I've spoken with the legal team. I might do it after that. It would look better if the university president answered questions. For now, if any reporters call for information, please direct them to this office. Understand?"

"Yes, sir."

"I'll take care of Wickingham myself."

⌁⌁⌁

Drayton spread his map out on the hood of his jeep. He and Harry studied it while Siscom readied the horses. The veterinarian lashed each person's sleeping bag onto the saddles and, when he finished, ambled to Harry's side.

It was another cloudless day with heat waves already shimmering off the desert.

"Horses are all ready," Siscom said.

"Okay," Drayton said, "we'll follow the tracks as far as we can then do what we can to pick them up if, and when, they disappear." He folded his map and walked to his horse. "Let's mount up. Got your tranquilizers, Gerald?"

"Right here," Siscom said, patting the leather pouch that was slung over his shoulder.

The group mounted their horses and headed out, with Drayton in the lead followed by Harry, Dixie, and Millie. Siscom brought up the rear. They plodded along, single file, following the large, human-like footprints. Harry tried to relax in the saddle but the constant rocking made that impossible. Flashbacks to Mongolia passed through his mind like a stream of pictures as he watched Drayton ahead of him.

They came to a shallow stream that zigzagged between two buttes. The footprints seemed to pause as there were a number of them at shoreline then headed along the edge of the slow-moving water. Drayton stopped and dismounted. The others followed suit.

"Look at this," he said, pointing to the group of tracks.

"Looks like they stopped here to drink," Harry said, "then continued on downstream."

"Any idea how old the tracks are?" Millie said. She knelt to get a closer look.

"The bottom of the tracks are dry," Harry said, "so at least a day, I'd say. Can't be sure, however. Bruce?"

"Hours to days would be my guess. Impossible to tell otherwise."

Dixie and Siscom splashed water on their faces and the group returned to their saddles. As they continued on, the slopes of the buttes, covered with rock and sand, were punctuated by stands of mesquite, Joshua trees, banana yucca, sagebrush, bitterbrush, and desert gooseberry. Spiny hopsage and evening primrose bloomed and dotted the hillock in pink and yellow. The water, thought Harry, allowed for all this vegetation.

The stream they followed was only two to three feet deep in its deepest regions. Mostly its depth ran only one to two feet. The water was clear and cold, languid, but sometimes it dropped over a series of boulders creating a series of eddies and currents. Drayton led the group along the shoreline until they came to a series of hot springs lined with more lush vegetation—moss and ferns. He stopped and motioned for Harry.

"I've lost the tracks," he said. "Harry, hop down and scout around up ahead and see if you can pick them up. The rest of you, spread out and do the same."

The hot springs were a series of small ponds that contained water whose temperature ranged from 120 to 150 degrees. The Washoe and Paiute tribes used the hot springs as campsites, villages, and sacred places. Early settlers in the 1850s claimed many of the thermal springs near the western Great Basin's Carson Range and built bathhouses and resorts. As rains fell on the surrounding peaks, it percolated into the rather porous sedimentary rocks. Descending through the rock, it picked up a variety of materials, everything from radium to sulphur. Also, as it moved farther beneath the surface, it heated up from the primal heat of the earth. Eventually, it encountered a large thrust fault, or crack. As water descended behind it, it forced the now-heated water to ascend along the fault line to surface as a hot or warm spring.

Most hot springs discharged groundwater that was heated by shallow intrusions of magma in volcanic areas. Some thermal springs, however, were not related to volcanic activity. In such cases, the water was heated by convective circulation—groundwater percolating down until reaching depths of a kilometer or more ,where the temperature of rocks was high due to the temperature gradient of the earth's crust—fifty-four degrees per kilometer in the first six miles.

Heat-loving microorganisms formed many of the colors in hot springs: bacteria, such as cyanobacteria, and species of archaea and algae. Many thermophilic organisms grew in huge colonies called mats that formed the colorful scums and slimes on the sides of hot springs. The microorganisms that grew in hot springs derived their energy from various chemicals and metals—potential energy sources included molecular hydrogen, dissolved sulfides, methane, iron, ammonia, and arsenic. In addition to geochemistry, the temperature and pH of hot springs play a central role in determining which organisms inhabit them.

"Don't you just love that smell?" Millie said, waving a hand in front of her face.

"The smell is a result of hydrogen sulphide, a gas similar to natural gas," Harry said from over his shoulder. "It results from anaerobic bacteria converting some of the dissolved sulphur in the water to hydrogen sulphide."

"Not my favorite smell," she said as she ambled around the springs searching for tracks.

Harry picked up a few tracks interspersed irregularly a good distance from the stream that emptied the hot springs.

The footprints, difficult to follow in the drier soil, led deeper into the gorge between the two buttes. Paiute Mountain loomed large in the background.

"Over here," Harry called out. He climbed back into his saddle, waited for Drayton to catch up with him. "They may be heading toward the mountain," he continued. "High elevation means cooler temperatures."

"It they get up there, they'll be harder to find," Drayton said. "Too many places to hide."

"They may be searching for a cave," Dixie said. "Any caves in that mountain?"

"I have no idea," Drayton said. "Never been up this way."

When all were mounted, Drayton began the trek upward away from the hot springs.

ℭℌℭℌ

Bernard Wickingham folded his paper and tossed it on his breakfast table. Sipping his morning coffee, he felt a familiar smugness, a satisfaction that things were going his way. His small apartment, located near the baseball park and football stadium south of Hunter's Point, gave an idyllic view of the bay. The apartment was expensive, more than he could afford on his salary, but a new, single faculty member at a university should have some of the finer things of life. He had worked hard to achieve his doctorate and his position at Cal Pacific.

The article covered the topic nicely without mentioning his name—the reporter had a certain flair in his description of the Yeti situation and who was responsible.

Wickingham took another gulp of coffee and put the mug in the sink. He tied his tie, grabbed his sport coat, and headed to work. While driving, he reflected on his wanting his own lab and Dr. Olson's refusal to find him space. It was difficult to work secretly in the paleontology lab where students came and went at all hours. Wickingham had managed a small corner set apart from the main lab but, still, it wasn't his own space. He had hoped that by being personable toward Olson's wife, Dixie, that, with time, the man might feel differently, but so far it had not happened.

An image of the tops of Dixie's breasts formed in Wickingham's mind as he pulled into the faculty parking lot. It was a thought that he carried to his office in the Science Building where he doffed his jacket and donned his lab coat. Sitting at his desk, he turned on his computer and began reading his email. As he scrolled through his messages, he paused at one that caught his eye. It was from his friend, a former graduate student colleague, now on the faculty at a university in Texas. Reading the email, a smile formed on Wickingham's lips and he let out a long, even sigh. He finally had some leverage. The email read:

> *Bernie,*
> *Good to hear from you. Yes I do have some information you might find useful.*
> *Your Dr. Olson does indeed have a past. Years ago he falsified some data that appeared in a journal article he wrote. His departmental chairman, a Dr. Julius Kesler, wrote a letter to the journal explaining the falsified data, citing a mix-up in transcribing the final paper for publication. The man's apology saved Dr. Olson's reputation and career.*
> *I have enclosed the article and Dr. Kesler's letter in the attached file. Hope this helps.*
>
> *Best regards,*
> *Boyd*

Wickingham settled back in his chair and smiled. How interesting. And to think, no one knew of this now that Dr. Kesler was dead, with the possible exception of Pauling and Dixie. But there was no need to involve the president or Harry for that matter. No, this called for more stealth. Going directly to Harry and confronting him might spell Wickingham's own termination but Dixie might be another matter. Wouldn't she do most anything to save her husband's career? Especially if he could produce some evidence that would prove that Harry acted with knowledge of the falsified data and that it was not the inadvertent mix-up as claimed by Kesler. She could pressure Harry for the space he wanted. And Harry need never know anything.

He knew blackmail or extortion didn't become him but he was desperate. He would have to give the matter his full and serious consideration.

Chapter 27

Calder climbed out of his sleeping bag, craving a hot cup of coffee. But the prospects were dismal, considering they were out in the middle of nowhere with limited supplies. It was close to dawn and, once he was up and around, Hardin stirred and got up, yawning.

Hardin ambled to the jeep and pounded on the window. "Hey, Williams," he called loudly. "Time to rise and shine."

The jeep door opened and the big fellow tumbled out, looking worse for wear and rubbing his eyes.

"I take it no snakes during the night?" Hardin said, laughing.

"Screw you, Deputy," Williams answered with a surly tone. His eyes shot sparks at Hardin.

Jessup joined the men and noticed the chopper still parked on the hard-packed desert clay. Its sleek fuselage glistened with dew.

"I'll wake the pilots," he said. "We can get them into the air before the sun's up."

Once everyone was awake, they formed a semicircle around Calder. He stuck his hands in the pockets of his rumpled pants and paced. The air was crisp with a few clouds hanging low. "Sorry there's no coffee, folks, but that's the breaks." He heard the pilots utter a quiet grumble, ignored it, and continued. "We haven't had any luck in finding these animals. We are low on food supplies and water. We can always send the chopper back for those items and stay out here for another few days. But the longer we go without any signs, the less chance we have of finding them. So, here is my suggestion. We continue with the search today, using the helicopter flying in a wide circle. This afternoon they can break away and fly to Elko for food and water—enough for another couple of days. If we've had no luck by then, we'll call off the search and return home. Any objections?"

Jessup looked at the chopper and back at Calder. "No, that seems reasonable, Buck. It's going to be rough going from here I take it. No horses."

"We'll go as far as we can. If we find them and can't get to them, we'll have to use the chopper. Is that possible, Malcomb?"

"Sure. It can hold another couple of passengers so we ought to be able to get to wherever they turn up."

"If they turn up," Hardin interjected.

"Right," Jessup said.

The pilots went to their aircraft and began the warmup procedures and soon had the rotors turning. The whine of its turbine made talking difficult. Hardin, Jessup, and Williams, climbed into the jeep with Calder at the wheel and, as the chopper lifted off into the growing light, they headed northwest.

The sheriff worried they were on a fool's errand, rattling around the desolate countryside, hoping to find animals who were either already dead or nowhere in the vicinity. What if they had gone east in the opposite direction than they originally suspected? They could be hundreds of miles from where the team was presently searching. He thought about Helen and the boys and wondered what they were doing. She was fixing them breakfast, most likely, and getting them ready for school. He missed her easy smile each morning. Maybe when this was over, they could take a short vacation together—him, Helen and the boys. Do some fishing. But no camping for a while. He'd had his fill of camping.

ℰↄℰↄ

Dr. Gerald Siscom sat in the saddle and bounced along at the rear of the column headed by Drayton. His experience with riding was limited to his teenage years, although he had treated many horses, during and after vet school. To him, horses were unpredictable and not one of the smarter of the barnyard animals. His horse, a large gray gelding, seemed to want to brush him out of the saddle because the darned beast ambled close to any tree or shrub, forcing him to grab the reins and turn the animal's head. His rear objected already and it wasn't noon.

He housed his tranquilizer gun in the scabbard and stored the darts in the pouch he carried. Although he'd spent the past three years at the Primate Research Facility, he had never met Harry or his wife until the Yeti arrived. Since that time, he came to like the man's easy demeanor, his relaxed way of handling problems. Once, Radner warned him to be wary of the man, but Harry's manner reassured Siscom that he knew what he was doing. And in Siscom's experience, staff meetings were always pleasant and efficient.

Siscom's role in the Yeti research was to sedate the animals, run the basic lab studies, and see to their overall health and wellbeing. Once the male, Bentu he was called, caught an upper respiratory infection and ran a high fever. The scientists and Radner were worried until

Siscom had given him an IV and antibiotics that aided the animal's recovery. Other than that one illness, his job was routine. He maintained a notebook on each animal, listing their vital signs, what was done to them medically, with dates and times. Sort of a clinical chart.

The maintenance of the Animal Care Unit was his responsibility, and he prided himself in the job he did. Under his watchful eye, the technicians kept it immaculately clean and the cages were hosed out and disinfected daily. He checked the air filtration system of the airlocks going to and from the unit regularly so no contamination from the outside was possible. Once, he had to fire a technician found circumventing the policies and who brought his lunch into the unit, something strictly forbidden.

When the alarm sounded with the Yeti's escape, Siscom was in his office down the hall from the unit. By the time he donned his coveralls and made it through the air lock, they were gone and Jimmy lay on the floor in a huge pool of blood. Both cage doors were open, a fact that Siscom couldn't reconcile. And Millie was gone.

He hurried through the exit air lock into the main building complex where sheer pandemonium greeted him. People ran in all directions, screaming loudly, their eyes wide with fright. The Yeti managed to get out of the Animal Care Unit, scurry through the main building, scaring everyone there, as well as those outside. By the time he bolted through the front door, they were nowhere to be seen.

He understood Millie's theory regarding the Yeti's intelligence and how they both might have escaped. He tended to agree with her. Working with the Yeti as he had, he also had a chance to observe them display a certain level of high intelligence. They seemed particularly adept at solving puzzles so, to Siscom, deducing how to work the lock on a cage wasn't difficult to believe.

He shifted his weight in the saddle trying to ease the aching in his back and rear. Finding these Yeti, he thought, might prove more difficult than originally planned.

ↄ∕ↄↄ∕ↄ

No amount of familiarity with horses enabled Dixie to appreciate their finer qualities. Despite her two trips to Mongolia and spending countless hours in the saddle, she despised the beasts. She and her husband agreed on that point. Her legs, along with her back, hurt and the constant squeaking of the saddle started to grate on her nerves. She looked over her shoulder and noticed that Millie seemed all in. Dixie reined up and fell back alongside her. "Need a rest?" she said to Millie. "I could sure use one."

Millie nodded, but didn't say anything.

Drayton called a halt so Dixie and Millie slid to the ground, stretched their legs, then sat on a nearby rock. Harry plopped down next to Dixie while Siscom went around and adjusted the cinch on everyone's saddle. Drayton paced ahead, following the tracks as Dixie drank deep from her water bottle.

According to Drayton's map, they were at the base of Paiute Mountain and its peak stuck impressively into the thin air. It was a rugged mountain, and the map showed several small lakes halfway up its southern slope.

"From the map," Drayton said, pointing, "there are two lakes up there. The tracks lead that way, up the mountainside, so the Yeti could be up there seeking water."

"And the cooler temperatures at the higher elevation," Harry added, rising and standing beside Drayton. "Let's eat something while we're here."

"I know this mountain has a year-round glacier near its summit," Drayton said. "Glaciers have long played a role in the geologic history of Nevada. In the past, glaciers were active in several areas of the state, leaving behind geologic evidence such as glacial deposits, mountain cirques, and glacial striations. Here in northern Nevada, evidence from glaciers during previous geological times is found all over these mountains. I remember reading that one of John Muir's assistants came to this area and conducted experiments on the glaciers."

Millie broke out the trail mix and jerky and they sat in a semicircle and ate in silence. Dixie studied the landscape and marveled at the vastness of the desert plain. "We going to head for those lakes?" she said. "It looks like quite a ways to me. And all uphill."

"The footprints go that direction," Harry said. "I vote to continue on."

Drayton frowned, nodded his head toward the horses. "We came to hunt these Yeti down and take them back," he said. "Mount up."

There was no trail to follow, just the occasional footprint in the sand soil, so onward they plodded, single file, gradually ascending Paiute Mountain. It was rough going, the horses stumbling as rocks slid out from under their hooves and careened downward. They inched their way parallel to the fall line and upward, using a zigzag pattern forming switchbacks. It was a longer route to the lakes, which was the way the footprints were leading, but much safer. The colorful sky pilot plant along with alpine daisies and dwarf sunflowers pushed their eager heads through cracks and crevasses between the rocks and under boulders. At this altitude, the air was fragrant and sweet so Dixie took the time to breathe deep the mountain's perfume.

Arriving at a narrow ledge, Drayton stopped to reconnoiter what lay ahead. The side of the ledge dropped several hundred feet straight down into a grove of Joshua trees.

Remaining in his saddle, he retrieved the binoculars from a saddlebag and scanned the mountain. Dixie watched him, wondering what the man was thinking.

"See anything?" Harry said.

"Nothing," Drayton said. "We'll keep going. Watch the side of the ledge."

Suddenly a woman's scream pierced the desert stillness. Dixie jerked her head around to find Millie missing from the back if her horse. She realized that Millie had fallen from her saddle.

"Harry!" she called. "Millie has fallen! Do you see her?"

Harry and Drayton reined their horses to where Dixie pointed. It was over the side of the ledge.

Dixie jumped off her horse, scrambled to the ledge's rocky edge, and peered down the side of the gorge. She saw Millie lying on a pile of rocks. She didn't move.

"Harry!" Dixie called again. "Over here!"

In an instant, Harry was at her side, along with Drayton. Siscom remained on his horse.

"I'm going down," Harry said. "Get me a rope."

Siscom tossed Harry the rope attached to his saddle and Dixie watched as he tied on end around his waist.

"I'll belay you," Drayton said. "When you reach her, dollar what her condition is."

"Will do," Harry said as he scrambled over the edge.

"Be careful, honey," Dixie called after him.

She watched her husband descend a step at a time down the craggy side of the mountain. It was slow and looked like an arduous task, but Harry finally made it to where Millie lay, still unmoving.

Harry quickly felt for a pulse and nodded, gave a

thumb's up sign. Dixie watched him check her over for injuries then shake his head. He looked up.

"She appears to be all right, no injuries that I can detect. But her face is flushed and she is extremely hot to touch."

"Heatstroke," Siscom ventured. "We need to get her out of the sun and cooled down. The sooner the better."

Dixie returned her gaze back to Harry and Millie. Her husband had Millie sitting now and the girl sported a weak smile. Harry tied the rope around her waist, helped Millie to her feet.

"She okay?" Drayton called.

"Seems to be," Harry shouted. "Just hot and a little dizzy. She feels she can climb so I'm going to help her on the way back up."

"Be careful, honey!" Dixie's voice wavered, betraying her concern.

Drayton kept taut pressure on the rope, gathering the slack as Millie climbed upward. Dixie could see Harry just below her, keeping a hand near her waist. Hand over hand Millie climbed. One slow step after another. Dixie was concerned about the redness in Millie's face. *I hope she'll be all right.*

At the lip of the ledge, Millie reached out a hand and Drayton took it, pulling her onto level ground. Millie lay on her back, lungs heaving, eyes wide, darting about. Dixie grabbed a water bottle and held it to her lips. Millie drank greedily.

"Careful," Dixie said. "Not so fast. Rest a while."

Harry appeared and jolted over the edge. He knelt beside Millie, felt her cheek.

"There's some shade over here," Siscom said. "Under a tall bush. Get her into the shade."

Drayton and Harry helped Millie over to the bush and allowed her to recline in the shade where the temperature was a good twenty degrees cooler. She continued to drink from the water bottle. Gradually, the red color left her face and she smiled.

"I think I just got overheated and fainted," Millie said.

"You probably weren't drinking enough water all along," Siscom said. "Bruce, we should rest a while until Millie is rehydrated and feels better."

"I feel fine," Millie said. "I'm sorry."

"No need to apologize," Harry said.

"We'll do as Gerald suggests," Drayton said. He went to gather the horses.

After an hour of rest and water, Millie felt much better. She refused to go back to the facility, stating the Yeti were her responsibility.

So they mounted up and Drayton continued on with the rest of the group plodding behind. Once they were beyond the ledge, he reversed course on a switchback, maintaining the path toward the lakes.

The higher they trekked, the rougher was the going—steeper and rockier.

Harry noticed that the air was thinner, the temperature a few degrees cooler. His horse seemed to be straining with each step. At a level area they stopped.

"Let's give the horses a breather," Siscom said. "The going gets more vertical from here."

Everyone dismounted and stretched their legs while their mounts regained their wind.

Drayton retrieved his binocs and scanned the hillside. Suddenly, he turned and shouted. "Up there!" He pointed to an area near the lakes. He still had the binocs trained in that direction as he spoke. "I see them! Two Yeti near the lakes! Harry, come here!"

Dixie's heart leaped into her throat as she watched Harry scramble up beside Drayton. He took the glasses and trained them in the direction Drayton still pointed.

She strained through the bright sunlight to see but the glare was too great to make out anything.

"Yes," Harry called out. "I see them. Gerald, up here."

Dixie couldn't believe their good fortune in locating the Yeti.

"Do they look all right?" she asked Harry, who continued to observe them through the binoculars. "I mean, are they moving?"

"They appear in good health, Dixie. They are just sitting in the sun right now."

Siscom arrived at Harry's side and took a look through the field glasses. He nodded. "They appear to be fine. Think we can load them on horses once I have them sedated?"

Harry let out a low whistle. "I don't know. We were planning on using the horse trailer but it's quite a ways from here."

"It's all we can hope for," Drayton said. "Maybe we could fashion a travois and drag them to the trailer."

At that moment the drone of a helicopter pierced the quiet. Squinting against the glare, Dixie noticed a black dot getting larger with each passing second. The others looked skyward at the sound. The noise from the aircraft's turbine boomed overhead.

"The strike force!" Drayton yelled. "It's the strike force chopper!"

"They'll kill the Yeti!" Millie cried. She stood to gain a better look at the helicopter screaming toward the mountain.

"Oh my god, no," Dixie muttered in a low voice. And she grabbed Harry's arm.

Chapter 28

It was past midnight. The sky was clear, the stars shown bright while a silver sliver of a moon hung on the western horizon. Johnson and Falco stood at the gate marking the beginning of the property belonging to Cal Pacific's Nevada Primate Research Facility. In the distance loomed Cinder Mountain, a dark foreboding mass. After driving most of the previous afternoon and evening to get to where they now stood, Johnson had parked the car and the pair surveyed the distance to the mountain.

"The facility is at the top of that mountain there," Falco said with an unbelieving tone.

"Unfortunately," Johnson said.

"I didn't realize the mountain was that large. It's going to be quite a hike. And then a climb. I wasn't prepared for a big job."

"Let's get going. The sooner we start, the sooner we can get back home." Johnson climbed over the gate, took the lunch pail containing the bomb from Falco, waited for his friend to join him, then the pair started off across the open meadow. The dry brittle grass crunched underneath their feet. A soft breeze blew in their faces.

Halfway across the meadow Falco stopped.

"I need a rest," he said.

"Not now," Johnson said, plodding on toward the dark mass of Cinder Mountain. "We can rest in the trees. Besides, we need to get this bomb planted before it gets light. I want to be far away from here when it goes off."

Falco shook his head and continued behind Johnson. Crossing the meadow meant they were exposed, there was no way to conceal their presence. Johnson hoped their dark clothing would help conceal their approach. Once he glanced back toward the gate. The car was nothing more than a dark silhouette. He doubted anyone at the facility could make out what it was.

He was having second thoughts about bringing Falco along, for the man was not in good enough physical shape for the climb that awaited them. Maybe Johnson would just leave the man in the trees while he proceeded ahead. He thought about Norma and what the future held for them. If she didn't come across with her promise of providing him with a nicer apartment, he would have to dump her. And once this job was finished, he would dump Falco as well. Maybe even take all the money for himself.

When they reached the foot of the mountain, they rested in the sanctuary of the forest before beginning the upward climb to the primate facility. Falco seemed to be doing better, he wasn't breathing hard, wasn't complaining. The initial ascent was rugged with numerous rock outcroppings blocking their way. Johnson scurried around and over them. They were in the middle of a forest and the sliver of moon offered meager light to illuminate their progress.

Higher up, the forest thinned out leaving large sections of mountain open to the sky. An owl hooted somewhere in the trees and crickets chirped a nighttime serenade. Johnson drank from a canteen, passed the water to Falco who sat on the ground. He scanned the area. Ahead, the climb became steep once again with huge rock outcroppings blocking the ascent. There was no trail.

Johnson led Falco over a series of boulders, the man wheezing behind him. Limbs and vines from the underbrush slowed their progress. At one point, Falco tripped over a root, fell to the ground with a *thud*.

"My legs hurt," Falco said. "This is a stupid way to earn money."

Johnson turned and glared at him. "Dammit, shut up. Go back to the car if you want to. Just shut up."

Near the summit the climb became easier. The underbrush thinned.

Johnson stood before a tall security fence.

"Quiet," he said in a hushed voice. "We're here."

Signs were posted on the fence every fifty feet. *PRIVATE PROPERTY! KEEP OUT!*

"This way," Johnson said, pointing to the north. "We'll follow the fence a ways. See if we can find an easy place to enter."

He led the way, stumbling along the fence line. Every few yards, Johnson stopped and peered through the fence into the dark void beyond. All was quiet. There was no movement.

Soon they came to a corner where the fence turned to the west. It was a heavy chain-link affair with razor wire along its top. Satisfied that no one was patrolling the area, the two men continued on. Once, through the trees, Johnson caught a glimpse of several buildings, each with a dim light in the window. After an hour of stumbling in the dark, they arrived at a large metal gate. A dark guard shack stood next to the gate. The road from the bottom of the mountain continued beyond the gate, and Johnson thought he could make out the silhouette of a building in the distance. The guard shack appeared deserted.

There was no one walking the facility grounds.

Everyone must be in bed. Johnson opened the lunch pail, set the digital clock's alarm, and handed it to Falco.

"Set it at the side of the gate. Be careful. It's armed."

"We're not going to set it off inside the compound somewhere?" Falco said.

"No, this will do. Norma just wants to make a statement. Doesn't want to hurt anyone. Let's go."

Falco took the lunch pail and set it behind a gatepost where it wouldn't be seen. The two men started back down the mountain.

❦❦❦

The chopper pilot squawked his sighting to Sheriff Calder and Sergeant Jessup who followed in the sheriff's jeep. The Yeti were halfway up the southern side of Paiute Mountain and appeared to be lounging in the sun. The pilot requested further instructions.

"Able Leader, this is Chopper One. Do you read?"

Jessup grabbed the radio and responded.

"Go ahead, Chopper One."

"Yeti sighted. Halfway up Paiute Mountain. Request further instructions. Sergeant, do we engage? Repeat, do we engage?"

"Negative, Chopper One. Meet us at Double Hot Springs," Calder said into the radio. "Sergeant Jessup and I will board your aircraft then get us back up there. Copy that?"

"Roger, Sheriff. Double Hot Springs. We can be there in five minutes. Will wait for you."

"Fine," Calder said and Jessup signed off. "Well, Sergeant, what do you make of that?"

"We'll finish them off before dark. That's good. I'm tired of all this chasing around."

Calder reversed his course and sped toward Double Hot Springs, a good thirty-minute drive over rough terrain. While driving, he hoped this was the right decision, not to let the scientists try to recapture the animals. He understood they were about to destroy valuable scientific specimens. But maybe it was a small price to pay for the innocent dead victims.

When they roared into the region called Double Hot Springs, so named after two large bubbling pools of hot aqua-blue water that extended to unknown depths, they found the helicopter perched nearby, its rotors slowly turning.

"Andy," Calder said, "come with Sergeant Jessup and me. Sergeant, can you have Williams take the jeep back to Elko and wait for us there? This shouldn't take long."

Jessup nodded and gave Williams his instructions. The man sneered and sulked to the driver's side of the vehicle. The sergeant gathered the shoulder-fired rocket, grenade launcher, and flamethrower and headed toward the chopper at a trot. Calder and Hardin climbed in behind Jessup, buckled themselves into their seats as the aircraft lifted off the ground, deliberately at first, then screamed northwest, climbing into the clear sky.

Calder watched the hot springs get smaller then disappear from sight. Ahead, he could see Paiute Mountain looming like the spine of a large animal, its peak dusted with snow. *A gray-bearded old man keeping watch over his vassals below.*

As he gazed out at the passing landscape, a thought once again struck Calder that he was speeding toward a rendezvous with destiny that would change the course of scientific understanding. Understanding of the human race. That's what Dr. Olson said they were attempting at the research facility. Calder had the sudden feeling that what they were about to do might hamper that understanding profoundly. If that were the case, he reasoned, then killing these animals would be a morally reprehensible act. On the other hand, these beasts had ravaged and killed several people, citizens of his county, people he had been elected by and sworn to protect. He had a duty to avenge their deaths and see to it that it never happened again.

"Sure we're doing the right thing here?" he asked Jessup. "I mean aren't we about to destroy scientific specimens"

"Look, Sheriff," Jessup said, coldly, "we're here to do this job. It's too late for such philosophical arguments."

"But we have the time, right now, to reconsider the appropriateness of what we're about to do. My gut says take them out but my mind tells me we should listen to the scientists."

"Why this sudden change of heart, Calder? Don't you remember that poor man behind the gas station in Grant?"

"Of course I do. But I've been thinking that these Yeti are not doing anything different than what you or I would do if the situation was reversed. Remember *Planet of the Apes*?"

"Are you kidding?" Jessup said with a sneer. "That was just a stupid movie. You can't be serious, Calder."

Calder stared out the chopper window as the ground shot by.

"Yeah, I know," he said. "Just a stupid movie."

They continued on in silence, all the while Paiute Mountain loomed larger. Calder's stomach churned with his newfound morality.

೮ා೮ා

Somehow word had filtered back to Cal Pacific University that the Yeti had been spotted and the strike force was closing for the kill. Dr. Bernard Wickingham sensed that soon the Olsons would be back in San Francisco and his laboratory would become a reality. Harry Olson possessed what Wickingham thought was rightly his—fame, a beautiful wife, and a position of authority at a major university. But he reasoned that these dividends would only come his way if he played his cards right. He salivated at the prospects of his upcoming talk with Dixie Olson. Okay, he thought, he was jealous, he could admit it to himself. Once he published his paper on the wooly mammoth, the world would recognize his intellect and talent. Cal Pacific was just the first step in a journey to an Ivy League appointment. Then he would show those who said he would never amount to anything.

❧❧❧

Harry craned his neck and sought to locate the helicopter in the brilliant sunlight. He heard the whine of its turbine but couldn't find it. Then a flash glinted off its fuselage and he saw it, like an ominous bird of prey speeding directly toward them. He shot a glance up the mountain.

The Yeti were gone, probably frightened away by the chopper's noise.

"Dammit," he muttered under his breath and kicked his horse to alongside Drayton. "Now what?" he screamed.

"Keep going," was Drayton's reply. The man urged his horse forward.

The security chief found a narrow trail and moved his horse onto it. At least the going was smoother, thought Harry, glancing over his shoulder toward his wife. She looked as if she was on the verge of tears, a blank look on her face, her eyes squinted and narrowed. Dixie held the saddle horn with both hands, a sign, he knew, of fatigue or pain.

He resumed his search for the Yeti, scanning the mountain hillside. They were nowhere near the lakes, although he couldn't be sure for the mountainous terrain partially obstructed his full view of them. Large rock outcroppings required that they steer a convoluted course around them, the lush vegetation dwindling as they moved higher. Unfamiliar with the countryside, Harry had no idea where the Yeti could hide, whether there were caves in the area or not. The Yeti's natural habitat was to live in the caves of the high Altai Mountains of Mongolia so finding one on this mountain would seem a natural instinct for them.

The lakes, mirrored gems with their inverse image of Paiute Mountain reflected in their quiet waters, seemed a special anchor of the alpine landscape. Their rocky or marshy shores, at any other time, demanded a few moments or hours of reverent meditation.

"They'll be seeking shelter," he said to Drayton, "a safe place away from us and the chopper noise. A cave system if they can locate one. Know of any up here?"

"No, I don't. Never been in this part of the state. Funny, I never felt the need to leave Cinder Mountain."

The helicopter buzzed low overhead and banked in the direction the Yeti were last seen. Harry saw Sheriff Calder in a rear seat but wasn't able make out the other occupants when the aircraft turned toward the lakes. When it arrived over the spot where the Yeti were last seen, it hovered, facing the mountain, gradually banking right and left as if to give its passengers a better view of what lay below.

"Need to hurry, Bruce," Harry said and he kicked his horse into a trot. They were still a long way from the lakes and the chopper but he pressed on, nevertheless. From his perch atop his horse, Harry watched the helicopter as it buzzed up and down the mountain slope, crisscrossing its flight path. *If the Yeti are still up there,* he thought, *they'll find them.*

But the Yeti never showed.

The chopper again hovered for several minutes then veered to its right and disappeared around the far side of the mountain.

"They are going to search the other side," Harry said. "Let's keep pushing."

"If they have moved to the other side of the mountain," Dixie said, her voice shaking, "we'll never reach them in time."

The drone of the helicopter decreased as it put distance between it and Harry's group. They pushed hard. The horses began blowing and panting.

"You mentioned you are relatively new to this area, Bruce. How did you get the job with the facility?" Talking helped take Harry's mind off his aching legs and back.

"It was pure chance that I stumbled onto it," Drayton replied. "Lots of jobs are available to ex-cops so I wasn't worried about finding employment—just wanted a good job with good people. Not long ago, I found it at the primate facility. Radner has been difficult to work with at times but overall I have enjoyed the work. It's certainly different."

"We scientists are indebted to folks like you, Bruce. With these large animals around, you keep everyone safe."

"Until now," Drayton said, shaking his head.

"Don't beat yourself up over this. This was the fault of a stupid graduate student, not you."

They were closer to the lakes now and Harry could

make out a flat area of the mountain next to a rounded knoll on the far side of them.

"Let's head for that flat ledge over there," Drayton said, pointing. He led the group in that direction.

The helicopter shot from behind the mountain, speeding in a low arc, banking hard. Its turbine screamed overhead, sending Harry's and Dixie's horses into a panic. As the chopper continued on, Harry managed to get his and Dixie's horse under control and pointed toward the lakes and a flat rock face forming a short wall under a rock overhang. A large hole was at its base. "See that?" he said. "They may have ducked in there. Looks like a cave or recess of some kind. They couldn't have gone far so they must be in there." He motioned Siscom to the head of their column. "Gerald! Get up here! And load that gun of yours!"

The helicopter set down on the flat expanse but kept its rotors whirling. Two men emerged and Harry could tell it was Calder and Sergeant Jessup. They carried large weapons.

What happened next occurred as if in slow motion. Harry watched, mesmerized. They were still too far away for Siscom to use the tranquilizer gun if the Yeti appeared—if they were even in that cave.

Crouching under the chopper's rotating rotors, Calder and Jessup approached the opening in a crouch, their weapons at the ready. Halfway to the cave, they hesitated, looked over their shoulders at Harry, then continued. The whine of the chopper's turbine echoed through the mountain valley below, causing a faint rumble in the distance. Drayton pushed his horse toward the helicopter, and the rest followed.

Then Harry saw them. Two large, brown, hairy creatures standing at the opening. They advanced several steps until they were in the bright sunlight. Calder and

Jessup stopped and shouldered their weapons. Both Yeti looked first at the approaching men, then down the hillside and Harry jerked when his stare met their red, glowing eyes. The larger of the two Yeti, Sasha he reasoned, tossed her head back, and roared. It was a roar that echoed down the mountain, pierced Harry's heart. It was if she perceived what was about to happen. It wasn't a growl he had heard before but a sound of incredible anguish. And resignation.

For Harry, time slowed. It was as if a slow motion movie played in front of him, each frame jumping to the next. His pulse pounded in his neck while he gripped the reins until his hands ached.

In unison, the Yeti advanced toward Calder and Jessup. In an instant, they raised their weapons and fired two rockets into them followed by grenades. A horrific explosion erupted and a fireball shot skyward. Black smoke billowed from the animals' charred remains.

Behind Harry, Dixie's scream echoed up the mountain.

"Noooooooooo!"

Chapter 29

At the exact moment of Dixie's scream, a deafening explosion rocked the plain. She jerked her head toward the sound and in the far distance saw dark smoke billowing up in the direction of Cinder Mountain.

"What the hell was that?" Siscom said.

"It came from the facility!" Dixie screamed and pointed to the top of the mountain. "My god!"

Harry scrambled to Dixie's side and stared at the rising black smoke.

"Damn," he said. "What in the world is happening?"

Drayton joined them, the small group stunned by what they had just witnessed—their Yeti executed and now an explosion at the facility. Drayton's mouth was open in horror.

"We need to get back there," he shouted. "Something terrible has happened."

They mounted and hurried back to their jeep. It was all Dixie could do to keep a lid on her reeling emotions. Tears streamed down her cheeks and she shot a quick glance at Harry. His jaw was set firm and his eyes flashed anger. "Harry!" she cried. "They did it! They killed our Yeti!"

"The bastards," Siscom said, his gaze riveted on the billowing smoke from atop Cinder Mountain. "I can't believe they did it."

"Everyone," Drayton said, "we need to get back to the jeep and back to the facility. Something terrible has happened."

The group began the descent to where they left the jeep and horse trailer. Dixie glanced over her shoulder and barely made out the charred crumpled remains of Bentu and Sasha. She heard the whine of the helicopter and watched it rise into the thin clouds and streak southward.

❧❧❧

Dr. Reginald Pauling stood in front of the group of reporters and television cameras, adjusted the microphone, and cleared his throat. The news conference was in the main parking lot of California Pacific University and was crowded with reporters and satellite trucks. The sun was near the horizon, the sky gray-blue.

Pauling adjusted his tie. "Ladies and gentlemen, I am Dr. Reginald Pauling, the President of California Pacific University. As you know, last week, two of our experimental animals—Yeti, to be specific—escaped from our Primate Research Facility near Elko, Nevada. Unfortunately, a number of people were killed during the week while they were on the loose.

"I am here to report that several hours ago a state police strike force located and killed both animals on the side of a mountain in northern Nevada. The search for the Yeti is officially over. The threat to the public is over. The animal's remains will be transported to the research facility where the facility's veterinarian will examine them.

"We at the university are devastated by the loss of human life and our thoughts and prayers go out to the families involved. However, this is also a serious blow to the scientific community. Losing potential knowledge of our human heritage and development is a sad event, but we understood the threat to public welfare and are supportive of our law enforcement officials.

"That is all I have at this time. There will be no questions. Thank you all."

"Dr. Pauling," shouted a reporter. "We heard that there was an explosion at the primate facility early this morning. What can you tell us about that?"

"I'm sorry," he said. "I have no comment."

Amid a flurry of more shouted questions, Pauling ducked into the Administration Building where campus security blocked entry by the reporters. He ambled up to his office and collapsed in a chair, poured scotch into a tumbler. After gulping down a swallow, he leaned back and massaged his temples. *Well, it's over. The nightmare is over without additional loss of life.*

His phone rang. It was Radner.

"Dr. Pauling," he said, "I saw the news conference and thought it went fine and you did a remarkable job."

"Thanks, Miles. What's the latest from your end?"

"They are bringing the Yeti carcasses here in the morning. According to Harry, there is not much of them left, however. I will email you the veterinarian's report as soon as I have it."

"What about the explosion, Miles?"

"As near as I can determine, it was a bomb detonated at our front gate. Nothing left of it but a mass of twisted metal. I have contacted the FBI and they are due here later today. Our security chief, Bruce Drayton, is returning with Harry. They should be back any moment now."

"I appreciate it. Anyone hurt by the explosion?"

"No, sir. Fortunately, it happened at a time when there was not much traffic in or out of the facility."

"Fine, Miles. Have Harry and Drayton call me when they get back. I wish to speak with them personally."

Pauling finished his scotch, stood, and gazed out his window. The sun had set leaving only purple hues in the darkening sky. He would appoint a committee to investigate the Yeti escape to be sure, giving a few of the appointments to well knowns outside the university in order that there be no accusations of whitewash or cover-up. He wished that Professor Kesler was still alive, as his reputation was such that there would be no questions if it was determined that the university was not culpable. Would the committee recommend the university close the primate facility? He hoped not, as it was the only one of its kind on the West Coast and gave Cal Pacific a certain degree of prestige. In addition, if the facility was kept open, he would definitely re-evaluate the anthropology department's selection process for sending graduate students to it.

He switched on the television across from his desk and noticed the Elko County Sheriff and someone from the state police holding a news conference. The law enforcement officials involved in killing the Yeti, he surmised. He muted the sound and watched the men in silence. Behind them was a large map of northern Nevada and the sheriff pointed to it during the conference. Obviously detailing what happened and how they tracked down the animals. He tried to make notes of what he would say to the board of trustees, due to meet in the morning, but had difficulty concentrating so he pushed the notepad aside. He clicked off the television and went home for the evening.

e∽ිe∽ි

Rupert Lowell and Nash Yarak lounged in Lowell's Burbank townhouse. They had just finished watching the news and Cal Pacific University's president hold the news conference describing the Yeti's escape from the primate facility and their killing. Lowell fixed drinks and handed one to Yarak. His friend's arm was in a cast and he himself was bandaged and bruised.

"Well, Nash," he said, settling into an overstuffed chair. "What do you think?"

Yarak shrugged then smiled.

"I think we barely escaped with our lives, boss. Those monsters are called Yeti, huh?"

"That's what they said. Some version of Bigfoot, I believe. And I thought all that stuff was just fairy tales."

"Apparently not," Yarak said, taking a sip of his drink.

"After the sheriff's office brought Terk's and Garby's bodies down from the mine, they kept asking me what had happened. I tried to tell them. They weren't forthcoming with information. Now we know the truth."

"Those creatures," Yarak said, "if I hadn't seen them with my own eyes, I would never believe they existed. And they escaped from a research facility, eh?"

"Apparently so," Lowell said, finishing his drink. He poured himself another. "Brought here from China or Mongolia, I understand."

"We left all our gear in the mountains, sir. Not to mention all that gold we took from the mine."

"Yeah," Lowell said. "Not to mention all that gold."

"We going back up there? To finish what we started?"

Lowell smiled. "But of course, Nash. But can we wait until we've healed? I need the rest."

❧❧❧

It was close to noon when Dr. Wickingham noticed

Dixie hurrying down the hallway toward her office. She looked haggard, as if she hadn't slept for several days. He caught up with her.

"Dixie?" he said, touching the sleeve of her lab coat. "You're back."

She turned without stopping and smiled. "Yes, Dr. Wickingham. Earlier this morning."

"Please call me Bernie," he said, following her into her office.

"Okay, Bernie. How are things here?"

"I would like to talk to you about something important. That is, if you have some time."

"Well, Bernie, Harry and I are due to meet with Dr. Pauling after lunch but I guess I have a few minutes. What's on your mind?"

Dixie sat behind her desk and Wickingham took the offered chair next to her. He sat quietly for a moment as if collecting his thoughts. The office was piled high with books and journals stashed every which way in bookshelves. She kept the door open.

"You know how much I've needed my own lab space—" he began.

Dixie nodded. "And how there's simply no room at present," she interjected.

"Dixie," he continued, as if not hearing her, "I need that space. I was wondering if you could have a word with your husband maybe—"

"Bernie," Dixie said, holding up a hand. "Harry can't create space out of thin air. Like I said, there is no available space. Believe me, he has looked."

Wickingham's eyes narrowed and the smile turned to a frown. He lowered his voice to barely above a whisper. "I hate to bring this up," he said in a slow drawl, "but I know of Harry's forging his data for the article two years ago."

"What?"

"I know, Dixie. He falsified data and Dr. Kesler fixed it after the article had been published. Saved Harry's bacon."

Dixie sat in silence, staring at the young faculty member. "I'm not sure I know where this is going, Bernie," she said, elbows on the desk. "But it doesn't sound good."

"Just as I said, I know. And if I know, others might find out."

"Bernie, this was all made right a long time ago. I am well aware of what he did. He has apologized and that is the end of it."

"Maybe not, Dixie. Like I said, Harry's credibility might be jeopardized if this became public knowledge. I mean beyond academic circles. If you could just help your husband understand how much I need that lab, I can assure you no one would ever need know his dirty little secret."

Dixie nodded in silence for a minute. "Yes, I understand now. His *dirty little secret* as you call it. This lab is important to you, isn't it, Bernie?"

"It is, yes."

"Well, I'll see what I can do." She stood, her brown eyes darker. "I'll be in touch, Bernie. Now, if you'll excuse me, I have work to do."

⌇⌇

That afternoon, Harry, Dixie, Radner, and Dr. Siscom sat in burgundy leather chairs in Pauling's office. Harry sipped a cup of coffee while Siscom thumbed through a series of typed pages. While they waited for the university president to arrive they chatted about the previous week's happenings.

When Pauling arrived, he took a seat and smiled at each of them.

"I asked you all here," he said, "to hear Dr. Siscom's autopsy report on the Yeti and discuss it before he finalizes it. Gerald, do you want to begin?"

Siscom cleared his throat and referred to the pages as he spoke. "First," he said, "the remains of both Yeti animals were almost completely destroyed, leaving behind only a partial skeleton consisting of a few bones and their skulls. Not having any other means for identification, I separated the charred bones based in size, figuring the larger ones belonged to the female. That included the skull."

Siscom hesitated while he glanced over a page and adjusted his reading glasses. "There was nothing unusual in the surface anatomy of the bones. Numerous fractures were obvious, many of them broken in half. There were many bone fragments that were unidentifiable as to which animal they belonged. The trauma involved was horrific.

"The skulls of both Yeti were relatively intact. All of the fur and skin had been burned. The larger skull, which I said must have been the female, had a frontal bone fracture extending into the parietal bone. I could see brain matter beneath the fracture line.

"Although significantly charred, the male skull was unscathed, no fractures were observed. Finally, I did a post-mortem examination on the brains of each animal. And here is where it gets interesting."

Siscom turned the page of his report and continued. "The brain of the female was normal. Much larger than a human brain but normal. However, not so with the male brain. In the anterior or front portion of the frontal lobe there was a large tumor. In the left frontal lobe. It was the size of a softball."

Dixie gasped and Harry let out a low whistle.

"Are you kidding, Gerald?" Pauling said, leaning forward on his desk. "For real?"

"Absolutely," Siscom said. "I examined it under a microscope. It was a glioblastoma."

"Speak English, Gerald," Dixie said. She squirmed in her chair, eyes wide.

"It's an extremely malignant cancer," Siscom continued. "And one this size is uniformly lethal. These are extremely aggressive tumors."

"You're saying the male Yeti had a huge brain tumor?" Pauling said.

"Yes. These cancers grow rapidly in all directions putting tremendous pressure on the surrounding normal tissue. Like I said, they are highly lethal."

"So, Gerald, could this brain tumor in the male explain his unusual aggressive behavior?" Harry had a notebook out and took notes. "Millie reported that Bentu acted aggressively toward Jimmy, the other graduate assistant. We assumed it was due to his harsh treatment of the animal but could it have been due to this tumor?"

Siscom adjusted his glasses again and glanced at everyone in the room. "It's possible, but we will never know for sure. The brain exists in a closed container, the skull, and as the tumor gets bigger, the skull can't expand. So the pressure inside the skull increases, the brain itself is compressed which compromises circulation and blood flow. It can be extremely painful as well."

"How long had he had this tumor?" Harry asked.

"No telling but he probably had it when he arrived here."

"And would have died fairly soon?" Pauling asked.

"Again, I can't say but in my opinion he had less than a year to live."

Harry massaged his temples and shook his head.

Siscom turned a page in his notes. "Frontal lobe tumors and dysfunction have been postulated as an etiology for sociopathic behavior, including murder. Despite the scientific evidence, the legal system has in large part failed to address the implications of frontal lobe dysfunction in the criminal process. Frontal lobe dysfunction does not fit neatly into either a diminished capacity or an insanity defense."

"Dr. Pauling," Harry said, "should we release this information to the press? What's your opinion?"

"Not at present, I don't think. Harry, I'm going to appoint a committee to investigate what happened and determine if the university was culpable. My feeling is that everyone is off the hook—this was a huge tragedy. But we'll let the committee decide how much information the public gets. How is this graduate assistant...what's her name?"

"Millie," Dixie said. "Millie Harbaum."

"Yes. How is Miss Harbaum doing right now?"

"She's holding up," Dixie said. "She bonded with Sasha, the female she was studying, so her death was a bitter blow. But she's strong, she'll be fine."

"Anything else, Gerald, with the report?" Pauling said, leaning back in his chair.

"That's it. Pretty bizarre, really. I must admit I liked these animals. They were strange, looked as if they had come from another planet, but I could see how you thought they were relatives of ours. When they first arrived, just their looks frightened me. How they could see right into your soul, like a beast from hell, like the asterian beasts in Dante's *Inferno*."

"I remember," Dixie said. "I still have nightmares of them from when I was in Mongolia. They have a way of getting into your psyche. But I wish it hadn't ended this way."

"Fine," Pauling said. "Now Miles, what have you learned from the FBI?"

Radner cleared his throat and sat up straight. "The bomb was a simple device," he said. "Plastic explosive with a clock timer. No fingerprints. But what with all the animal rights protestors of late, they think the bomb might be related to them. They have several leads which they are following at present."

"All right, I think we are done," Pauling said. "Unless anyone has something else they would like to add. If not, Gerald, put that report in its final form and get it to me tomorrow." Pauling stood. "Now, all, let's get back to work."

Chapter 30

Bernard Wickingham sat in Dr. Pauling's outer office, wondering why he had been summoned so early in the morning. When he arrived at his own office earlier, there was a note on his computer stating that his presence was required in the president's office immediately. The tone of the note was more on the line of an order and along the way Wickingham worried what the reason might be.

The door opened and Pauling stood in the doorway.

"Please come in, Dr. Wickingham," he said. His tone was a formal monotone.

Wickingham passed Pauling, entered the office, and stopped in his tracks. There, in a chair next to the large desk, sat Dixie. She smiled when she saw him. His knees went weak and his stomach turned upside down. Suddenly, he was nauseous.

Pauling crossed the room and took his usual seat behind his desk. He motioned to an empty chair. "Please, Doctor, have a chair."

Wickingham gulped and sat. His pulse raced.

"Dr. Wickingham," Pauling began, "Dr. Olson here has come to me with a most disturbing complaint concerning you. She states that yesterday you approached her with the notion that she help you obtain lab space. That she try to influence her husband in rearranging the laboratory assignments to your benefit. In other words, to pressure her husband to get you a lab. In return, you promised not to divulge certain facts about her husband, that you claimed to have, which might prove embarrassing to him. Do I have this correct so far?"

"Dr. Pauling, I…I…I…" Wickingham said, struggling to find the words.

"I take it by you hesitancy, Doctor, that I have the facts right."

Wickingham shot a quick glance at Dixie who sat silent, a small smirk on her face.

"Well, Dr. Pauling, I wasn't…"

"Weren't what?"

"I think you—and she—have this all wrong. I wasn't trying to pressure her. I merely said—"

"In a court of law, Dr. Wickingham, it's call extortion. It's something we don't tolerate at this university or among our staff."

"Dixie," Wickingham blurted out, "I'm sorry. I didn't intend for you to take it the wrong way. I merely—"

"Enough, Doctor. You are still in your probationary period, correct? Yes. Doctor, as of this moment you are no longer employed by California Pacific University. Your termination is effective immediately. As per the terms of your probationary period, you can be terminated without cause at any time. You are to turn your keys in to security, along with your ID. Then you are to report to HR and sign the necessary papers in order to receive your final paycheck. I will entertain no objections. Good day, sir."

Pauling stood and Wickingham followed suit. His legs felt like Jell-O, his head swam. He thought he might faint.

As he stumbled to the office door, he noticed Dixie out of the corner of his eye.

She sat, still silent, with the same smirk on her face.

❧❧❧

Harry pulled the steaks off the grill and brought them into the house. The setting sun cast deep shadows over San Francisco Bay to the east of his and Dixie's San Mateo home. Gathered around the large dining room table were his wife, Siscom, Drayton, Radner, and Millie. Harry had mixed drinks for everyone, and they had spent the last hour rehashing the events of the previous week. He felt close to them, a feeling kindled by communal suffering.

As they ate, the discussion about their experiences continued, with Drayton making his point. "Frankly," he said, "I'm glad it's over. I'm not the camping type."

"I feel so sorry for Jimmy," Millie said. "His death—so senseless."

"If he had followed our guidelines," Radner said, "he would be alive now and this whole tragedy would not have happened."

"Yes," Millie said, "but..." Her voice trailed off and tears formed in her eyes. It was obvious she agonized over Jimmy and his family. "I feel so sorry for his parents."

"Yes, we all do," Dixie said. She sat next to Millie and gave her a sympathetic pat on her arm.

"And we all can be grateful that the board of trustees took the advice of the investigating committee and allowed the facility to remain open," Radner said, beaming. "And that I and Harry still have a job at Cal Pacific."

"I'll second that," Dixie said, which produced much laughter from the group.

"As tragic as the loss of life of both people and the Yeti is," Siscom said between mouthfuls, "the world has lost something equally valuable. And that is future scientific knowledge those animals might have provided. Who knows what contributions their lives at the facility could have provided?"

"Well said, Gerald," Harry said. "Collecting and preservation of physical specimens is an integral, irreplaceable element of biological sciences. There is hardly a branch of biology that does not rely on the examination of organisms' bodies, be it for the purpose of their identification, understanding of the functions of their respiratory system, or the speed of transmission of neural signals. Museum collections, where specimens are preserved for future scientists, are also a special, important case. There, specimens are often deposited not for a particular, clearly defined research project, such as when a geneticist examines thousands of fruit flies to measure the expression of a particular gene. Rather, collections serve as both a documentation of the current state of species composition in a particular time period or an area, or as a library of morphological and genetic diversity across a wide range of species.

"We cannot anticipate what questions will be asked, and answered, using specimens deposited in such collections. For example, the ban on the use of DDT, a horrible environmental pollutant, was based on the discovery made in ornithological collections that bird egg shells had been getting progressively thinner, thus leading to high mortality of birds, ever since the chemical began to be used. The spread of chytrid fungus that was killing amphibian species across the globe was understood only by examining specimens dating back a hundred years."

"Very interesting, Harry," Radner said.

"My point is that having the Yeti in our possession

was of great scientific value, even if immediate gains were not realized."

"We had discovered the entire Yeti genome," Millie said.

"A great advance to be sure," Harry said. "But having them where we could continue to study them was the greatest advance, and to lose potential knowledge is sad, very sad."

"But aren't specimens lost all the time?" asked Siscom. "Sold to collectors or on the black market?"

"It is an odd situation. Even that a tiny scrap of bone or tooth fragment might be of immense value to someone if it provides evidence of a new pattern of evolution or provides data for geochemical analysis, yet it is something that even most paleontologists might throw away as worthless. These things really are priceless, and worthless, and it's sometimes odd to think of them in that sense, but it is true, and profoundly so in some cases.

"This contrasts strongly with how people view fossils and scientific specimens. While it's true that something like a Yeti skeleton is clearly worth a ton of cash, that's not true of most. But people hear about the expensive ones and even a good dinosaur tooth can set you back tens or even hundreds of dollars from a collector, so the image builds up that they are all valuable.

"If they aren't, why do people spend thousands and thousands to travel the world and scour the Earth for them, ship them home, prepare them, and store them? This can and does lead to the false assumption that all fossils are valuable and, as a result, people expect money you don't have and can't pay and don't want to pay for something or even access to something that is not actually valuable in the first place."

"What my husband is trying to say is that these specimens are both priceless and worthless. In and of themselves, they are not worth much at all but, to us scientists, they are priceless for the information they contain."

Dixie smiled and nodded at Harry.

"Well said, my dear," he replied.

"But even at a more basic level," Millie said, "the loss of such specimens creates a major stumbling block for paleontology. If a previously studied and published fossil has been stolen and sold off, then the specimen is off limits to researchers who want to take a fresh look or check up on old data. The fossil has effectively disappeared from the literature as it's no longer open to study. To me, it's a matter of reproducibility. If a specimen like the Yeti skeleton can't be permanently stored and cared for in a museum, then no one can re-examine or check on what has been gleaned from it."

"Fossils are part of a natural history heritage that belongs to everyone," Radner said. Destroying them in any way not only steals them away from science, but prevents researchers from translating discoveries made from them into the inspiring visions of our past and what our future may hold. It is a loss to humanity."

"The good news," Millie said, "is that we have the Yeti's genome and blood stored in a freezer. At our leisure we can study, compare, and hopefully understand their relationship to we humans."

"In the case of our Yeti, there is more good news," Harry said. "We know that they are living, breathing hominids, existing right alongside of us. So it would be possible to go back to Mongolia and return with another pair. We have the facility. We have the expertise. We have the personnel. It would be possible."

A buzz went around the table.

"How about it, Millie?" Harry continued. "After you earn your doctorate, would you be willing to become Dr.

Radner's assistant at the primate facility? Help us if we manage to bring back another pair of Yeti?"

Millie's eyes turned wide and bright. A broad grin crossed her face. "Gee, Dr. Olson." She giggled. "Nothing would please me more."

Dixie sank deep into her chair. *Oh brother. Here we go again.*

About the About

Richard Edde was born and raised in Oklahoma. After graduating from Central State College, he attended the University of Oklahoma College of Medicine, where he earned his medical degree in 1971. After spending a few years in family practice in two rural Oklahoma towns, he completed a residency in anesthesiology. Following a long career in academia and private practice, he retired to devote time to writing. His first novel, *The Photograph*, was released in 2014. Dr. Edde resides in eastern Oklahoma with his wife.